SINS AND SECRETS

KIRA COLE

1
____

BILLIE

"We are calling to inform you Mr. Arturo Carbone has been in an accident and has been admitted to our urgent care."

My entire world comes to a screeching halt as I pull my car over to the side of the road and stare at my phone in shock. The nurse's words play over and over again in my head but I can't make sense of them.

"Miss? Hello? Are you still there?"

"Wh-what? Yes, yes. I'm sorry, who is this again?"

"This is Nurse Hopkins calling from General Hospital. Is this not Billie Carbone, daughter of Arturo Carbone?"

This cannot be happening.

"Yes, I'm Billie. I'm sorry. Can you tell me what happened? How is he?"

"I'm sorry, ma'am. We are unable to give further information at this point. We are calling you because you are his emergency contact. If you want to come over, I'm sure the doctor will be able to provide you more details later tonight."

"Thank you. I should be there shortly. Can you please at least tell me if he is going to be okay?"

"I'm sorry, miss, but the doctor will have more information for you."

I fight the urge to scream and instead take a deep breath. "Alright. Thank you. Who do I ask for when I get there?"

"Doctor Michaels is the one handling your father's case. He's finished with your father's surgery and will be heading into another, but he should be done by the time the tests come back."

Surgery? Fuck, that's not good.

I know this life is dangerous, especially for the Consiglieri for the *famiglia*, but Papa was supposed to be at home.

I hate this life. Why couldn't he have listened to me?

"Thank you." I look at the little speakerphone icon still glowing brightly. "Is there anything I should be prepared for when I walk in?"

"I really can't discuss anything more with you. Doctor Michaels will have more information for you later tonight."

"Look, I know that you're doing your job, and I appreciate that, but this is my father. Isn't there anything else you can tell me about how he's doing? Please? Something?" I hate begging, but Papa is my world. He's the only parent I've ever known. I can't lose him now.

"I'm sorry." The nurse doesn't say anything else, disconnecting the call. I stare at the phone in disbelief.

Papa can be dying right now and this bitch just hung up on me.

I toss my phone onto the passenger seat with my wallet and try to remember how to breathe.

This isn't the first time that my father's been close to

death. Nearly dying every year comes with the territory of being the consigliere to the most dangerous man in Atlanta.

It's time to be done with the mafia for good. This time, I'll make him listen.

For years I've been telling him that he's getting too old to keep following younger men and being the first one into a fight. He doesn't see it that way. He's always thought that it's an honor to be as close to Alessio Marchetti as he is.

I know better, though. Being close to Alessio is a death sentence. Always has been, always will be.

After calming my racing heart, I pull away from the curb and head to the hospital. Throughout the entire drive, all I can think about is how I'm going to save my father once he gets better.

This life is killing him. It's killing me. We have to do what we must to survive, but the cost is getting too high to sustain.

The drive to the hospital is short, but the walk to the ICU feels unending. I glance at the names on the doors, looking for my father's room. Finally, I see one door shut at the end of the hall.

Nurses pass me as I look at paperwork sitting in the file holder beside the door.

Arturo Carbone.

My pulse is pounding when I open the door and walk into the room.

As I stare at my father lying in the bed, looking fragile and like a shell of himself, I want to scream.

He's covered in bandages with wires and tubes running back and forth from his body to the machines.

Seeing him like this makes me want to throw up.

We should have left the mafia a long time ago. We should have packed our bags and run the moment I was old enough to help support us. I should have made Papa see things my way.

"Papa, please come back to me, okay?" I whisper. "I need you to get well fast so I can get you out of this." My voice chokes as I hold back tears.

There are too many machines connected to him. Everything around him is either beeping, filling him with fluids, or monitoring something.

It's overwhelming. This is the worst that I've ever seen him.

"I was wondering how long it would be before you got here," a deep voice says from behind me.

I wipe the tears away quickly before turning to face Alessio. He stands in the doorway, arms crossed, brow furrowed. My gaze drops to the way his tailored suit hugs his body, highlighting every firm line.

I always found his dark hair, blue eyes, and well-groomed beard attractive.

Even when I want to kill him for the trouble he has put my father through.

"What happened to him?" I ask as I head to the door. I glance over my shoulder at Papa again before leaving the room. "The nurses won't tell me anything."

The corner of his mouth tips up but there is still a haunting look lingering in his eyes. "Why do you assume that *I* would be able to tell you anything?"

My blood is boiling. "This is all your fault," I say pointing to Papa's room, "so stop playing these fucking games. Just tell me what happened to Papa."

He arches an eyebrow. "Careful, Billie. You may be Arturo's daughter, but you are still a subordinate. I will tolerate the tone only this once given the circumstances, but you will *not* make a habit of speaking to me this way."

Argh, I could kill him right now.

But if I did that, I would have a mafia after me. Getting Papa out of this life is going to be hard enough as it is. I don't need to add a mob boss murder to the list of reasons people are going to want me dead.

It almost kills me, but I have to play by his rules. For now.

"I'm sorry. I'm just worried about Papa. He's too old to be getting attacked."

Alessio frowns and stands taller, his shoulders stiff as he glares down at me. "Your father knew what he was getting into."

"It's nothing to be too worried about. A job went wrong. The men who attacked him are now dead."

I cross my arms, trying to hold myself together.

"But what's happening to him now? You have to know something! You're a powerful man. There is no way that my papa is your consigliere and you know nothing about his condition. Please?"

Alessio studies me for a minute, his gaze traveling up and down my body. Heat floods to my core and my cheeks warm as I try not to look at him.

Why can't you just get rid of this damn crush? He's nineteen years older than you. He's Papa's best friend.

Papa, who is fighting for his life.

I feel sick. I shouldn't be thinking about what Alessio has always done to me when Papa is in the hospital.

"Beneath all those bandages, he's pretty badly beaten, but like I said, nothing you need to worry about. I made sure he has the best care available."

His tone is final, so I nod, keeping my head down and allowing my blonde hair to fall like a curtain in front of my face.

I'm still as worried about Papa as I was before this conversation, but Alessio is a dangerous man, and causing more trouble will only get us under permanent surveillance. I don't want that. I can talk to the doctor later and avoid prolonging this conversation.

As I head back into my father's room, I can feel his gaze burning a hole in my back. I try to keep myself looking small and meek — like a woman who has been thoroughly chastised — until the door is closed behind me.

The moment I'm alone with Papa, I drop the act and stride over to the seat beside him, taking his fragile hand in mine.

God, I hope he pulls through this.

He looks so bad. His face and knuckles are bloodied and bruised, and I suspect, so is the rest of his body.

Everything is going to be okay, Papa. I'm going to make sure that this never happens to you again.

EMILIA IS WAITING FOR ME WHEN I GET BACK HOME several hours later. She meets me in the driveway with a sad smile, pulling me into a tight hug the moment I step out of the car. Her flowery perfume wraps around us, washing away the scent of antiseptic and blood that's been invading my senses for the last several hours.

"How is he?" she asks, stepping away from me. "Is Arturo going to be alright?"

"Sorry I scared you with that text," I say, leading the way into the house. "I would have told you more at the time if I could have, but it's a lot to process."

"Come on, you can tell me all about it over dinner and a glass of wine. I made chicken parmigiana."

Emilia loops her arm through mine and tows me to the kitchen, though all I want to do is go to bed.

Being in this house without Papa doesn't feel right. He should be here right now, singing along to the old Italian songs I've heard throughout my entire childhood. We would talk about my business plans while he cooked, always planning for a future that may not come.

"Papa is in a coma. They don't know when he's going to come out," I say as she pours me a glass of white wine. I take the glass and down it all before handing it back to her for a refill. "A job that went wrong was what Alessio told me. The men who attacked him are dead, but what good will that do if he doesn't come out of the coma?"

Emilia refills my glass before pouring one of her own. "I'm sure that Arturo is going to pull through. He always does. That man is a tough bastard to kill."

I laugh and nod, even as my vision starts to blur with the tears pooling in my eyes. "I know he is. And as soon as he gets out of that hospital, I'm getting us out of here."

Emilia's eyes go wide, and her mouth drops open. She takes a long sip of wine before going to the stove. Her entire body is tense as she puts some of the food on plates and brings it to the island.

"You know that trying to get out is more likely to get you killed, right?" she says, her voice soft as we dig into our meals. "Besides, what makes you think that Arturo would leave this time? He's never wanted to before."

I lean against the counter as I cut my chicken into small pieces. "I know all of that, but I still have to try."

"The only way out is death." Emilia shakes her head. "Billie, it's too dangerous. Your papa is the consigliere. He doesn't get to leave. Not without a special pardon from Alessio. It's treason."

"If he stays, he is likely to die just as easily. And with all the shit that's going on among the capos and soldiers right now, this is going to be the only chance I have to get him out. You know that all the tension among the ranks is going to come to a head sooner or later. If Papa is better by then, the chaos of what is happening will be enough to allow us to disappear."

"*If* your papa even wants to. And what about money? You don't have enough to make that happen."

I shrug and look down at my food. My chest constricts. I know she's right. If I touch any of the money Papa has for working for the mafia, they will call it theft and add on yet another reason to come after us. Kill us.

There is no way for us to start over if the mafia is hunting us.

All my dreams of a normal life, settling down, having a family, opening a resort will go down the drain. I won't ever get to see Papa living a life without stress and the threat of being killed around every corner. And that's all I ever wanted for the two of us.

"I have to find another way to earn a lot of money in a short amount of time. Something that is going to be enough to get us overseas and off the grid. When I finally make my move, I want me and Papa to disappear completely."

Emilia moves the pieces of chicken around on her plate, biting her bottom lip. When she finally looks up at me, there is hesitancy shining in her eyes.

"What is it?" I ask, reaching for my wine.

"I may know of a way that will get you at least two hundred thousand dollars. Though it can go as high as a mil."

"Really? Tell me!"

"I don't know, Billie, it's dangerous."

"I'm willing to do anything. Please."

Emilia frowns and runs her hand through her auburn hair. Huffing, she says, "There's this auction…"

I frown. "Auction? I have nothing—"

"Yourself," she says, cutting me off. And my jaw falls to the floor. "You would be selling yourself to a man."

"What the hell? Emilia, what are you talking about? How would this help me?"

"There are contracts you have to sign. You can say yes or no, but the bottom line is, you would be at the mercy of whoever bought you for at least two months."

"Two *months*?" I'm not even sure I could do one *night*. How can I expect to last two months under someone's thumb? "What would I have to do, do you know?"

"No. But it will most likely involve having sex with your buyer. Which, by the way, you have no way of knowing who it would be."

I'm looking at her, and this is all making me sick, but the image of my papa in that hospital bed suddenly reminds me what is at stake.

I need to save him. Get him out of this life.

Make sure he has a life. A long one.

Breathing deeply, I know I really don't have a choice. Two hundred grand would buy my freedom.

"I don't care." I take a sip of my wine, trying to stave off the fear. "I'm willing to do anything to get out of this shit. How do I sign up for the auction?"

"You don't. It's invite-only." Emilia turns around and grabs her purse off the counter. She takes out her phone and pulls up an email. "I got this from one of my friends. Invites are going to be sent out in a few days but there is no way to know if you're on the list unless you get the invite."

"Do you know who decides who gets the invites?" I ask as I skim through the email.

She just shakes her head.

Nothing is truly said in the email that gives away who is running the auction or what you need to do to be invited to it. Hell, the email barely even acknowledges that there will be an auction. Fuck.

"So, there's nothing I can do but wait and see?" I groan and run my hands down my face, feeling more helpless than ever.

I could go to the casinos and gamble in a desperate attempt to make thousands of dollars fast, but I've never been very good at it. I could run favors for other members of the mafia or some of the affiliated gangs, but it would get back to Alessio and make him suspicious.

If I can't be in this auction, I have no idea what else to do.

"Everything is going to be okay," Emilia says, taking her phone back and slipping it into her purse. "I'll talk to the person who told me about the auction. I'll try and see if there is any way to guarantee an invite."

"Thank you. I really appreciate it." Emilia is an amazing friend. One I cherish more than anything.

And then it hits me, "You know helping me is going to be just as dangerous for you. If you get caught helping me, Alessio will have you tortured for information and then they'll kill you."

Emilia shrugs. "Alessio Marchetti already took away the people in my life who mattered to me the most. What more do I have to lose? My own life is a small price to pay for this."

The tears start rolling down my cheeks as I round the

counter and pull her into a tight hug. "You're the best friend that I could have ever asked for. Thank you."

Emilia hugs me back, her embrace so tight I'm sure that there will be bruises in the morning. Right now, it's exactly what I need.

Somehow, I'm going to save me and Papa.

2

ALESSIO

Pulling open the front door and stumbling on dead bodies while going out for my morning run wasn't what I had pictured for the day. I look down at the blood staining my shoes before I crouch down beside the dead men.

One look is all it takes to tell me that these men are two of my most trusted capos. Their eyes have been pulled out and most of their fingers are mutilated.

My stomach lurches.

Dead bodies are nothing new to me, but it still doesn't make seeing them any easier. Especially when they are the bodies of men I grew up with.

If they are here on my doorstep instead of buried somewhere that nobody will ever find them, then it's a message to me.

Yet another message that I don't need from Paolo Marino, the ringleader in the circus of problems the *famiglia* has been having lately.

Every time I turn around, he is testing my control again.

When he left with over a dozen men to try and be my

competitor, I slaughtered the men but left Paolo alive out of a sense of duty.

A few weeks after those men died, Paolo started recruiting men outside the famiglia. I have no doubt he has spies inside as well, though I haven't been able to root them out yet.

He began playing his petty games, sending message after message but none was as brutal as this.

Murdering my dead brother's best friend is something I haven't been able to bring myself to do, but this time, he crossed a line. After this, brother's best friend or not, Paolo is going down.

These men supported me without question when my father died ten years ago, and I came into power.

I was young and they were two of only a handful of people who didn't fight me every step of the way. They were there for me even when it was clear this life wasn't my dream.

This life was never what I imagined for myself. It was supposed to belong to my brother until he died. I was the spare. The one who was going to start his own business and make millions of dollars a year.

The one who wasn't going to be involved in the mafia. Who didn't have to kill people for a living.

Guess the joke is on me.

I'm going to find whoever did this and I won't rest until you both have justice.

I pull out my phone. My first instinct is to call Arturo. Normally, he would be the one to handle the bodies, ensuring that they were both given a proper burial. However, he is teetering on the edge of death. I suspect Paolo had a hand to play in that as well, though I have not been able to find any evidence yet.

"Davide," I say as soon as the call connects. "I need you and the doctor to come to my house immediately. Ricardo and Dario are dead."

Davide is quiet for a moment, shuffling around in the background. "I'm on my way and I texted Doc. He's going to meet me there."

"I want you to gather whatever information you can on Paolo Marino and his hideouts. While Arturo is in a coma, you are to be the acting consigliere."

"Thank you, sir. I will bring what information I already have and touch base with several of the capos on my way over."

"See that you do," I say, heading inside and grabbing a throw blanket from the storage ottoman in the living room. "I want this handled as quickly as possible. Paolo has been making a fool out of me for too long now. It is time that this comes to an end."

"Yes, sir."

I end the call before draping the blanket over the two dead men. As I stand, I look out over my property.

It is large and surrounded by trees. Just beyond the line of trees is the rest of the compound.

The majority of the *famiglia* lives outside the compound but I made sure when I became their leader that I had enough room to house everyone if I needed to.

However, I built my house segregated from the rest. A good leader cannot be too involved with his people. They must still fear and respect him.

At least that's what my father used to say before he died twelve years ago. He left my older brother in charge of the *famiglia* back then. I was supposed to have my own life. Then Enzo died and it was up to me to take charge of an operation I never wanted.

Somewhere on the other side of those trees, someone is out to get me. Men I'm supposed to trust with my life are doing what they can to bring me down.

Working for Paolo.

Because there is no way that Paolo would have been able to bring two dead bodies — the bodies of two of my men — to my doorstep without inside help.

I have been slacking. But no more. I'm going to hunt them down and make them regret the day they were born.

I sit on the step beside the bodies, not caring about the blood that stains my clothes. As I watch for Davide and Doc, I sift through everything I know about Paolo's operation. It isn't much, but I know that he is going to keep coming at me until he gets what he wants — control of Atlanta.

The roar of engines racing through the compound brings me back to the situation at hand. Davide is the first to park his car and get out, hurrying over to me.

"I spoke to a couple capos. There might be a way to get inside Paolo's operation for information in two weeks," Davide says. Glancing down at the bodies, he adds, "Do you want me to talk to wives and inform them of the tragedy?"

I shake my head as I stand. "No. I will handle that personally. What's this about a chance to get inside Paolo's operation?"

Davide nods as Doc backs up a black armored vehicle that was once an ambulance.

Doc doesn't say anything to either of us as he gets out and gets ready to transport the bodies.

"Paolo is hosting an auction. Apparently, he's done it before, about six months ago."

"When he started this bullshit." I run a hand through my hair before I think about the blood that is staining my hands. I can forget about my run, but I'm still going to need to shower before I head to the casino for the day. "What is he auctioning off?"

"Women."

I see red. While the *famiglia* may not have the best reputation for how they treat women — something I try to fix — they would never think of auctioning them off like cattle. Just the thought makes me sick.

"And you think that attending this auction will be a good chance to see who he has working for him," I say, pushing past the nauseous feeling.

My father used to say that I was too soft for a life of crime. There are some days when I think he was right, and I should have never taken over after Enzo died.

However, the proud man that lived inside me couldn't let the family business go either.

Davide nods. "I think that it will be the best chance to see what he's up to for a long time. There's an auction in two weeks. Plenty of time to come up with how best to infiltrate his territory."

I shake my head. "No. I will be going in alone. Until I know who is working for Paolo and who isn't, I cannot trust anybody to have my back. Arturo is in the hospital despite the details of the arms run being a secret shared only by a select few."

A select few who are now being tortured and killed for their part in what happened.

"I'm going to get cleaned up," I say, watching as Doc loads the bodies into the repurposed ambulance. "And then I'm going to talk to the wives before going to the casino. See to it that these men have a proper burial arrangement. Spare no expense, whatever their wives want for them. Make sure the wives are both paid as well. We need to provide for them now that their husbands no longer can."

"Yes, sir." Davide pulls out his phone and starts sending messages.

I watch the ambulance take off before heading back inside my house to get cleaned up. Today is going to be a long day. I can't talk to the widows covered in their husbands' blood.

This is the part of my job that I hate the most.

IT'S LATE THAT NIGHT WHEN I GET HOME. THE MOON IS hanging high in the sky and the stars are shining. I had spent more time than I cared to admit at the hospital, trying to talk this entire situation over with Arturo, though I know he cannot say anything.

When I first took over the mafia, he took me under his wing and showed me that there was more than one way to be a good leader.

I don't know how to continue leading without him at my side.

Right now, I have no choice. Hundreds of people count on me.

Falling apart is never an option.

And then there's Billie, who didn't say anything to me when she arrived to visit her father.

What a shame, I think as I strip down and get in the shower.

There are times when I don't know what to think about Billie. She grew from a young girl to a beautiful woman in the blink of an eye.

That tongue is going to get her in trouble one day, though.

Instead of giving me hell — like I thought she would — she glared at me and disappeared into her father's room.

I hadn't missed the look of desire that had flashed through those pretty green eyes when she looked at me.

It is a look that she gives me every time she sees me. One that shows me her childhood crush developed into something more.

Not that I would ever go there with her. She is Arturo's daughter and I'm far too old to be hooking up with a woman who is only twenty-four. Nineteen years is a larger age gap than even I am willing to cross.

Still, there is no harm in imagining her on her knees as I get in the shower.

I groan, my hand wrapping around my hardened cock as the hot water cascades down my back. I run my thumb over the head as I picture the way her mouth would open while her thighs parted.

Her pussy would be dripping, waiting for me as her tongue darted out to lick the head of my cock. Those full lips would part, taking me in a little at a time while her hands roamed her body.

I could see her now, pinching her nipples between her fingers, moaning around my cock as I wrapped her hair around my fist. I would be slow with her at first, enough to tease her into wanting more.

The real fun wouldn't start until saliva was dripping down her chin and her fingers were thrusting in and out of her tight little pussy.

I moan, bracing one hand against the wall while I stroke the other up and down my cock. I grip it a little harder as I picture the way I would thrust my cock into her, harder and deeper until I was hitting the back of her throat.

She would come on her fingers as I fucked her throat, her moans only making my cock harder.

Finally, that sharp tongue would be silenced as she tried to swallow more of my cock than she could manage. She would be so eager to please me, her fingernails digging into my thighs as she tried to take me deeper.

I can even hear the sounds she would make as I came in her mouth, keeping my cock in place until she had swallowed every last drop and licked it clean.

My hand moves faster up and down my cock as I imagine the way her tongue would drag along my length.

She would live to please me if I had my way.

I groan as I come, white ropes splattering against the wall. My hand keeps pumping until there is nothing left but the image of Billie swallowing my cock burned into my memory.

3

———

BILLIE

EMILIA HUMS ALONG WITH THE MUSIC PLAYING IN THE grocery store as we travel up and down the aisles. She grabs a couple of boxes of sugary cereal and tosses them into the cart.

"I don't see why the hell the women still have to take turns making the capos dinner every week," I say as I grab a box of biscuit mix. "I have enough to do between looking after my father and running errands for Davide. Now that he is the acting consigliere, he is twice as far up my ass to get things done."

Emilia rolls her eyes. "Because heaven forbid, we get rid of a tradition that was put in place over forty years ago. Women are supposed to honor the capos for keeping them safe, or some bullshit like that."

I pretend to gag. "Outdated nonsense."

"So, Davide, huh? He's cute." Emilia wiggles her eyebrows. "I know he's always been a pain in your ass, but maybe you should give him a chance. He's definitely not the worst man in the mafia."

"Hell no. I need a man who is going to take control.

Even if Davide is my boss, I think he nearly shit himself when I told him I couldn't go on a coffee run yesterday."

Emilia laughs and leads the way to the meat section. "Alright, I'll give you that. You are also a massive pain in the ass and it's going to take a brave man to deal with you all the time."

"What about you?" I ask, bumping my hip into hers as I reach for the steaks. I eye the amount still remaining in the showcase and hope it will be enough to feed the capos tonight.

"What *about* me?" Her cheeks turn a pale shade of pink as she helps me load the steaks into the cart.

"Are you seeing anyone these days?" I pile more steaks into the cart. "You haven't said anything about anyone since you dumped that last piece of shit."

"I've been seeing someone, I think. I don't know. It's complicated with him. I think we're both just looking for a little fun and that's all that it's going to be for now. I don't have time in my life for another person."

I eye her for a moment, wondering if this man has the potential to be more than a little bit of fun. For her sake, I hope not. I love Emilia like she is my own sister, but she has the worst taste in men. Far too often, she dates a man because he charms her for the first week or two.

When he starts acting like an ass, she stays and insists that they are in love.

I've tried everything I can to help her, but none of it works. At this point, I've settled for being there when she needs me but largely keeping my opinion to myself. She doesn't listen to it anyway.

All I can do is be her friend and hope that it's enough.

"I got you something," Emilia says, changing the subject as we head off in search of the ingredients for lasagna.

She reaches into her purse and pulls out a little black envelope. I take it from her and open it up, seeing a date and address embossed in gold on the black paper.

"What is this?" I ask her, holding out the envelope.

She whispers, "It's the invitation to the auction." Emilia smiles as my heart pounds in my chest.

Oh, my god.

I put the invitation in the back pocket of my ripped jeans.

"You'll have to pretend to be me, but they should let you in. Everything is anonymous so all they have is a name. One of the girls I work with was invited, but she had to pass it up. She was in their other one, so she recommended me as her replacement, and they took me up on it."

"You're kidding," I say, staring at her in disbelief, joy and dread filling me in equal parts. "There is no way that you got an invitation that fast. Holy shit. This is amazing, Emi. Thank you so much."

"Don't mention it." She grabs a couple of massive packs of ground beef and tosses them in the cart. "And I really do mean, *don't* mention it. The auction is supposed to be a secret. If you want this to work, you can't breathe a word of it to anyone."

"I won't." I smile and grab a couple of packs of bacon. "Holy shit, I might be getting out of here soon. Two hundred thousand dollars is more than enough money to disappear."

"It is." Emilia takes the list from me and crosses a couple of items off. "What are you going to do once you leave?"

I shrug. "I haven't thought that far ahead yet."

"You probably should."

"Once I get home, I'll start trying to figure everything out."

Nothing about the escape is going to be left up to chance.

If I go through with this, I will have to be at the beck and call of whoever buys me, for several weeks. But after that, I'll be two hundred kay richer and free to leave.

Oh, shit. I'm going to have to let some stranger touch me.

My skin crawls. Never in my life did I think that I would get to this point.

Maybe there is a way to be more of a maid. I don't want to sleep with a strange man — especially not for money. I'm going to do everything I can to avoid it, but I don't know what kind of man is going to buy me.

I need to prepare myself for the worst-case scenario.

"Are you sure that you want to do this?" Emilia asks, concern in her eyes as she looks at me. "If you don't, we can find another way."

I smile and shake my head. "I have to do this. I appreciate it, though. Auctioning myself to a man may not be something I look forward to, but it's the fastest way to get the money I need to start our lives over."

"If you're sure."

"I am," I say, though I've never been less sure of anything in my life.

What I am sure of, though, is that my plan needs to be good enough to get me and Papa far away from Atlanta before Alessio even realizes that we're missing.

Emilia starts to talk about the dance classes she is teaching at a studio in the city while we gather the rest of the ingredients. Her chatter is a welcome distraction from everything else going on in my head.

By the time we finish getting the groceries and loading

the car, I've nearly forgotten about the invitation burning a hole in my back pocket.

"Do you know what you're going to wear to dinner yet?" Emilia asks on the drive back to the main house at the Marchetti compound.

"Something that shows off my boobs and ass." I grin at her and turn down the music. "I'm only half kidding about that. You know that the capos will leave us alone if we give them something to look at."

Emilia sighs and leans her head back against the seat, looking out the window at the trees as we pass. "Sometimes, I dream about what life would be like outside the mafia."

"You know, you could come with us."

Emilia shakes her head and gives me a sad smile. "You know I can't do that. Someone has to stay here and cover for you. Besides, this life is all I've ever known. If I keep doing right by the mafia, eventually I'll get to live out my own dreams."

"Or you'll be trapped here like everyone else who believes that there's a better way to live life here. Alessio doesn't give a shit about his people. If he did, we wouldn't be serving the capos like they're gods."

"You know that this is just temporary. Our turn to feed them only comes up once every couple of months. It isn't that bad."

"We're going to keep a running tally of how many of them grope or hit on us tonight and then you can tell me if it really isn't that bad."

My stomach rolls just thinking about it. The weekly capos dinner is like an excuse for them to all act like animals. Not that they need the excuse. I don't know if those men have ever been respectful of anyone other than themselves a day in their lives.

Might as well use it as a preparation for what's to come, I guess.

Emilia's lips press together in a thin line as I turn up the music.

We may not fight often, but this is one of the things that we do argue about. She is content to live life with the mafia, never making waves, and I want more for myself.

I want to be seen as a person instead of a maid or a commodity.

As backward as it may be, selling myself is the one thing that's going to give me a life outside of being property to Alessio and his men.

I guess I need to be willing to be sold as property to stop being property. Can my life get even more complicated?

* * *

MEN LINE THE TABLES IN THE DINING HALL, LAUGHING and drinking as women rush around and deliver plates of food to the tables. I scowl as I dodge another set of grabby hands to deliver two beers to a couple of men.

"You know, that really is a pretty dress on you," one of the men says, his hand sliding up my thigh as I put his beer on the table. "If you like, I would love to show a pretty little thing like you what a good time is."

"Go to hell," I say, grabbing his hand and pulling it off me. "Have a nice dinner."

I take off before the man can do anything to me. Talking back to the capos is asking for trouble, but sometimes they deserve it.

I'll be damned if I let these assholes take advantage of me, though I know it's coming. With Papa in the hospital, most of the men who want to try something will see me as vulnerable. They think they won't have my father coming after them if they mess with me.

I disappear into the kitchen to look at the leftover food and see what can be packed up. The end of the night is coming fast, and soon I'll be able to go home and forget that tonight ever happened.

"You know," a deep voice says from behind me. "You should really respect the capos more. They are doing their best to keep you safe. If one of them wants something from you, then you really need to do your best to honor it. Why, I bet a dirty little whore like you makes a game out of getting on her knees for the capos."

I don't bother to look at the man, instead listening to the sound of his footsteps on the tiled floor. He paces around the area behind me, putting himself between me and the block of knives.

After taking a deep breath, I turn around to look at him. I hold my head high, determined not to let this man see the fear that is running through me. If he does, this is going to get much worse.

I have to keep my head about me if I want to get out of this kitchen unscathed.

He grins and takes a step closer to me. "I want to hear how you are going to make it up to me. You should have learned to mind your manners by now. I know your father would have taught you better than this shit."

"Well, you'd be wrong," I say, my voice strong and clear. "Get out of here before I make you wish you had never come in here."

The man throws his head back and laughs like it's the funniest joke that he's ever heard. "Do you really think that you're threatening, little girl?"

"Fuck off."

His eyes narrow and he takes slow steps toward me like a predator hunting his prey. His hands curl into fists at his side. "You're going to regret talking to me like that. Do you really think anyone is going to come in here and save you? Me and the boys have been talking about the way you run your mouth for weeks."

"Good for you. If you come any closer, I'm going to make sure that you can never have children."

I glance around the room, trying to figure out if I can get out of the kitchen without putting my hands on him. The moment that I try to fight back, it's going to be a meeting with Alessio.

I don't know how that meeting would go, but Alessio isn't known to be the kindest man out there.

He laughs and lunges at me. I jump to the side, ducking beneath his arm as I move. He slams into the counter as I spin around and reach for the nearest thing I can find. I heft the weight of the frying pan in my hand, glaring at him as he stands up.

"You bitch." He gives me a wild grin. "You're going to regret that."

"Fucking try it," I say, crouching slightly, prepared to run or fight.

He lunges at me again and I swing the frying pan hard. The pan collides with his face and the sickening crunch of his nose breaking fills the room. Blood pours down his face as he staggers back.

The man spits blood onto the floor and shakes his head. "You're going to fucking regret that."

He storms out of the kitchen, forcing his nose back into place. I take a deep breath, keeping the frying pan in hand as I walk over to the knives. I pull the largest one from the block, ready in case he comes back with some of his friends.

Footsteps echo outside the door before Davide enters the room with the man trailing behind him. Davide looks exhausted as he stops in front of me and crosses his arms.

"Really, Billie? You broke his nose?"

"Bastard was trying to assault me. You're fucking right I defended myself."

Davide sighs and pinches the bridge of his nose. "You know that any fighting has to be brought in front of Alessio. Let's go."

I glance at the man who tried to attack me before putting down the knife and the pan. Though I know it's a bad idea, I flip the man off before following Davide out the side door. As soon as the door is shut behind us — the man still inside — Davide turns to me.

"Really, Billie?"

"You already asked that," I say as I continue walking by him. If I have to meet with Alessio, I might as well get it done sooner rather than later.

"Don't you have a sense of self-preservation? Arturo is in the hospital. The fear of what he could do to the men isn't going to stop them anymore. In their eyes, he is as good as dead for the time being."

"Davide, I know what I'm doing. We both know that I could have killed that man if I wanted to. All I did was break his nose."

He falls into step beside me, tension rolling off his body in waves. "I know Arturo trained you to be as deadly as he is, but I don't need dead bodies while I'm acting consigliere. Please keep the violence to a minimum."

I shoot him a glare. "I'll do my best but I'm not going to let those bastards assault me because they think they can. And to be honest with you, if I hear of them trying to assault any other women, I'll kill them. I don't give a fuck."

Davide's eyes widen slightly, the familiar fear shining there. He shakes his head as we get into a car and drive toward Alessio's private office. He keeps his home and his office segregated from the main building of the compound, preferring to be as isolated as possible.

It's fitting for a man as cold and distanced as he is.

"Billie, you need to be careful." Davide's words are a warning that I doubt I will heed.

"I know you might mean well," I say, my tone cold as I cross my arms. "But like I said, I'll defend myself if *anyone* tries anything against me. You may be the acting consigliere and I appreciate the concern, but I can handle myself. And I'll kill if I have to."

Davide's mouth presses into a thin line and he grips the wheel until his knuckles go white. Every now and then, he looks in my direction before changing his grip on the wheel.

At least he's smart enough to know I mean what I say.

4

———

ALESSIO

I don't know what I'm going to do about Billie. The call about her fighting with Roman, one of the older capos, is enough to give me a migraine. I don't know what she's doing but this isn't the first time she's tried picking fights with people since she found out her father is in the hospital.

It's like the woman has a death wish just because her father is sick.

As I wait for Davide to arrive with Billie, I pace back and forth across my office. I'm going to have to deal with Roman as well, but if I don't pull Billie into the office first, then Roman will start shit with the other capos.

I have enough drama going on at the moment. I don't need Billie to start civil wars with my capos.

How the hell am I supposed to deal with her?

Especially when I agree with what she did. Roman has had a broken nose coming for a long time. He just picked the wrong woman to try and push his luck with. He should have known that Arturo taught her how to handle herself.

It's the first report of attempted assault for him, though,

and it will be the last. I may be lenient on some rules, but trying to sexually assault anyone is a death sentence.

"Davide, leave us, please. Go get Roman. I wish to deal with him next."

Davide nods and closes the door. Billie perches herself on the edge of a chair and crosses one leg over the other. She looks down at the ground, though I can practically feel the anger radiating off her.

A million different thoughts of what I could do to her right now flash through my mind.

Most of them involve spinning her around, bending her over my desk, and hiking that short dress up over her curvy hips.

Get your shit together. You can't think about her like that.

"Alright," Billie says, as she looks up at me. "I know that I shouldn't have broken that piece of shit's nose. I can't apologize to him, though. Please don't make me."

"Billie, you know how to conduct yourself. Why are you behaving this way? Do you have a death wish that I don't know about? I'm not a patient man and I'm not going to continue to allow this behavior from you."

She raises an eyebrow and shrugs. Her arms cross, pushing her breasts together. The low neckline would easily be pulled out of the way if I wanted to taste her.

I'm a fucking goner. There is no coming back from this. I'm going to an entirely different circle of hell for thinking about Arturo's daughter this way. Fucking my hand to thoughts of her is bad enough.

What's worse than hell? That's where I'm going.

Her green eyes narrow as she glares up at me. "Or what? You're going to kill me? For defending myself against someone who wasn't going to take no for an answer? I could have done a lot worse. I *should* have done a lot worse."

"He is going to be dealt with for trying to hurt you. I have a zero-tolerance policy for that shit and I will not allow it to continue. However, you have made a point of being defiant with a capo. I don't tolerate violence among the *famiglia*."

"He treats people he thinks are beneath him like property."

"That still doesn't excuse the way you are speaking to me," I say, my voice low as I invade her personal space. "You were raised in this life, and you know the expectations. If I have to beat them back into you, I will, but I really don't want to do that, given who your father is."

Billie scoffs and puts her hand on my chest, trying to push me back a step. "I know what the rules are. I'm sorry. It's been a hard week."

"Here's the funny thing," I say, leaning into her touch as my cock strains against my black pants. I keep it away from her, knowing that if I feel her body fully pressed against mine, I will lose all semblance of control that I have. "I don't think you are sorry. I think that there is a part of you that is craving the punishment. You want a reason to feel shitty about something else."

"You think you know me, but you don't. I don't crave anything." Her voice is slightly breathy as she looks up at me. Heat shines in her eyes and her fingers curl slightly against my chest. "I *am* sorry, though. I know that this is putting you in a difficult position. I shouldn't have spoken to you like that. Papa may be in the hospital, but I should remember myself."

"Tell you what," I say, already knowing that I'm in over my head with her. "In the privacy of my office, you can say what you like, and we will not have a problem. I understand that what is happening with Arturo is a lot and you need a place to vent. You can't take it out on the capos. I don't want to hurt you if I don't have to."

Thank you." She frowns, dark bags beneath her eyes and the exhaustion on her face. "But I'm not a rat. Venting to you is like signing my death certificate. These men already disrespect women. What do you think will happen if I come to you with my problems?"

"Then I will deal with them," I say. It should be obvious to her. "I'll keep you out of it."

She gives me a bitter laugh and shakes her head. "You just don't get it, do you?"

"Excuse me?"

"I'm not going to keep biting my tongue right now. You say that your office is a safe space to talk, so let's talk." Her eyes narrow as her gaze drifts up and down my body, lingering on my mouth for a little too long. "You've always been in a position of power with the *famiglia*. You were one of the heirs. You have money. You didn't have to be worried about being killed for breathing the wrong way. You could pay to take care of any problems you had. Or kill them. You never would have been brought into a meeting and told that snitching was the same as having a safe space to vent."

Scowling, I shake my head. "What was that little quip you said about not knowing you? I'm sure that the same applies here. Make no mistake, Billie, this offer is only being extended to you because of who your father is."

"And I will not be taking you up on that offer." Her hand flattens on my chest, and I know that she can feel my racing heart.

Being so close to her, hearing the sharp tone in her voice, as if she is barely holding herself back from unleashing everything that's on her mind, is a turn-on. I want her and I fucking shouldn't.

"You should think about what you're saying."

"I would rather die than sit here and vent to you. I'm not a snitch. You can take your offer and shove it."

There it is. Her breaking point. I've pushed her far enough that she's done playing nice.

Heat radiates between us as her gaze drops to my mouth once more. It is an invitation that is getting harder and harder to resist.

Especially when she looks at me like she wants to fuck me.

I exhale hard, knowing that I should take a step back. Instead, I press my body flush against hers.

"Billie, don't say shit you don't mean. Right now, you're tiptoeing across a very fine wire."

Her devilish smile is going to be my undoing. Billie leans back, the neckline of her dress pulling lower and showing me more of her body than I should see.

"I'm not saying anything I don't mean." Her tongue darts out to lick her bottom lip. "I happen to like playing with fire. And I could use a distraction right about now."

"That is not what this is," I say, my voice husky as I reach up to wipe a streak of mascara away from the corner of her eye. "I told you that you could speak freely in here. I know that you're going through a lot. But I'm not about to be a distraction for you."

She chuckles and hooks a leg around my hip, arching back and grinding herself against me. "Are you sure about that? You seem like you might like it."

As much as I want to push her away and tell her to get out of my office, I can't. I want her and she is offering herself to me, even if she is going to regret it in the morning.

Ever since she came back from university two years ago, she's been a wildcard. Every time I think I'm close to understanding what is going on in her head, she changes the game.

Maybe this is just another game for her. Distract me so she can do something when my guard is down.

I shake the thought from my mind as she moves back on the desk and hooks her other leg around me. The skirt of her dress falls around her hips as her toned thighs squeeze my hips. I groan, the last shred of self-control I have gone.

My mouth captures hers in a searing kiss as my hand closes around her neck. If this is what she needs to distract herself from her life, then I am more than happy to oblige.

She moans as my tongue tangles with hers. Billie fists my shirt and pulls me closer, as if there is a way to get rid of the non–existent room between us.

Her body is hot against mine and my cock throbs at her core.

My hands move up and down her thighs, fire igniting everywhere I touch. I groan as I grind into her.

Her little moans only drive me on as I grab her hips and pull her harder against me.

Billie's fingers sink into my hair as my teeth sink into her lip.

As I roll my hips, pressing my cock harder against her pussy, her legs tighten around me as she grinds onto me.

I kiss my way down her neck, sucking and biting on the sensitive flesh until she is writhing against me. Her fingers make quick work of my buttons, popping them open. She slides her hands over my shoulders beneath the shirt, her nails digging into my back.

It's only the sharp bite of her nails into my skin that reminds me who I'm about to fuck on my desk.

I jump away from her like I've been burned, buttoning up my shirt. Billie slides off the desk and combs her fingers through her hair. Her eyes are wild as she looks at me and her already full lips are slightly puffy.

Why the fuck did I have to pull away from her?

"I think that it's best you leave," I say, my voice gruff as I look at her. "My offer still stands, though. If you need to talk about what is happening with Arturo, my door is always open."

Billie shakes her head. "I think it's better if we aren't alone with each other again. I appreciate the offer, though. I'll do better with the capos, but I'm not promising not to break another nose."

I chuckle, though tension floods the room. "Thank you for that. Your punishment for speaking to me the way you did and causing issues with the capos is to clean the main house for a week. I want that place as clean as a hospital."

She winces and it's only then that I think about my poor choice of words. Billie shifts her weight from one side to the other before giving a sharp nod.

"Well," she says as she heads for the door. "I'm going to leave now. Thank you for not beating me."

The devilish smile that she gives me over her shoulder has all the blood in my body rushing south. I groan and adjust my cock before sitting on the edge of my desk. A few moments later, Davide walks into the room with Roman behind him.

"Roman," I say, reaching to the other side of my desk and pulling a gun out of the top drawer. "Let's go for a walk, shall we? I believe I have a lesson to teach you and the other capos about what will happen if you put your hands on a woman."

"It was that bitch's fault." He looks between me and the

gun with wild eyes. "I didn't do anything that she didn't want."

"Wrong fucking answer," I say, flicking the safety off the gun and aiming it between his eyes. "I was hoping to do this outside, but here works too."

The gunshot rings out as the bullet plants itself between Roman's eyes.

"Take his body and get rid of it. Make sure the capos know what will happen to them if any of them decide to pull a stunt like this," I say, barely glancing at Davide as blood drips down the wall. "And then call a team to get this cleaned up. I'm heading out."

Davide nods, already on his phone. I turn the safety back on before tucking the gun into my holster.

As I step over the dead body, I give it a final kick.

Nobody will fuck with Billie again after this.

ARTURO IS STILL WRAPPED IN BANDAGES AND ATTACHED to several different machines as I sit in the chair beside his bed. The steady beeping of his heart monitor is the only thing that lets me know he's still alive.

Seeing him like this is difficult. I may have killed all the men who are responsible for his state, but I still blame myself. He was out on a routine arms' run that he never should have been on. The lack of trust I have in my men — while proven to be a good thing — still got one of my best friends put in the hospital.

If I had been there, I might have been able to save him.

If someone else had gone on the arms' run, Arturo wouldn't be the one on the brink of death.

Billie wouldn't be driving me insane with her antics.

While I anticipated her behavior, I'm still not thrilled it's happening. I don't want to be the bad guy when she is already upset about her father, but she isn't giving me much of a choice.

It's hard to be the villain when I've known her throughout her entire life. I've seen the way she handles loss and pain.

The only difference is that Arturo isn't around to channel some of her angry energy into something more productive.

I'm out of my depth when it comes to her, and I don't know what I can do to help.

"You need to wake up soon," I say as I lean forward and cross my arms on the edge of the bed. "I need you to do something about your daughter. She is testing the limits of what she can get away with. I don't know what to do with her."

I leave out the part about dry-humping her on my desk and everything else I've imagined about Billie. Arturo doesn't need to know the things I would do to his daughter if I was given half a chance.

Guilt claws at me as I look at him, wondering how he would react if he knew something had happened with Billie. I doubt that he would think twice about killing me. Billie is the love of his life, and she always has been.

"You know, I had to get rid of Roman. I know you never liked him. He tried to go after Billie. You would be proud of her. She broke his nose with a frying pan."

I chuckle and drum my fingers on the bed. What else do you say to a man who is in a coma with a traumatic brain injury?

"She is going to be the death of me if you stay in this coma much longer. I told her that she had someone to talk to if she needed it, but if she's anything like you, she's going to bury that pain away."

I sigh, my shoulders drooping as I take in all the machines for the millionth time since Arturo entered the hospital. I'm paying for the best care that money can afford, but the doctors still don't know if he's going to survive.

"You know, if you don't make it through this, I promise to make sure that Billie is taken care of. She'll have a position of power within the mafia. I think she's earned it after all these years. She could become a consigliere if she wants it. Davide would be happy to share."

Though I think I know what I'll do to take care of her, I know that if Arturo dies, there will be no saving Billie. She is unpredictable and wild.

If her father dies, she will hit the self-destruct button and take down everyone in her path.

I'll do everything I can to keep that from happening. I owe it to Arturo.

5
———

BILLIE

I sit in the back of the car, glancing at Emilia in the mirror. She offers me a reassuring smile as we move through the line of traffic to Club 666.

The hair on the back of my neck stands up as I get the sense we're being watched. When I look over my shoulder, nobody is there. At least, nobody I can see.

We're in enemy territory. Paolo Marino is going to have men in the shadows, watching for any sign of trouble.

"Everything is going to be fine," Emilia says, turning down the radio. "You are dressed to kill and the men are going to be falling all over themselves to get a shot at you. You're definitely going to bring in way more than the minimum bid."

"I hope so," I say as I smooth down the material of the black silk slip dress I'm wearing. "I've spent the last week lying low since my meeting with Alessio."

Emilia shakes her head. "I still don't know why you thought that picking a fight with a capo would be a good idea. If you had just been quiet and kept to yourself, you would have drawn less attention to yourself."

I shrug and look out the tinted window at the people milling about in the street hoping to get into the clubs that lined it. "I told you. There was no way that I was just going to allow that man to put his hands on me. Breaking his nose wasn't the worst that I could have done. Besides, I got a proper chewing out from Alessio afterward."

"And now that you're following along with his punishment and acting like the perfect little mafia member, he really doesn't suspect anything." Emilia laughs and shakes her head again. "Sometimes I can't believe the things that you come up with."

"A girl's gotta do what a girl's gotta do to survive. I need to get out of here. He went easy on me and I'm grateful for it. I know that it could have been worse. That's exactly why I'm doing this. Why I'm trying to get out of this life. A woman shouldn't be punished for defending herself, even if the punishment is as simple as mine has been."

The car inches forward in traffic. Emilia pulls up alongside the curb, the Club 666 sign glowing neon pink against the dark night. She takes a deep breath and turns off the car before twisting to face me.

"Last chance," she says as I take out the invitation. "Are you sure that you want to do this? There is still time to back out. I'm sure that we could find another way for you to come up with the money you need to leave."

"I don't think there is." I pull out a small compact mirror from my purse and adjust my makeup. "Not this fast anyway. I'm going to do what I must to keep my papa safe. If this is the best way to do it, then that is what I got to do."

Emilia nods and reaches back to take my hand. She gives it a quick squeeze. "You call me as soon as you can and let me know what's going on. If anything happens to you, call me and I will make Davide come get you."

I laugh and squeeze her hand back. "Everything is going to be fine. You don't need to worry about me. I know how to take care of myself."

"I don't care." She gives me a stern look. "Promise me that you're going to call me if you need help. I don't want you to feel like you're trapped in whatever you get yourself into."

As I put away my compact, I squeeze her hand again. "I'm going to call you if I need to. I promise. I won't do anything stupid, and I know that you'll come get me if I ever get in over my head. It's only going to be two months, though. I'm sure it will be fine." I need to believe this.

"Stop dismissing the danger, Billie. You could die. You need to be careful with what you're doing. I don't want to bury my best friend."

"You're not going to bury me. I will call you as often as I can." I hope I get to do that much, at least.

"Good." Emilia's eyes water and she lets go of my hand to swipe away the tears. "I love you, Billie."

"I love you too." I give her a smile before opening the door and stepping out onto the sidewalk. "Thank you for this. You don't know what it means to me. I'm so lucky to have a friend like you."

Emilia waves a hand, already biting back more tears. I swallow the lump that rises in my own throat before shutting the door.

As I spin to face the club, I hold my head high. I'm walking into the lion's den, and I need to be prepared. Not only have I no idea what's waiting for me, other than being sold for two months, but there is a chance that some people could recognize me. This whole auction would be done for me if that happened. These people have to think that I'm Emilia.

If they don't, I'm dead.

I stride toward the door, my heels clicking against the cement. There are a few muffled protests as I pass several people waiting in line and head straight to the bouncer. The man crosses his arms, his biceps bulging as he looks down at me.

"Back of the line," he says, his voice gruff.

"I have an invitation," I say, reaching into my purse and pulling out the little black envelope.

The bouncer takes it and inspects the invitation before nodding to the man who stands just inside the doorway. The man nods to me and turns, disappearing through the first door that leads into the club.

I smile at the bouncer before following the other man into the club. There is one door that leads into the main club, the music pounding and strobe lights flashing. The man leads me to a small hallway on the right.

We descend a dark staircase lit only with warm red lights that glow along the roof. The man stops at the bottom of the staircase and pulls out a key, inserting it into a lock that I can't see on the black wall. Another door pops open and softer music escapes.

"In here," the man says, looking back at me.

I nod and follow him, the door closing behind me with a loud thud.

As we walk through this new part of the club, I try to take in all of my surroundings. Black suede booths surround the perimeter of the club, glossy black tables spread through the middle. Men and women in expensive suits and dresses are talking to each other.

Masks made of lace and leather conceal their identities as they move about the room and mingle. I glance at a few of the people, trying to figure out why they seem so familiar.

"Mr. Marino, she's here for the auction," the man says as we reach the other side of the room.

My breath hitches as I look at Paolo Marino. Though I knew he was the one running the auction, I didn't think that I would see him here. I was hoping that he would be nowhere near me if I'm being honest.

He is the one person who might be able to blow my cover. He's known me for my entire life, and once upon a time, he was close friends with my father and Alessio.

I tip my chin upward, trying to look more confident than I feel. "Hello."

"And who are you?" Paolo asks, smirking and crossing his arms. "I can't say that I remember sending you an invite."

"Emilia Bugia." I put on my best sultry smile and hold out my hand. "It's a pleasure to meet you. Thank you so much for inviting me to this event. It means the world to me."

It takes everything in me to bite my tongue and keep my smile in place as I face the man I suspect is behind my father's beating. I need to get into this auction and Paolo is what stands between me and my chance at freedom.

"Pleasure to meet you, Emilia," he says, drawing out the name. "I trust that you know the rules of my auction?"

"I've heard of them but I could use a refresher."

"Excellent," he says, holding out his arm for me to take. "Let's go into the room to get ready and we can discuss the rules while we're in there."

I loop my arm through his, feeling like I'm going to throw up. He leads me through another door to a room with a dozen other women wearing nothing but lingerie and heels.

"You're going to have to get changed. We have a

wardrobe over there if you didn't bring something of your own." Paolo nods to a clothing rack in the corner. "House takes a fifteen percent cut of whatever money you bring in tonight. You'll get the rest of the money in weekly payments until the end of your contract."

"And the contract is only for two months, right?" I ask as I drop his arm and rummage around in my purse for the lingerie I bought just for tonight.

"Just for two months, although if you wish to make any arrangements outside of that, it's between you and whoever buys you tonight." Paolo leans against one of the couches in the dressing room, his gaze roaming up and down my body.

The look he gives me is almost predatory.

Oh god, I hope he doesn't bid on me because if he is the one that buys me, I'm not sure that I'll be alive when the two months are up.

As if being at the auction in his club wasn't already bad enough.

If anyone from the Marchetti mafia finds out that I'm in Marino territory, I'm dead. Or at the very least, tortured for information. Hell, I'm sure that Alessio would be the one to do it.

I can picture it now, him towering above me as he pulls out my fingernails and demands insider information.

I take a deep breath, trying to calm my racing heart. I need to make it out of this night alive and with as few problems as possible. That means that I need to get out of my head and into the mind space of the woman who is willing to do whatever it takes to save her family.

"Get ready," Paolo says, standing up and hooking one of the thin straps of my dress with a finger. He pushes the strap down my shoulder, making my skin crawl. "You're going to have to sign several contracts before you go on stage and then there will be a final one once you are bought, outlining what you will be used for."

Used... I'm going to throw up.

"Alright," I say, trying to stop my stomach from tossing and turning as I look around for somewhere to change.

There is a curtain pulled across a small corner of the room. It's going to do little to hide my body from everyone else, but it's enough.

Paolo leans forward and kisses my cheek quickly before leaving the dressing room. Several of the other women in the room are glaring at me. I give them a polite smile before going to change.

This is going to be one hell of a night.

I hide behind the curtain, shimmying out of the dress and into the green lingerie that matches my eyes. I pull the garters up my legs and connect them to the slim gold belt that circles my waist.

As I stuff my dress into my purse, I try to take a deep breath. I need to convince myself that everything is going to be alright. If I don't, I know I'm going to get on the stage and freak out.

But I have to do this for me and for Papa. We need out, and this money will be our key to freedom.

I adjust the sheer emerald bodysuit over my body, making sure that my breasts are pushed up high, as I fight my instinct to run.

While I have no problem showing off my body, this is another realm of uncomfortable. I'm going to be showing off my body in front of a room full of strangers, dangerous people who want to purchase me.

I step out of the changing area and head to a small woman at a desk in the corner. She hands me and another woman a pile of paperwork.

"There's still half an hour until showtime," the woman says. "You need to go through this paperwork and sign off on all of it. You have until you sign the contracts to back out. If you don't sign the contracts or back out before you are called to the stage, then you will be barred from all future auctions."

I nod and accept the paperwork and a pen, finding a quiet corner in the room to read over everything.

Though everything about this auction is terrifying, there is a small rush of excitement that goes along with it.

For the next two months, I'll be a toy for someone, but I'll be building my way out of the mafia.

That thought alone is enough to make me feel like I'm walking on air as a woman leads us to the door to the stage.

However, as I stand at the end of the stage, the gravity of what I'm doing hits me like a runaway freight train.

In a matter of an hour or two, I'm going to sell myself to a man I don't know. I'm going to commit to spending the next two months with him, doing whatever he wants, when he wants it.

Ohgodohgodohgod! I think I'm going to throw up.

"Are you alright?" one of the other women asks, her tone hushed as a name is called over the speaker. "You look a little green."

I nod and take a deep breath. I just have to keep reminding myself that I'm doing this for Papa and my dream resort. I'm going to give us a chance to start over with our lives.

This is the only way to get what I need as quickly as I need it.

"I'm okay, thanks." I rearrange my curls, pulling some over my shoulder. "I just don't know what to expect. This is my first time here."

The woman gives me a sympathetic look. "Most of the men are going to want you to sleep with them. It will be required in the contract. You will have some room for negotiating. The men who run this club may be monsters, but they want women to keep answering the invitations. Advocate for yourself. Decide what you're willing to do and for how much money. The worst that happens is that the purchase will fall through."

"What happens if the purchase falls through?"

My stomach is tossing and turning as I look at the curtain that separates the dressing room from the stage. I bite my bottom lip, taking another deep breath as I try to calm my racing heart.

I just need to get through tonight without throwing up onstage.

"They don't invite you back and you're blacklisted for other auctions." The woman smiles as the first person is called to the stage. 'Don't worry, honey, everything is going to be fine."

I might have believed her. However, it's hard to think that everything will work out in the end when I'm standing at the lowest point of my life.

6

─────

ALESSIO

I HAND THE BARTENDER THE THREE THOUSAND DOLLARS I promised him before slipping inside the back door. Though his fee is high, the value of what I will be getting tonight is much higher. The music is pounding loud in the background as a man stands near a door hidden on a black wall, letting other men in.

As another group of men approaches the door, grinning and speaking amongst each other, I slide into the back of the group, nodding along like I'm listening to them, even though I'm trying to take stock of everything in the club.

People are milling about, doing laps around the entire place. They look like partygoers who are just searching for a table, but I catch a glimpse of a gun as one of them passes.

Paolo has this place filled with people who are ready to defend him. Coming here alone was a terrible idea, but it's one I'm committed to now.

The man outside the door lets us in. I follow them into another section of the club before breaking away. I keep my hands in my pockets and stay in the darkest parts of the room as I look around at the tables and people milling about.

"And now, it's time for our first woman. Lorelei is a petite blonde who loves to have a good time. If she isn't out at the club, she is partying on a boat. Bidding starts at two hundred thousand dollars."

I take a seat at one of the empty booths in the corner. A woman with a glass of champagne and a bidding paddle on a tray appears at my side. She puts the paddle down on the table before handing me the glass of champagne.

Her cheeks turn a bright red when I wink at her and hold the glass up in a silent salute. The waitress gives me a flirty smile before heading back to the bar.

Maybe that will keep her from trying to figure out who I am and running her mouth to her boss.

As more names are called and women walk across the stage, I take a look around, searching for anything that I might be able to use against Paolo. There are dozens of successful men and women spread throughout the club, but most of them are keeping to themselves.

Exposing the auction would make me more enemies than it would friends. The men and women here know what they are doing and what goes on in a place like this. If I were to out them in hopes of ruining one of Paolo's businesses, that would put me on a blacklist throughout Atlanta.

To my left, people are passing around a mirror with white powder, but none of them are connected to Paolo beyond being here to buy a woman. At least, not that I'm aware of.

"You should have seen her," Paolo says from somewhere behind me. I glance over my shoulder and see him sitting at a table a few feet away with a woman. "She's definitely not the kind of person we get in here often."

"Isn't she the daughter of that consigliere?" the other man asks, his voice soft. "You know that you're going to be playing with fire if you bid on her. Should Marchetti find out that she is spending time with you, both of you would be dead."

Paolo chuckles. "She will not just be *spending time with me.* She will be mine to do with as I please. And let me tell you, those two months will be spent with her on her knees."

The men laugh as my stomach starts to turn. If they are talking about me and a consigliere's daughter, Billie has to be here somewhere.

I fight the overwhelming urge to get up and go look for her. If Paolo sees me here, it will start a war between our people. Though, that is his goal to begin with.

If people are going to die, I don't want all their blood on my hands, though. I will not be the one to instigate the war.

Especially when I'm alone in a club that belongs to the enemy.

He would kill me before I finished standing.

Instead, I cross my arms and lean back in my seat, hoping that Billie isn't stupid enough to enter herself into something like this.

"Alright," the auctioneer says, his voice carrying through the room. "We have our last woman for the night. Emilia is a firecracker both in the streets *and* between the sheets."

I breathe a sigh of relief. Billie knows better than to come to a place like this. It's the one saving grace I have at this moment. I don't know what I would do if I saw her standing on the stage, wearing skimpy lingerie like all the other women had.

I might kill the first man to bid on her.

I'm about to get up and sneak out when the click of

heels against the stage draws my attention to the stage. My mouth drops open as Billie stands in the middle of the stage, looking like sex and sunshine at the same time.

Her blonde hair shines under the lights. The green lingerie she wears leaves little to the imagination. Men start bidding immediately, their paddles raising high in the air.

I can't tear my gaze away from her. All I can think about is sliding those garters down her long legs with my teeth. My cock hardens as I raise my paddle.

"Five hundred thousand," I say, lowering my voice an octave. I don't want Paolo to recognize me before I get Billie out of here.

"Our current bid is five hundred thousand. Do I hear five hundred fifty thousand?"

Paolo laughs and raises his paddle. "I'm willing to do just about whatever it takes to get that beauty into my bed."

I see red as I stand up and raise my paddle. "Two million."

It is more money than anyone else has spent that night, but it is worth it to keep Billie away from Paolo. It is also more than Paolo can afford to spend. His mafia is still new. He can't treat two million dollars as if it is nothing more than five hundred dollars.

However, my family is old money. They have been running things in Atlanta for decades. Two million dollars is nothing to me.

Especially when it means keeping her safe.

Billie looks around the crowd, her eyes wide. I'm careful to keep my face in the shadows, making sure that she can't see me as the auctioneer asks for more bids.

"Well, if nobody is willing to top that, then the beautiful Emilia is sold to paddle number eighty-one. Sir, please go through the red door on the left side of the room to begin contract negotiations."

I hurry away from the table and across the room before Paolo has a chance to see my face. I don't know how long the contract signing is going to take, but I need it to be quick. I follow a few other men and women through the red door to a room where a dozen desks are spread throughout, people sitting behind each one.

"Eighty-one?" a man says, standing up from behind one of the desks and waving his hand. "This way please."

As I make my way over to the desk, I wonder what the hell I have just done. Before I arrived at the club, Davide briefed me on the auction.

Two months where I'm contractually bound to another person. A person who is agreeing to do whatever I want, whenever I want.

Somehow, I have a hard time imagining Billie being willing to spend the rest of her life in lingerie.

That is your best friend's daughter. Get your shit together. She is untouchable.

"Is this your first time at the auction?" the man asks as he pulls out a small stack of paperwork. "I'm Geoff and I'll be guiding you through the contract negotiation."

"It's my first time, though I have heard that the women who are sold are obligated to follow a contract."

"They are. I will meet with you on your requirements for the contract, and then I will meet with the woman you purchased to go over them. She will deny anything that is a hard limit for her, but beyond that, yes. She will be obligated to do whatever is in the contract. You will be required to pay a fifty percent deposit before she is allowed to leave the club with you."

"That's fine," I say, pulling out my phone for the first

time that evening. I send a message to Davide, organizing the transfer of funds from me to Club 666. "Done."

Geoff hands me the contract. I flip through it, carefully reading each line. I wouldn't put it past Paolo to sneak clauses to benefit him in there. I fill out the page with what I expect Billie to do.

I keep my requirements neutral. Cooking for me once a week to give my chef a break, cleaning my home, working for my casino if asked. Living in my home for the duration of the contract Most of the tasks align with what I would ask of a maid or personal assistant.

Though I want her, I'm not going to sign a contract that forces her to fuck me.

If she ever does — and that is nothing more than a fantasy — then I want it to be on her terms.

The rest of the contract is straightforward, outlining what I can and can't do as well as what constitutes a breach of contract. I sign the last page as my chest constricts.

This is really happening. I bought Billie for two million dollars.

Two months of her by my side, tempting me every single day.

I'm about to hand the contract back to Geoff after signing it when I flip back to the requirements form.

Sex will only be had if she begs for it.

I don't know what depraved part of my brain compels me to write it into the contract. Perhaps it's the thought of her begging me to fuck her that excites me the most.

Billie has never been the kind of woman to beg. The thought of her getting on her knees and begging me to fuck her has my cock straining against my pants.

"Would you please tell her to meet me outside?" I ask as

I stand up and fix my suit jacket. "I have a call I need to take in a few moments and my reception is not good down here."

Geoff nods. "As soon as we are done, I will send her your way with two copies of the contract."

"Thank you, Geoff," I say, holding out my hand. He shakes it before sitting back down to review the requirements page.

I duck my head and leave the club, trying not to be seen by Paolo or any of his people in the process. I've already made it this far and I don't want to be caught now.

While I might not have gotten the information I came for, I'm going home with a much better prize.

This might just be the final straw that breaks the camel's back for her.

As I lean against the brick wall, watching the street, my cock throbs. Thinking about the way she would try to prove herself to me. She will try to play the game, but she isn't going to win.

In a few years, I have no doubt that she will be able to face down some of the most dangerous men and women in the world. She's smart and she's the kind of person who will do well in a life of crime.

She's the kind of woman who doesn't allow others to tame her. Wild and free is how Arturo has always described her. The docile young woman she presents to me most of the time isn't the person she truly is.

Others may not be able to tame her, but I'm looking forward to trying.

7
———

BILLIE

"This way," Geoff says, standing up after I've signed my name to the contract. "Please wait by the door while I make two copies of these. One will be for you and the other will be for the man who purchased you."

"Where is he?" I ask, proud when my voice doesn't waver even though it feels like my entire body is shaking.

It was too bright on the stage to see the crowd. I have no clue who bought me for the next two months or why they were willing to spend millions of dollars to do so.

"Outside. I'll take you out to meet him and then you're on your own after that."

I nod and try to take a deep breath as I stand up. My contract could have been worse. Even though the man is willing to pay an obscene amount of money for me, he wrote in the contract that I had to beg for sex if I wanted it.

There is going to be no chance of that. I don't want to sleep with a man who is willing to buy my time.

As I stand by the door, I keep trying to remind myself why I'm doing this, but nothing is chasing away the disgusting feeling that crawls through me. If there was another way to get the money as soon as I needed it, I would have done it.

However, this is the best chance I have.

I need to keep reminding myself of that if I'm going to get through the next two months. While the man who bought me might have written in a clause about sex, I'm sure that he will try to push it. Most men do.

"Come this way," Geoff says as he hands me both copies of the contract.

He leads me back through the club and out the front door to a sleek black sedan with windows tinted so dark I can't see inside of them. The back door opens and my mouth drops open.

"This is the man who bought you. Good luck, Emilia. You should see the first half of the money minus the club's cut by tomorrow morning."

"Thank you," I say, trying to ignore the way my heart races when Alessio's gaze drags up and down my body.

He looks at me like a man starved as I stride toward the car, trying to pretend as if I've never met him before. How he got into the club and through the auction without being recognized, I don't know. Security is tight, but here he is, without a gun pressed to his head.

"After you," Alessio says, standing to the side and gesturing to the car. "It's time to head to your home for the next two months."

I bite back the nervous laugh that threatens to bubble to the surface.

What does he mean? Will I be locked up? Trapped in the compound, away from the main house where most of the other members of the *famiglia* are?

I would be isolated from everyone I know.

At least I know what kind of person I'm dealing with.

Except this time, if I want to get paid, I'll have to let him control me. Own me.

God, how good it would be to be owned by him.

Stop that!

I duck to get into the car and slide across the leather seat. He follows and shuts the door behind him as the driver presses a button to engage the partition between the front and the back.

"Care to tell me what you're doing here tonight?" Alessio asks, his hand resting on the seat beside my bare thigh.

"I thought it would be fun to go home with someone for once. It's not as if I can bring anyone back to the compound ever." I shrug and lean back in the seat, stretching my legs out and crossing them at the ankles.

"And two months with a man who could make you do whatever he wanted seemed like a good way of getting what you wanted?"

I shrug, hoping he doesn't see through the lie. "It was as good a plan as any. See someone for two months, make a lot of money, and then I can carry on with my life."

"That was stupid, Billie. And you know it. Who knows who you would have been going home with if I hadn't been there?"

"Paolo Marino. He looked like he was doing his best to make sure I would be leaving with him."

Alessio sighs. "You make that sound like it would be a walk in the park. Paolo has always been a brutal man with a wicked imagination. The things he would make you do would make you question if you were even human anymore."

"I appreciate the concern," I say softly, trying to toe the line between assertive and docile. "But I knew what I was doing when I went into that club tonight. Paolo is no worse than the rest of the men in the mafia."

"And you think that's a fine way to live your life?"

I play with the hem of my dress. "It's the way I live now. I'm no stranger to brutality, Alessio. I've even killed my share of people."

He falls silent for a few minutes as we drive out of the city and down the winding road that leads to the compound. It's still nearly half an hour away by the time his hand lands on my leg, his thumb drifting along my skin.

Sparks ignite everywhere he touches, and I don't know what to think of it. The touch is casual from him. Almost caring even.

Though I know that would be going too far. Men like Alessio only care about themselves and their best interests.

I put my hand on his and move it off my lap. "We're not going to have a repeat of last time. That was a mistake."

He chuckles lowly, the sound sending heat flooding to my core. I clench my legs together, trying to ignore the way I ache when I hear his laugh. It's rare, but it fits him.

Smooth and sexy, like he knows exactly what it does to me and he's going to keep doing it.

"You seem to forget that you signed a contract stating that you would be willing to do whatever I want. Right now, this is what I want."

"Sex is not happening. I'm never going to beg for you."

He looks at me fully, arching an eyebrow. "I doubt that. You think I didn't see the way you pressed your thighs together? You think that I don't know that you're soaking wet for me. Hell, Billie, I bet you're thinking of the way my cock would stretch you to your limits right now."

My cheeks warm as I look at him. "That wasn't what I was thinking about."

But now it is.

He smirks, his hand climbing higher up my leg. He slides his hand beneath the hem of my dress, his fingers just grazing against my inner thigh. My pussy pulses at the thought of those fingers inside me.

"You didn't deny the rest of it, though. That's what I find the most interesting," Alessio says. "I'm going to be drawing up a new contract later tonight. A supplemental one to what we signed at the club. One that says you'll keep everything about this a secret for another half a million dollars."

My mouth drops open as he grazes a knuckle up my slit, pushing against the silky material of my thong. He leans back in his seat, the front of his pants strained by his cock. My tongue darts out to lick my bottom lip.

"See something you like?" he asks, his voice husky as he slides my thong to the side and slips a finger into me. "And for what it's worth, you might not be begging yet, but you certainly aren't complaining."

My eyes squeeze shut for a moment as he thrusts slowly, his thumb pressing against my clit with each thrust. "This is a mistake."

"If you want more, Billie, all you have to do is beg for it. Beg for me to pull out my cock and let you straddle my lap."

I look at him. "Not going to happen. We're not having sex."

"You're right. We're not. I said that I wouldn't have sex with you unless you begged for it. However, this doesn't count as sex unless you come. And guess what, Billie? You haven't been a good girl. You don't deserve an orgasm."

His fingers move faster inside of me, thrusting harder and deeper. I moan, rocking my hips to meet his thrusts.

When his thumb presses hard against my clit, my pussy starts to pulse.

"Like I said," he says as he withdraws his fingers. "You might be soaking wet, but you certainly don't deserve to come."

The car comes to a stop and the drivers get out. I hurry to adjust my dress, pulling it down just as the door opens. Alessio gets out of the car and holds his hand out to me. I scowl before putting my hand in his, playing the part that I'm expected to play.

"I'm not going to do anything to you from now on that you're not begging for," Alessio says as he holds my hand and leads me to the front door. "That was just a taste of what you're missing out on."

I take a deep breath, trying to slow my racing heart.

I can still feel his finger inside me. He plays me so easily that, in a matter of seconds, I was ready to come.

I knew these two months would be hard, but I had no idea I'd be fighting my own body and my craving for this man. Fuck.

I am so far over my head. Why did I agree to this?

My stomach is rolling as I count my breaths and try to pay attention to what's going on around me. I can't have a meltdown when Alessio is watching.

My entire body feels like it's on fire as he leads me through the tall wooden doors and into the front hall. I look around at the dark gray walls and white furniture.

Everything about his home is sleek and modern. It's not the kind of house I would expect a bachelor — especially one of his age — to live in. I was expecting to see furniture that didn't match and hadn't been updated in years.

In my head, there wouldn't have been any art or warmth

in his house, but the subtle wood accents and abstract paintings prove me wrong.

"Nice house," I say as I look around. "It's hard to believe with all the time that Papa has spent over here, I've never seen the inside of your home. Just your office and the main house on the compound."

"I don't like having people in my space. That's why you're going to be signing another contract that swears you to secrecy about this entire thing. If anyone asks what you're doing with me, you're to tell them that you're my personal assistant. Understand?"

"Yes."

"Good," he says as he makes his way to the kitchen. "Did you have anything to eat? I know when my father died, I had a hard time eating."

There is a sharp pain in my chest as I take a seat at the kitchen island and run my fingers along the butcher block countertop. "I had some lunch. Couldn't really eat before the auction."

Alessio nods and opens the fridge, digging around in it until he pulls out a box of pizza. "It's not much, but this is all I have right now. Taking over grocery shopping is going to be one of your tasks. My chef will write you a list tomorrow of everything you're going to need to get for him."

"Okay," I say as he opens the box. I grab a slice of pizza and take a bite. "This is the best pizza I've had in a long time. Thank you."

"You're welcome. I'm going to have a room prepared upstairs. As you know, I like my privacy. The only other people who work here are my chef, Rodrigo, and my housekeeper, Annette. You'll see both regularly and they will assist you with anything you don't know how to do."

"Alright."

Inside, I'm freaking out — It's going to be a lot harder to plan my escape when I have to live in his house. Hopefully, he is never home or wants very little to do with me.

The edging incident in the car was just a show of power.

He's testing me to see how far he can push me until I break.

I'm not going to let it happen, though. Getting through the next two months is the only thing that matters.

I finish my pizza and yawn. "Do you mind if I go to bed? It's been a long night."

Alessio nods and leads the way through the house to the staircase. "Did you bring anything to sleep in? You're going to be living here for the next two months."

"I could just live at my own house."

He shakes his head. "Not happening. If I need you to do a task for me in the middle of the night, I don't want to waste time trying to get in contact with you and then waiting for you to get over here. For the next two months, this is your home."

Even though I want to argue with him, I know there is no point. It is a clause in the contract after all, but it was worth a try.

Either way, going along with what he wants is the best way to keep suspicion off me. I play his game for the next two months, get more money than I've ever had, and then move on with my life.

It's a simple plan, but nothing in life is ever as simple as it seems.

"This will be your room," he says after we climb two flights of stairs. "You will be responsible for this area of the house at all times. The housekeeper will not be coming up here."

"Alright. Thank you." I look around the loft area.

Though there is no door to the loft, the room stretches into what looks like a studio apartment. There are two doors on the other side of the loft that I assume lead to the bathroom and closet. Large skylights line the sloping roof and even more windows line the walls.

In the morning, this room will flood with natural light. My bedroom at home doesn't have nearly as much space or light in it.

If this is where I have to sleep for the next two months, this might not be so bad.

The room is decorated much the same as the rest of the house, with dark moody tones and accents of white and wood.

"I'll be back in a minute," Alessio says, turning to head down the stairs. "Take a look around and let me know if there is anything you're going to want changed or added. I'll have my driver take care of it in the morning if there is."

His footsteps echo back down the stairs as I walk through the loft. I run my fingers along the white leather couch in the seating area and look up at the massive television. I get the feeling that a lot of nights are going to be spent up here watching movies.

There are bookshelves lining the wall with the doors and more books than I can count. I smile and walk along the length of one of the cases, running my fingers along the spines of the books.

When I peak inside the doors, I find a closet that's larger than my bedroom at home, lined with shelves and areas for hanging clothes. A massive island with dresser drawers sits in the middle of it all. Getting ready in here each morning is going to be like a dream come true.

I make my way into the bathroom, my jaw dropping when I see the freestanding tub in front of a massive window. The window overlooks the backyard, and the tub is a deep and long oval, giving me more than enough room to properly relax.

As I walk back out into the main room — already dreaming about the showers I'll be taking beneath the rainfall showerhead — Alessio walks back up the stairs.

"All I have is a couple old shirts, but this one should be fine for tonight. I'll send Beck with you tomorrow to collect everything you're going to need." He holds out a shirt and a shiny black card. "This is also a card for you. If there is anything you need while you're here, please charge it to this."

I raise an eyebrow as I take the shirt and the card. "Thank you. This is very kind."

"If you're going to be living here, I'm going to make sure that you're taken care of," he says, something a little off about his tone. His gaze rakes down my body before he looks away. "Well, I hope you have a good night. Get some rest."

It's the *get some rest* that bothers me the most. I know what kind of man he is, and it isn't the kind who gets someone an old shirt to sleep in. Alessio has never been the kind of caring man who would instruct someone to get some rest.

None of this is right.

"Thank you," I say as he turns and leaves the loft.

I wait until his footsteps on the stairs fade before heading into the washroom. There are enough toiletries stocked to get cleaned up before pulling on the shirt Alessio handed me.

The scent of his cologne still lingers in the material,

reminding me of the way the scent wrapped around me in the car.

My core aches as I get into the bed, relaxing back into the plush mattress. I grab a remote from the bedside table and hit a button that turns off the lights.

Left in the darkness, my mind races. Each thought keeps turning back to the way Alessio's hands felt on my body in the car. I can't get the feeling of his fingers as he pushed deep inside of me out of my mind.

My fingers drift down my body, teasing my nipples through the thin material of Alessio's shirt. I picture his fingers in place of mine, rolling the sensitive buds into stiffened peaks. I let out a soft moan as I picture the way his mouth would close over one nipple and then the other, taunting and teasing me until I was writhing beneath him.

He would lay me out on the backseat of the car, his hands still massaging my thighs as he nipped at my nipples. He would trace patterns across my collarbones with his tongue. I could feel his hot, wet mouth against my collarbone, sucking on the skin until he left his mark.

The thought of him marking me sends shivers racing down my body.

I dip one hand between my legs, sliding my fingers along my wet slit, imagining they're Alessio's. He would push my dress up around my hips, kissing his way down my body until his mouth covered my clit.

As my fingers swirl around the sensitive bud, I think of his tongue and the feeling of his rough hands on my smooth skin. He would grip my thighs, lifting my legs over his shoulders while his tongue teased me closer to orgasm.

I moan as I press harder against my clit, my fingers moving faster. My pussy pulses as I imagine Alessio pulling out his cock. I could see him stroking it as he looked down at me, groaning as he lined his cock up with my pussy. I moan as I picture him sliding his cock into me, stretching me as far as he could.

My orgasm comes hard and fast the moment I picture him driving himself into me over and over again, burying himself to the hilt.

I moan as I come down from my high before the guilt starts racing through me.

I just got off to the man who bought me for the summer. The man I'm supposed to hate for what he's done to my family. My father's best friend.

As I get up and make my way to the bathroom for a cold shower, I know that this is going to be a long summer.

I just need to do what Alessio wants and stop using thoughts of him as orgasm fuel.

8

———

ALESSIO

"I WANT YOU TO ADD IN A CLAUSE THAT ALL HER expenses will be paid for. I don't want her to have to worry about a thing while living here. She is to have access to her own account which will have a thousand dollars a week deposited into it. That will be in addition to the money that she will receive upon completion of the contract from Club 666."

I pace back and forth across my office. Leaving the house this morning had been hard. Last night, I heard Billie moaning my name. An hour in a cold shower later still had me wanting to sneak up there and make her beg for what she really wanted.

Leaving the house was the only way to put some distance between us.

I will get a little bit of a reprieve when I head to The Fortuna later today. There is business I need to take care of that has to be done there. It's been a couple days since I last checked on my employees.

While they are capable people, money doesn't launder itself.

There is no trusting anyone in a business like mine. Left alone too long, even people I think are loyal have the potential to turn against me.

"Alright," Mason says as he types in the clause to the new contract he is drawing up. "Are there any situations in which you would like to take this allowance away from her?"

"No. She keeps the allowance, even if the contract is terminated early. Her family is going through a rough time right now and I need to make sure that she is taken care of."

Mason nods. "Alright. Is there anything else?"

"I think that everything we've gone over this morning covers it. The contract will end on September first, the same day as the original contract. We've added in the secrecy clause and the lie that she is expected to tell. We should be covered from that angle."

"Alessio, I've known you a long time and I'm going to be blunt," Mason says as he finishes off the contract and hits print. "Arturo is going to kill you if he finds out that something is going on with his daughter. You know that the moment he wakes up from that coma, he's coming after you."

"Arturo may be a lot of things, but he isn't stupid. If he so much as thinks about killing me, then I will kill him first."

"And as your lawyer, I didn't hear that." Mason shakes his head and gets up to grab the contract from the printer. "Everything is ready. If you want to call her to the office, then we can get the paperwork signed."

"You better keep your mouth shut about this too," I say as I pull out my phone. "You and Billie are the only ones who will know the truth about what is going on. If I even hear so much as a rumor about me and Billie, I know where to look."

Mason nods and sits back down at the desk, going over the contract one last time. I find Billie's number and hit the call button, listening as it rings over and over again.

"Hello?" Her voice is raspy with sleep. "Sorry, I didn't realize it was so late in the morning. Is there anything I need to do? Beck isn't still waiting for me, is he?"

"No. I left Beck's number on the counter so you can call him when you're ready. I need you at the office to sign the new contract. Call Beck and have him bring you over here immediately."

I hang up and tuck my phone back in my pocket. As Mason reads over the contract, I pace over to the window. As I look out at the compound, I see several of my men training with Davide.

The problems with Paolo are going to come to a head sooner or later. Everyone who can fight is going to be training multiple times a week. This *famiglia* will not be going down without a fight.

I head over to the computer and pull up my schedule for the day. I have a meeting in three hours at the casino with a man looking to start an account with me. Arms and cocaine are his interests, and though Jovan, the leader of the cartel in Miami, recommended him, I still want to check this man out for myself.

Expanding the business is in my best interest, but not if I'm going to be doing business with a man who will turn against me.

Or is working for the cops.

Though the cops in Atlanta tend to turn a blind eye — at least the ones I pay do — they are still a concern. The federal agencies have been after my family for a long time.

The women in the *famiglia* are rushing around the

compound. Most of them are headed about their daily lives, taking care of children or on their way to their jobs.

When my great-grandfather first established the Marchetti mafia, he insisted that women would not be equal to the men. The pattern continued with my grandfather and my father. My brother, Enzo, had wanted to change the pattern.

Sadly, he didn't have the time.

I've been trying to change the way things work, but each time I do, I'm met with more resistance. Paolo Marino being the biggest irritant.

I'm going to have to kill him sooner or later.

Enzo wouldn't want me to kill Paolo. He would want me to find a way to save his friend. To make him see the way that things should be, instead of the way that things have been.

He would want me to do everything in my power to try and fix Paolo.

There is no way to do that, though. Paolo doesn't want to see the world change. He doesn't want a mafia where women are considered equal. He would rather kill people on sight and keep women silent — left at home to raise children and cook meals.

It's not what Enzo wanted and it's not what I want for my *famiglia,* but changing things is going to take more time. It can't be done overnight, especially with a man like Paolo lingering around the edges of my territory and pushing the boundaries of my patience.

"Mason, you used to work for my father. What did you think of his leadership?" I ask, turning to him and crossing my arms.

"Your father was a brutal man. He was cold and

detached with everyone. He killed first and never asked questions. He kept the mafia in line, though. When others tried to tear the *famiglia* apart, he kept it together."

"That isn't an opinion," I say as there is a knock at my office door.

"Your father was a man who led with fear. While I may not have approved on all accounts, there is no denying that a few of his methods were effective."

I nod, trying to digest that information to figure out what I think about it. Several times in the last few weeks, I have been told that I'm nothing like my father. The older capos like to throw it around as if it is some kind of insult.

I like to think of it as a compliment.

"Come in," I say, looking toward the door. It opens and Billie walks in, still wearing her dress from the night before. "Good morning. If you want to take a seat with Mason, he'll go over the contract with you."

"Morning," she says, her voice soft.

She makes her way over to the desk and takes a seat beside Mason. Their heads bend together, and he starts going over the contract with her. While Mason may be my lawyer, I know that he is going to make sure the contract is in her best interest as well.

He may have worked for my father, but he isn't interested in taking advantage of people the same way my father was.

I head out into the lobby, closing the office door behind me seconds before my mother storms in. Her head is held high, and she looks like she's ready to start a fight as she drops her purse on the couch and crosses her arms.

My father may not have held women in high regard, but my mother liked to give him a run for his money in the privacy of their home. She may be docile in public, but behind closed doors she has no problem pushing her agenda and running her mouth.

Some days, I think that I need to get my mother in line, but I'm the only one she has left now that Enzo and my father are gone.

It's why I allow her to push and pull the way she wishes.

"Who the hell is the little whore that was walking out of your house in that slutty little dress this morning?" she asks, her voice raising. "Alessio, have I taught you nothing? You do not allow random people within your personal space, and you certainly do not leave trollops in your home alone."

"Ma, what were you doing at my house? You're supposed to call me before you come over. You know that I'm rarely there."

She raises an eyebrow. "Don't take that tone with me, boy. I'm still your mother."

"And I am still the head of this *famiglia*. There are other people in this building and I'm only going to tell you once to remember your place." I stand taller and look down at her. "Don't worry yourself with who was at my home."

If she didn't recognize Billie, then she was still a good distance down the driveway. That's a saving grace. I don't need my mother to know that Arturo's daughter was in my house. It would only lead to more questions that I would never be willing to answer.

She nods once, though her arms are still crossed and her mouth is set in a thin line. Ma may not be pleased, but she is going to behave.

"There is nothing going on with that woman. A friend is in a tough position and needed a place for his daughter to stay while he travels for business. She's much younger than me, Ma."

Her arms drop to her sides and her frown deepens. "How are you ever supposed to find a wife if you have another woman living with you?"

I throw my hands up in the air. "Ma, I don't understand. First, she is a whore and now she is a problem?"

"Alessio, you need to think about settling down and starting a family. You're forty-three. Don't you think that it's time you get your life together? I'm not getting any younger and I want grandchildren."

I take a deep breath, trying not to explode. This is the same argument that we always have. I'm tired of going around in circles with her, but it seems to be all she wants to do.

"Ma, I appreciate your concern with my love life, but it's not happening. I have too much that I need to do. There isn't any room for a woman or a family in my life. Not for a long time if ever."

"It's always about business with you." Ma shakes her head and clicks her tongue. "I wish that you would learn that family is what is important in life. You think that these men will continue to respect you without a good woman at your side?"

"I don't need a woman to win the respect of the men. I'm their leader."

She grabs her purse. "You're going to regret not taking my advice one day. You need to find a woman to love you. Someone kind and understanding of the life you lead."

"And one day, I might find that, but right now is not that day. Now, if you'll excuse me, Ma, I have to finish with my meeting in the other room and then head to The Fortuna."

"You and that damn casino," she mutters as she turns and heads out of the office building.

As the door closes behind her, I groan and run my hands down my face.

The battle about a wife may be over for now, but I am far from winning the war.

9

____

BILLIE

I STARE AT THE TWO CONTRACTS ON THE DESK IN MY room. They've been sitting there for the last two days, a blatant reminder of the mess that I've gotten myself into.

I've been doing everything I can to avoid Alessio, which has not been very hard, since he's barely been home.

When I was at his office the other day, I asked for time to consider the contract. Alessio was kind enough to allow me two days to look it over and think about the new clauses.

While the allowance is nice, and keeping the secret would be easy, I keep wavering on the other line he worked in there.

Though Billie must beg if she wants sex, she is permitted — and encouraged — to initiate any other physical activity that she may want. However, while she is under the terms of the contract, she is not permitted to be with anyone else — man or woman. If there is something Billie seeks, she will come to Alessio Marchetti directly.

Two months with nothing but my hand and a couple vibrators to keep me entertained.

When Beck and I grabbed my clothes from my home

two days ago, I made sure to slip my vibrators into one of the suitcases. There is no way that I can survive two months of being close to Alessio and thinking of the way he turns me on without being able to get myself off.

I'll be damned if I go to my father's best friend and beg for sex.

Though I told him I needed time to consider that single clause, I know that there is no true consideration to be had. While the initial contract is going to provide me with more than enough money to start my life over, an extra five hundred thousand is nothing to turn my nose up at.

I would be able to do a lot more with both my dream resort and Papa if I agreed to the extra money.

With a sigh, I get off the couch and walk over to the desk. Opening the top drawer, I find a pen. My hand shakes slightly as I flip through the new contract to the final page.

After taking a deep breath and a moment to still my hands, I sign my name to the line at the bottom of the page.

Here goes nothing, I think as I grab the contract and head to the stairs.

I search the house for Alessio only to realize that he isn't here. There is no note about him working from his office on the compound or going out on an arms or drug run. That leaves the casino.

I'm not going all the way there just to leave him a contract.

After dropping the contract on the kitchen island — our standard place for leaving notes — I sit outside on the porch swing. I look through my phone at the notes I took while at the hospital with Papa last night. His doctor thinks that there may be some hope of him waking up soon, but there is no way to know for sure.

I had been able to hold in my tears until I left the

hospital last night. Beck was kind enough not to mention the tears streaming down my cheeks as we drove away. Instead, he turned up the music, playing one of my favorite songs, and drove me back to Alessio's house.

The early morning sun is already warm against my skin. The day will be scorching.

I scroll on my phone for a little bit, replying to messages from a few of my friends, before the heat finally gets to me.

That pool has been calling my name since I got here.

I race up to the loft to get changed before heading outside. The water is blue and inviting, shining beneath the hot sun. I smile and drop my towel onto one of the loungers before approaching the edge of the pool.

After adjusting the black bikini strings on my hips, I jump in. The cold water rushes up, cooling me off. When I swim back to the surface, a sense of relief fills me for the first time in weeks.

As I float on my back, staring up at the clouds, I try to let go of everything bothering me. I need a little break, to *not* think about everything going on in my life.

I close my eyes as I float, dragging my hands through the water and propelling myself through the deep end.

"There you are."

Opening my eyes, I see Alessio standing at the edge of the pool. He has his suit jacket slung over one arm and the sleeves of his gray dress shirt rolled up. My body tenses at the sight of him, imagining the way it would feel to rip that shirt open and trace his muscles with my tongue.

Down, girl. Nothing good is going to come out of lusting over Alessio.

His gaze drags along the length of my body, his jaw clenching. My entire body feels like it's coiled tense and ready to strike. As I look at him, all I can picture is his fingers pulling the strings of my bikini until the fabric falls away.

Get your shit together.

When he looks away from me, I swim to the other side of the pool and climb out.

I can't be around him when I feel like I'm going to get naked if he looks at me the right way. Before he can say anything else to me, I take off, needing a moment to myself to cool down. If he wants to talk about the contract, I need to have a clear head.

I hurry by him and into the house, heading straight for the kitchen. As I pour myself a glass of water, Alessio walks inside. He doesn't look at me as he heads up the stairs to his bedroom.

When he comes back out a few minutes later, he's wearing nothing but a pair of swimming trunks.

If I wanted to drag my tongue up his body before, I really want to do it now.

I take a bite of the apple in my hand, trying to keep my composure as he crosses his arms and stands in front of me. He raises an eyebrow as if waiting for me to say something but when I don't, he nods.

"Alright, so this is how it's going to be? I'm the big bad monster that you avoid for two days in a row? And then when I do see you, I get the silent treatment."

"I'm sorry. I was just having a snack. Got a little hungry while swimming."

He rolls his eyes as if he can see straight through the lie. "Join me in the pool. I want to talk to you."

"Do you mind if I finish the apple first?"

Alessio presses his mouth into a thin line for a moment. "You're going to be here for two months, Billie. While we are alone, I want you to speak to me freely. I don't want any of this cold and distant crap."

"Okay. Well then, I'm going to finish this and then I'll meet you out there."

Alessio nods and leaves the room, stepping out onto the back patio. I watch through the sliding glass door as he walks to the edge of the pool. I take in the way his back muscles flex as he raises his hands high above his head before diving it.

It feels like a pit has opened in the bottom of my stomach as I watch him glide through the water. My core clenches at the sight of him.

I never thought that I would be attracted to an older man, but there's something about the way he carries himself that's intoxicating. When Alessio steps into a room, he commands it. Everyone's attention is on him.

I take a few moments to finish my apple before heading outside. Alessio is still swimming laps as I stand at the edge of the pool and stare at the way his body moves through the water.

"See something you like?" he asks as he stops swimming to tread water. He runs his hand over his hair, slicking it back. "Get in the water, Billie."

I stare at him for a moment, the command sending a rush of heat straight to my core. If he keeps talking to me that way, I don't know how long I'm going to be able to hold out on begging him for sex. Between the way he looks at me and the way he bosses me around, he's wiggling past my defenses.

I can't let him. I have to see this through for the money. This is nothing but a stupid little crush powered by lust. Just do what he says and stop thinking about sleeping with him.

Easier said than done.

The water is cool as I jump in and swim to the surface. Alessio is still treading water, a few feet between us. He studies me with a strange look on his face before looking up at the clouds drifting across the sky.

"So, you graduated university a couple years ago," he says, glancing back at me. "What did you study there?"

"Business. With a minor in English."

"Why business?" He floats on his back, his eyes closed. I grab one of the inflatable loungers from the shallow end of the pool and climb onto it.

"I want to start a business someday."

He hums and drifts across the water. "What did you plan to do for the summer? Arturo mentioned that you used to do nannying, but you weren't interested in doing that again this summer?"

"I'm done with watching kids." I smile to myself as I cross one leg over the other. "I love them, but it's a lot of work. The money is good, but I would rather spend time doing something that would propel me forward in my career."

Alessio glances at me before ducking beneath the water. He swims to the edge of the pool and pulls himself out of the water to sit on it. "Our lie is that you're my personal assistant for the summer. Would you like to make that true? I have an internship available, and if you're looking to get into business, this could give you a leg up."

For a moment, I don't know what to say to him. It's the last offer that I was expecting from him. I didn't think that I would spend my summer doing anything useful to my career after I did the auction. I thought that I would be spending my summer doing everything that someone else wanted me to do.

Working for Alessio would be the chance of a lifetime.

The Fortuna is a well-known and popular casino. It brings in billions of dollars a year. I would hopefully get to make connections with other people in the business world while I was there.

It would be stupid to throw away an opportunity as good as that one, though being closer to Alessio is going to be a problem.

He already turns me into a horny teenager when he appears in my line of sight. Spending an entire summer working in an office and living with him is going to drive me insane.

The little crush will finally go away when I leave the mafia, though.

The job would only help me once me and Papa leave.

"I don't want to take away an internship from someone who has earned it," I say, though I want the internship. I don't want to be the reason why someone else loses a job they already lined up.

"The internship hasn't been posted yet. If you refuse, I'll be posting it on Monday morning."

I bite my bottom lip, trying to stuff down the nerves, before nodding. "I would love an internship."

"Good." Alessio stands up and grabs my towel from the lounger. "I've got another meeting to attend at the compound office. The chef is preparing dinner but you will be dining alone again tonight. Is the second contract signed?"

If he's going to a meeting at the compound's office, there is a shady business deal going on. One that I stay far away from.

I may already have enough crimes under my belt to be arrested for, but I don't want to add any more. Especially not when I'm about to be free from the mafia.

Stay out of jail. Escape without dying.

Though it's a short list, the tasks are hard to accomplish.

Just two months. Just two more months, and hopefully Papa will be awake and stable enough to move. Hopefully he listens to me this time when I tell him we need to move.

"Yes. I put it on the kitchen counter." I pull myself away from my thoughts to give him a small smile. "I think I'm going to stay out here for a while longer."

"I'll let the chef know to come get you once dinner is ready."

Alessio disappears into the house as excitement about the internship starts to course through my body. I couldn't ask for a better experience to get me prepared for running my own company.

However, the way that the opportunity fell into my lap makes me feel a bit suspicious.

Does Alessio know what I'm trying to do?

I roll off the floater into the cold water, trying to shock away the suspicion. There is no way that he knows what's going on. I've kept everything a secret.

Maybe he is just a man trying to do something nice.

While I don't necessarily believe that either, it's got to be closer to the truth than his knowing about my plan.

Everything is going to be fine, and if it isn't, all I have to do is run like hell.

As I get out of the pool, I make a mental note to find somewhere on the property to hide some of the money so I can grab it if things go wrong.

Though Alessio doesn't know what I'm up to, I need to be ready to leave at a moment's notice if he ever does find out.

10

ALESSIO

Monday mornings deserve their own circle in hell. Even though I've been working since I was fourteen — first for family businesses and then for my own company — they never feel any better.

It feels like I have to use all my willpower to drag myself out of bed. At least two cups of coffee have to be consumed before I can even think about heading to The Fortuna.

However, this morning is different. This morning, I wake up to the sound of Billie's screams echoing through the house.

Her shrill scream has me jumping out of bed and grabbing my gun. I flick off the safety and head downstairs, gun pointed at the floor. As I walk down the stairs, I'm careful to avoid the floorboards that squeak.

I don't know what is going on downstairs or who might be in my house, but I'm not taking any chances.

The shrieking turns into sobs. I turn a corner at the foot of the stairs and see Billie covered in blood and bent over a body in the front hall. Her shoulders shake as I turn the safety back on and tuck my gun into the back of my waistband.

Through the window near the front door, I see my security detail starting to circle the house. If there is someone at my house, they'll find them. Right now, I need to focus on Billie.

"What's going on?" I ask, my tone soft as I watch her try to give compressions to a man who is clearly dead. "Are you alright? You're covered in blood."

Billie doesn't answer me, trying to give the man breaths before starting compressions again. Blood continues to seep out of a gunshot wound, pooling onto the floor.

"Billie, he's gone. I'll call the doctor but you need to step away from the body. He's gone."

She looks at me over her shoulder, her glare chilling me to the bone. Billie says nothing as she turns her attention back to the man, still trying to save his life even though it's useless.

I step around the blood to get a look at the man's face. My stomach turns when I see the blank gaze of my youngest capo. His face is pale, though there's an old bruise still on his cheek.

"Billie, he's gone. You need to let him go. I'm going to call the doctor and he will come to get the body. I'll make sure that he has a proper funeral, but you need to *let him go*."

She ignores me again, still giving CPR. I sigh and pinch the bridge of my nose. I don't know how to help her right now.

"He's not gone," she says, her voice a little more than a growl. "I felt a pulse. He's still alive."

I know she's wrong and there is nothing that she is going

to be able to do about it. No matter how many times I tell her that he's gone, she's not going to believe me.

As she continues compressions, I send a message to the doctor. I won't be able to bear the look on her face if I don't. She'll be crushed to think that I didn't do everything in my power to get someone here to save him.

I can't hurt her like that.

It doesn't matter that he's already gone.

"The doctor will be here in a minute but I'm going to get Davide to take over compressions. The doctor can't see you here and you need to get clean."

Davide walks through the front door as I'm talking and looks down at the body. "There's no sight of who did this outside, but the others are going to scour the compound."

"Good, take over compressions."

Davide raises an eyebrow, his mouth opening slightly. I shake my head before he has the chance to say what we both already know.

"The compressions need to be done until the doctor gets here and can get him to the hospital," I say as Davide kneels beside the body and gently takes over from Billie.

She sits back on her heels, looking lost.

My heart aches for her as tears run down her cheeks. Though I might not remember the man's name, I remember seeing him grow up. He was Billie's best friend, and I was sure that at one point Arturo told me that they were dating.

I couldn't imagine being in her position in that moment. I've seen people I love die, but I was turned off to the emotional impact when I was young. My father made a point of beating it out of me, making sure that his son would never show weakness.

Arturo was a kinder father than mine ever was.

"Come on," I say, leaning down to wrap an arm around

her waist and pull her to her feet. "You need to come with me. We have to get you cleaned up. I promise that Davide is going to take good care of him until the doctor gets here. You have to come with me, though."

Davide looks at me over his shoulder before his gaze darts to Billie. I can see the question there, but it's one that I'm going to do my best avoiding.

"This is between us, and you aren't to breathe a word of it to anyone," I say to Davide as I pick Billie up. She buries her face into my shoulder, her sobs soaking my skin.

"Yes, boss," Davide says.

Billie continues crying as I carry her up the stairs. She takes deep breaths, trying to calm down, but each time she nearly gets a hold of the sobbing, it starts all over again.

"It's going to be okay," I say as I carry her into the loft.

She doesn't fight me as I place her on the edge of the bathtub and crouch down in front of her. I run my thumbs beneath her eyes, trying to wipe away some of her tears but they just keep coming. I don't know how to help her and it's tearing me apart inside.

There is nothing I can say to her that is going to ease the pain that she's feeling right now. She needs Arturo here. He always knew what to say when things were going wrong. He would be the one to calm her down and get her cleaned up. He would make sure that his daughter was taken care of.

He's not here, though, and he will never forgive me if he finds out that I left his daughter to suffer alone.

He won't forgive me for the thoughts I have about his daughter either — though I have no intention of ever letting him find out about those.

"We need to get some of this blood off you," I say as I stand up and turn on the shower. The water cascades down, steam fogging up the glass that surrounds it.

Billie grips the edge of the tub like it's the only thing keeping her connected to this world. I stare at her.

I'm going to have to drag her in there and hope that the water breaks her out of her state of shock.

I take the gun out of my waistband and set it on the counter. Though her sobs stop, tears still stream down her cheeks as I help her to her feet and guide her into the shower. Her hands grip my forearms as I back up into the shower, stepping beneath the spray and bringing her with me.

Pink water coats the tiles, heading for the drain. Billie looks at me, her blonde hair hanging in her face. I push the hair away from her face and grab the shampoo. I squirt some into my hand before working on the blood staining her hair.

The suds turn pink as I try to get as much blood out of the strands as possible. Once I'm done with her hair, I work on her arms, taking my time to massage the soap into her skin.

"He's dead," she whispers as she blinks slowly. "Matt is dead."

Matt. I have to remember that name.

"I'm sorry," I say softly as I pull her soaked shirt over her head and toss it into the corner. I try not to look at the way her lace bra hugs her breasts. My hands ache to touch them, but now isn't the time. "I know he meant a lot to you. I'm going to find out who did this to him and I'm going to make them pay."

I don't bother to tell her that I know who did this. It would only upset her more.

Instead, I help wash the blood from her body before getting her changed into a soft pair of pajamas. She doesn't say anything else to me as I put her in her bed and sit on the edge, working a towel through her hair.

I grab a comb from her nightstand and untangle her hair, waiting for her to say anything to me. Her gaze is a million miles away as I finish with her hair and put the comb away.

"I have to go see if Davide has pulled any footage from the cameras. If you need anything, call for me or get the housekeeper and she will come find me, alright?" I stand up and bend over in front of her, trying to get her to look at me.

When she does, there is nothing but a haunted look in her eyes. Though I know that this isn't the first time she's seen death — not even close — this death is hitting her hard.

I don't know how to make her feel better. If I could take away even a little of her grief, I would, but since I can't, the best I can do is make Paolo pay for what he's done.

After watching Billie for a moment longer, I walk to the stairs. When I glance over my shoulder, she is disappearing beneath the covers. I sigh as I walk downstairs, wondering if I am completely fucking up her life.

If I didn't make her live here, she might not have seen the dead body of the boy she used to love. Hearing about his death would have been easier than trying to save an already dead man.

Guilt gnaws at me as I head back to the body. While I do have to check with Davide about the security cameras, I need to know if Paolo left any clues on the body.

"Is the doctor here yet?" I ask as I enter the front hall and see Davide watching security feeds on his phone.

"Yeah. He's outside and waiting for the okay to move the body."

"He'll have it in a minute," I say as I crouch beside the body. My stomach lurches as I look down at the dead young man.

Seeing the people I'm supposed to protect end up dead

is never easy. I don't know how my father or brother were able to grow so cold and numb to it.

I run my hands over his body, feeling for anything that might be in his pockets or clothing. There is something hard in the pocket of his jeans that catches my attention. I reach into it and pull out a piece of paper that's been folded into a tiny square.

When I unfold the paper and look at it, the world stops.

"How the hell did he get this here without anybody noticing?" I ask as I look up at Davide. "You better find something. I'm not going to continue playing this game with him."

I stand and walk into the kitchen, the paper still in my hand. I lean against the counter and look at the picture printed on the paper again. My head hurts and anger courses through me. When I find Paolo, I'm going to make him pay for everything that he's done.

I crumple the picture of Billie sleeping last night and tuck it into my pocket. The red writing that is scrawled across the picture is burned into my mind. Paolo wants to claim her as his. He wants to make our war into a game with Billie as the prize.

It's not going to happen. There is no way that I'm going to let Billie ever be with that man.

She's mine.

11

BILLIE

THE WHITE STONE EXTERIOR OF THE FORTUNA looms above me as I stand on the bottom step and look up. I take a deep breath, trying to calm my nerves. It's been a long few days and pulling myself together this morning took more effort than I ever wanted to admit.

Seeing Matt's dead body two days ago had been too much. I was sure that it was going to be the moment that broke me. I still feel horrible for not being able to save him. I could still feel his blood coating my hands as I gave him compressions over and over again.

Though I knew he was dead as soon as I saw him, I never would have forgiven myself for not trying to save him.

He was my first love. Our relationship ended on good terms years ago. We still spoke to each other every couple of months. I was at his wedding.

Now, he's gone, and I have to figure out how to go on with my life without one of my best friends.

Except I already know how to go on. I have to stuff my emotions far beneath the surface and hold my head high. I have to walk into The Fortuna and pretend that nothing is wrong, despite the fact that my entire life is falling apart.

You can do this. Working with Alessio is going to be good for your career. You just have to hold yourself together until bedtime and then you can throw yourself a pity party.

After taking another second for myself, I walk into the casino with an easy smile on my face. I glance around, taking in the expensive white stone floors and black marble walls. Gold accents surround me, making the otherwise basic color scheme pop.

Everything about the casino screams wealth. From the high-end machines to the staff who are all walking around in designer suits and cocktail dresses. It's clear that no expense is spared when it comes to giving the clientele a luxury experience.

"Pardon me, miss, is there anything I can do to help you?" a man in a pale gray suit asks.

"Actually, yes, thank you." I smooth my hands down the sides of my black pinstripe pants, trying to dry the sweat from my palms.

There is nothing to be nervous about. This is just going to be another job.

Except this job comes with a boss who makes me think about the way it would feel to have his hands running over every inch of my body.

It has the kind of boss who makes me want to get bent over a desk and have my hands tied behind my back with a tie.

"I'm here to meet with Alessio Marchetti. I'm his new assistant."

The man smiles and holds out his hand. "Carson Danvers. I'm the general manager of the casino. I was told to be on the lookout for you, but nobody warned me that you would be so beautiful."

His smile turns predatory as his gaze rakes over my body. I bite my tongue and fight to keep the smile on my face. I need to make a good impression here.

Working at the casino is good for my career. I need the experience here to help me when I start my own resort.

"Right this way," Carson says, grinning as he puts his hand on my lower back and tries to steer me toward the elevators. "You know, there's a great little club that just opened up recently. You should go with me. I'd be able to show you a good time."

"No, thank you." I keep my tone cool but polite, trying to diffuse the situation the best I can. "I have a lot going on in my life right now and I don't have much time for going out."

Carson frowns and shakes his head. "Do you not know how this works? I'm the manager and if you want things to go your way, you'll think twice before turning me down."

A throat clears behind us. "She said no."

I look over my shoulder and see Alessio standing there with his arms crossed. His button-down shirt is taunt across his biceps. Heat floods to my core as he glares at Carson. There is something about the way he looks when he's angry — like he will do anything to defend me — that turns me on.

Maybe it's the fact that we both know I can take care of myself but he is giving me the option of allowing someone else to take care of me that has my pussy pulsing.

The protective side of Alessio is far more of a turn on than I ever thought it would be.

"Sir," Carson says, stuttering over the word slightly as we turn to face Alessio.

"No need to say more," Alessio says, his tone dark as he

glares at Carson. "You're fired. I will not have you treating other staff members or the clientele in such a manner. I've listened to you from the moment that Billie walked in and all you have done is set a terrible image for the company."

"Sir, please. It wasn't what it looked like."

"Mr. Marchetti," I say, not sure how formal to be with him at work. "There is no need to fire Carson. Everything is fine and I'm not upset."

Alessio raises an eyebrow as he looks at me. "The final decision is mine. I have zero-tolerance policies surrounding this kind of behavior. Carson, security will escort you to the staff lounge to gather your things."

I watch as a security guard peels himself from out of thin air and appears beside Alessio. Carson hangs his head and walks with the security guard to a door behind the front desk.

Alessio scowls and reaches forward to press one of the buttons for the elevator. When the doors slide open, he still says nothing, waiting for me to get on.

The ride up to his office floor is silent and filled with tension. When the doors open, he leads the way through the open office area. My heels click against the pale wood floor as I follow him to the opposite wall. He stops in front of a towering glass door and opens it, holding it for me to step inside.

"This will be your office," he says, his voice gruff. He crosses his arms and jerks his chin at a door to my right that's nestled between two windows. There are curtains drawn across the window so I can't see inside. "And that's my office over there."

"Nice office," I say, running my fingers along the top of the dark wooden desk. "You know, you really didn't have to fire Carson. He was being creepy and definitely crossing a line, but I'm not going to make any friends by getting the general manager fired on my first day here."

Alessio closes the door behind us before taking a step toward me. "Why are you defending him?"

"I got someone fired on my first day here. He might have deserved it for being a creep, but one conversation with me wasn't enough to go on."

Alessio walks closer, forcing me to step back until I'm trapped between his body and the desk. Heat flows between us and pools in my core. I stare up at him, watching the way his gaze drags down my body and settles a little too long on my mouth.

"It was more than enough to go on. I have a zero-tolerance policy with my staff and harassment. Which is what he was doing."

"Funny that you seem to care so much here, but when we're at the compound you don't give a shit."

Alessio's nostrils flare as he invades my space entirely. The look in his eyes is deadly while the scent of his cologne is intoxicating. Everything about Alessio is dangerous and I hate that it excites me.

I hate the way he makes me feel like I'm walking into an inferno and loving every minute of it. I hate that a single look from him can soak my panties.

Most of all, I hate the way I allow him to see me fall apart.

I give him too much power in my life.

"Let's get this straight right now," Alessio says, his tone low and dark. "You are not to mention our lives outside of the casino. I do not want my businesses to be more entangled with each other than they already are."

"Says the man who uses his casino to launder money."

Alessio's hand wraps around my throat. My pussy

clenches as I picture him thrusting into me while tightening the grip on my throat. My core is slick against the silk material of my underwear.

For just a brief moment, I consider closing the distance between us. My heart pounds against my ribs and I grip the edge of the desk, trying to keep myself steady.

Something snaps in Alessio when his eyes lock with mine.

"I told you to watch your mouth," he says, his voice a growl that sends a shiver down my spine. "You never fucking learn."

One second, he is just a man trying to intimidate me, and the next his mouth is on mine and his hand is flexing around my throat.

I moan into the kiss as his tongue tangles with mine. He nips at my bottom lip as he unbuttons the blouse I'm wearing. His hands slip beneath the fabric to cup my breasts through the lace bra.

My back arches as he runs his thumbs over my nipples, teasing them until they are stiffened peaks.

"I'm going to teach you what happens when you don't want to be a good girl and listen to me."

"I thought you said that you weren't going to fuck me unless I begged you too," I say, breathless as he sucks on the sensitive skin at the base of my neck.

"This isn't fucking you, Billie, but if you want me to bend you over that desk and bury my cock in that tight little pussy of yours, then you're going to get on your knees and beg for it."

"Not going to happen."

He chuckles, sliding the shirt off my shoulders and letting it fall to the ground. Alessio makes quick work of the bra clasp, undoing it and dipping his head down to suck a nipple in his mouth.

My fingers weave through his hair, pulling him closer to me as I arch my back. He teases the other nipple between his fingers, sending a cloud of lust through my body. I moan as he switches sides, biting and flicking his tongue until my hips are rocking forward into him.

I'm aware that someone could walk in and catch us, but it only turns me on more. Knowing that we could be caught at any moment — that he's willing to risk it to fuck me — has my pussy aching for relief.

Alessio pulls away from me, taking a step back. "Take off your pants."

"I'm not going to do that," I say, wanting to see how far I can push him before he takes control again.

"I said, take off your fucking pants, Billie. If I have to be the one to come over there and do it for you, then I'll tease you until you're on the edge. I'll make you fucking desperate to come for me every single day this summer. And then, just when you think that you're finally about to get some relief, I'll leave you high and dry."

"And how does that benefit you?" I cross my arms, pushing up my bare breasts and grinning when his gaze drops to them.

"I can still go out and fuck whoever I like after."

I shrug, smiling as I feel wetness coating my thighs. "I could do the same. Hell, I could finish myself off."

Alessio glares at me. "Not if I tie you to the bed and leave you there. Last chance, Billie. Take off your pants or I'm going to make you wish that you had behaved."

I slowly run my hands down my body, rolling my nipples between my fingers. My core clenches at the lust that shines in his eyes as he watches me unbutton my pants and slide them down my legs. I leave the heels on as I perch myself on the edge of my new desk.

The wood is cool against my ass as I spread my legs. Alessio arches an eyebrow and grabs one of the chairs in front of my desk. He pulls it over and sits down, leaning back and watching me.

"I want you to tease your clit," he says, his voice gruff as he undoes his pants and pulls out his hardened cock.

Fuck, I want that in my mouth.

I swirl my fingers around my clit as he grips his cock. His hand slides up and down the length, his thumb swirling over the head. I picture my tongue tracing the same path as his hand as I move my fingers faster against my clit. My pussy starts to pulse as I lean back and brace myself with one hand against the desk.

Everything about this feels wrong, but it only makes my pussy that much slicker.

"Put your fingers in your mouth and taste yourself," he says as he tightens his grip on his cock. "Show me what a filthy little whore you really are."

I stare at him for a minute, my mind short-circuiting at the way he speaks to me.

"Billie." He gets out of his seat and shoves my hand out of the way, plunging two fingers into me and massaging my inner walls. He pulls his fingers out and holds them to my lips. "I told you to taste yourself. Lick my fingers like you're going to be begging to lick my cock."

My tongue darts out and swirls around his fingers, tracing the seam between them the same way I plan on tracing the vein that runs the length of his cock.

"Beg for it, Bille. Beg for me to slam my cock into you. We both know you want it."

I want to tell him that this is wrong and that we should

stop, but I want it too much. Alessio has been the source of my wet dreams for far longer than I would ever care to admit. He's been the one I've pictured slamming into me from behind or shoving his cock down my throat for years.

"Please fuck me," I say, begging in a voice that I barely recognize as my own. "Please fuck me. I need your cock."

Alessio chuckles and weaves his fingers through my hair. He pulls me to him, his mouth colliding with mine in a searing kiss. My core clenches around his fingers as he thrusts into me. He rocks his fingers deeper and deeper as he bites down on my lip.

"Be a good girl and come for me," he says, crooking his fingers.

He pulls my hair, forcing my back into a deeper arch. I bite down on the moan that threatens to escape me. There is no way that we can get caught before I get to feel his cock stretching me.

My legs shake as my orgasm comes hard and fast. Wetness soaks his hand, and he keeps thrusting his fingers into me, drawing out my orgasm for as long as possible.

"Stand up and turn around," he says, stepping back slightly and gripping his cock.

I hurry to turn around, bending over the desk and arching my back. Alessio groans softly as his hand sinks into my hair once more. He pulls my head back with one hand and grabs my hip with the other as his cock slides into me.

Alessio rolls his hips, sinking himself deeper until he's buried to the hilt. My pussy pulses around him as he starts to thrust. His hard cock fills me in ways I didn't know possible, stretching me to my limit.

The desk bites into my hips, creating a slight pain that only adds to the pleasure.

Alessio rocks his hips faster, thrusting harder and faster

as his cock starts to throb. His grip on my hip is bruising as my pussy clenches down around him.

"That's right, Billie," he says as he slams into me. I hear a crash as something falls to the floor. Moaning, I push back onto his cock as he pulls out completely before slamming back into me. "Milk my cock with your tight little pussy."

His hand leaves my hair to slide around my body. His fingers press against my clit and it's all it takes to send me over the edge. Alessio groans, thrusting faster as I come on his cock.

"Turn around," he says, pulling out of me. "And get on your knees."

I do as he asks, running my hands up his thighs before wrapping one around his cock. He pulls my hand off his cock before taking both of my wrists in his hand. Alessio holds them above my head as he shoves his cock into my mouth.

I hollow my cheeks and try to keep up with him as he thrusts, his cock throbbing. He rocks his hips, driving himself to the back of my throat as he comes.

When he pulls out, he looks down at me and shakes his head. His eyes are wide as he takes a step back and tucks his cock back into his pants. My tongue darts out to lick my bottom lip as he seemingly pulls himself together.

"I'm sorry. I shouldn't have done that. I lost control. It was a mistake and it's not going to happen again." Alessio clears his throat and looks at the broken picture frame on the ground. "Once you're dressed, clean that up and then I want you to look through the calendar and prioritize my meetings and events for the next two weeks. Send it to me when you're done."

He doesn't look back at me as he strides over to the door to his office and disappears inside.

I take a deep breath and fight the tears that threaten to fall. Though the sex was the best I've ever had, I know he's right and that it can't happen again. Our relationship is complicated at best.

While he may be the only man who seems to know my deepest fantasies without me telling him, it's not going to happen again.

It would have been one thing to call fucking in his office a mistake and then instructing me to get to work. I could have handled that. I know that we shouldn't fuck. That my father could kill Alessio if he ever found out.

The apology is what cut deep.

All it translated to was that I'm not good enough for a man like him. That he's sorry he ever took it that far with me.

My stomach tosses and turns as I get dressed before stooping to clean up the glass. I pick up the picture that had been in the broken frame, turning it over to see a young Alessio staring up at me. Beside him is my father, both men laughing like they've just heard the best joke in the world.

As I toss the glass into the garbage can, I can't stop thinking about what I've done.

Though I can't bring myself to regret the sex or the way I feel about Alessio, I can't ruin his friendship with my father. Especially when I'm only here for another couple months before I leave.

I just have to keep my head about me for the next two months and then I can move on with my life.

12

———

ALESSIO

"How did the strike go?" Jovan asks, his voice raspy on the other end of the call. "Did you do enough damage to deter the little shit?"

I chuckle and lean back in the seat of my car. "I've heard that it went well but I'm on my way there now. Paolo's largest importing ship sank, but several of his men and two of mine are dead. Davide is organizing a team for the recovery of my men's bodies, but it should still be a few hours yet. We have to steer clear while the coast guard launches their investigation."

The car comes to a stop at the edge of a pier. The driver drops the partition and I lean forward to look between the seats and out the front window.

"Looking at the wreck now," I say, watching as Paolo stands on another pier, pacing back and forth while shouting at someone. "Paolo is here as well. Angry. He's going to strike back soon, and I have no doubt that the loss of life will be even greater."

"Have you thought about getting in contact with Christian Herrera?"

"I thought he was still laying low in Colombia for now?"

"It's been years since he went down there. When he heard that Paolo was setting up camp in the no man's land your mafia and his cartel have between Nashville and Atlanta, rumor is that he came back."

"How reliable is this rumor?" I ask, though I'm dreading seeing Christian again. We've been tentative allies at best. He stays out of my way and I stay out of his.

"Well, I was speaking to him yesterday," Jovan says. Something bangs in the background, and he sighs. "I swear Hadley is doing everything she can to annoy me today."

I laugh and roll my eyes. "She is a little spitfire and you do have your hands full. How are mama and baby doing?"

"Still a few months left, but she's started the nesting period. If I have to rearrange the house one more time, I'm going to go insane."

"But you would do it anyway. I've never seen any man so whipped in my life." My tone is teasing as I motion to the driver to leave the scene.

The last thing I need right now is the authorities approaching my car and sniffing around in my business.

The driver presses a button and the partition slides back into place. I run my hand through my hair as Jovan shouts something I can't quite hear to Hadley in the background. I hear something that sounds a lot like *fuck you* and start laughing.

"So, her temper is still going strong," I say, grinning as I shake my head. "You're going to have your hands full soon. I'm willing to bet that your child is going to be a little replica of Hadley."

"Heaven help us all," Jovan says, though I've never heard him sound happier. "You know, one of these days, you're going to find a woman who is going to wrap you around her little finger and there's going to be nothing you can say or do to prevent it."

There is no way that I'm going to tell him that woman already exists. Admitting that Billie has me wrapped around her finger — especially when I should be staying away from her — is only going to get me in trouble.

Although, the trouble might be worth it for the sex we had. Guilt still gnaws at me for fucking her in my office, but I can't bring myself to regret it.

I want her.

I groan and tilt my head against the back of the seat. "I don't need that in my life right now. With all the shit that's going on, I need some time to get the business under control before even thinking about allowing another person to get close to me."

"Alessio, I know that you've been through some shit, but it's time to move on with your life. You're allowed to be happy."

"How about we talk about Herrera instead. You said that Christian had come back because Paolo was moving back into his territory. Does that mean that Paolo is recruiting from his territory and mine?"

"Good to know that you aren't just a pretty face. Sometimes I wondered about that."

"Shut the fuck up." I drum my fingers on the armrest and look out the window as we get on the highway and start heading back to Atlanta. "I have enough on my plate without you taking the piss out of me too."

"How is Arturo doing?"

A lump rises in my throat as I think about the state of my best friend. "We don't know if he is going to be able to pull through yet. He's still in a coma and it's looking more likely that he's going to stay that way. If that happens, then I have to talk to Billie about what to do with him and she's not going to like that at all."

"You make it sound so cold," Jovan says, the sympathy clear in his voice. "You know that you are allowed to feel things, right? You might not be able to do so around the people you lead, but in the privacy of your own home, you can."

"No good would come of me focusing on how I feel about the entire situation. Emotion is a weakness. You know that as well as I do. I'm not in the business of being killed because I was too wrapped up in my own emotions to deal with the things going on around me."

Jovan sighs. "One of these days, Alessio, you're going to have to bend before you break."

"We can revisit that flawed idea once I'm done dealing with this business with Paolo. However, I don't think that is going to be happening anytime soon since he seems hell bent on pushing all my buttons."

"Well, you know if you need my help, I'll be there with some of my men. Rio can handle things here on his own for a bit."

"I know and I appreciate that. Right now, I have it under control — at least as much as I can. I think you're right about calling Christian, though. Paolo is only growing his mafia. He's gathering low-level criminals and gang members. There is no sense of honor or family in what he's doing."

"Herrera is likely going to be his next target if he's not getting anywhere with you. I know the last time we spoke, you didn't want to kill him, but have you given any more thought to that?"

I cross one leg over the other, trying to get more comfortable for the long drive that's ahead of me. "I have.

Killing him is going to be the only way to end this problem. I've let him live for too long. Now it's time to put him down."

"Are you going to be able to do that? He was like family for a very long time."

"And then he betrayed us." My hand clenches into a fist as I think about finally killing Paolo. "There is no mercy for someone willing to turn against their own family."

Especially not when he has his eyes set on Billie.

THE SUN IS SETTING AS I WALK BACK TO MY HOUSE from the office space on the compound. Though it's a long walk, I have plenty of time to think through the problems that are plaguing my life.

When I got back to the compound, I sat Davide down for a long talk about the sinking of Paolo's largest drug importing ship. We started preparing for the counterattack that we know will be coming our way.

It's only a matter of time before he strikes out and I want as few casualties as possible.

I stuff my hands in my pockets as I walk along the worn path through the trees. It's the same path that I've taken nearly once a week for the last two decades. I built my house as soon as I could, away from everything else to have some peace and quiet.

On days like these, I am reminded of how nice it is to have my home and my office for mafia dealings separate. While I bring work home with me, there is no person invading my space and asking to speak about drug or arms dealing. No mention of money laundering or the prostitution rings I keep trying to shut down.

I hum to myself as I continue down the path, the silhouette of my house starting to rise up on the horizon. Billie is sitting outside on the front step when I get closer, a sketchbook in one hand and a pencil stabbed through the messy bun on top of her head.

Though I want to ask her what she's doing, it's best if we talk as little as possible after what happened between us in the casino the other day.

I shouldn't have bent her over the desk and fucked her like she was just some woman I picked up at a bar — even though I could tell she enjoyed it as much as I did.

I certainly should not have been fucking my best friend's daughter. It was wrong on all levels, but it was impossible to resist her. Especially when she was trying to get under my skin.

"I thought you were going to be gone longer," Billie says, closing the sketchbook and looking up at me. "Davide said that you would be gone until tomorrow."

"Got lucky and finished what I needed to get done early."

She nods and stares at me in the most unsettling way. I stand straight and try not to look like she's bothering me, but it's as if she can see right through me.

Billie shuffles over and pats the spot on the porch beside her. I raise an eyebrow and she shrugs.

"You look like you need someone to talk to," she says, her voice soft as she watches the sun dipping closer to the horizon. "I've been told that I'm a pretty great listener."

As I sit down beside her, I go back and forth about telling her what's on my mind. Her father is my consigliere. Billie has heard a lot in her time with the mafia and I know that she keeps her mouth shut. There is little worry about her feeding information to my enemies, but I still don't know if I can trust her.

My gut says yes, but there have been so few of those people in my life that I doubt my feelings.

If you can trust Arturo, you can trust Billie.

At least, I want to be able to trust Billie. It will be nice to have someone to talk to that I don't need to worry about.

The part that concerns me is that she's always been a bit of a mystery to me. Add that to the fact that she was in Paolo's club for an auction, and it makes me a little suspicious.

I could only tell her a little about things that are going on until I know if I can trust her.

"You don't have to talk about it if you don't want to," Billie says, a sweet smile on her face as she leans against the steps and looks up at the sky. "It's a beautiful evening."

"It's not that I don't want to talk about it," I say, sighing as I run my hand through my hair. "I don't know if I can trust you."

"Blunt." Her tone is teasing as she glances over at me. "It's alright. I know that telling you that you can trust me isn't going to help you figure it out, but for what it's worth, I dislike Paolo far more than I dislike you."

I laugh, feeling a little more at ease with her. "I guess that's fair. I know what I'm like. I'm not going to make an apology for it either. It's kept me alive for this long."

"I suppose that's the best that anyone can hope for." She crosses one long leg over the other, her skin glowing golden beneath the setting sun.

"The problems with Paolo run deeper than most," I say, taking a flying leap and making the choice to trust her.

"More so than him trying to destroy you and the people

who follow you?" Billie looks over at me, and for a moment, I picture a different life.

One where I'm sitting on the porch and we're talking about something trivial instead of the man I'm going to kill.

It's the life I've always wanted for myself. Sitting on my porch and talking to someone else about my day. The mafia left far behind me.

That's another world, though.

"He's starting to move into Herrera's territory in Tennessee. Which means that he's now got at least two states full of gangs and low-level criminals flocking to him to try and climb their way up the ladder."

Billie nods like she understands where this is going. "Papa told me a couple weeks ago that Paolo was going to become a problem. He's always said that Paolo was nothing but trouble, though. Even when I was little, he told me to stay away from him at meetings."

"Yeah, Arturo always had a better feel for people." I cross my arms and lean back slightly. "It's hard. He was my brother's best friend. Enzo made me promise before he died to make sure that Paolo didn't get himself into a lot of trouble. I feel like I've failed him, but I don't know what else I can do."

She shrugs. "I don't know if there is anything that you can do at this point. Some people don't want to be saved and you have to accept that about them."

"You seem to know a lot for someone as young as you are."

Billie rolls her eyes. "Please, I'm barely younger than you."

"Twenty-four is a lot younger than forty-three." Even as I say it, I know it's the harsh reminder that I need to stay away from her.

I allowed myself to lose control the other day in my office, but it can't happen again. Billie is too young to get caught up in this shit.

Sometimes I wonder why Arturo never sent her away like so many other parents have done. Yes, things were different while my father and brother were alive, but once I took over, he wouldn't have been met with a fight if he said he wanted to keep her safe.

Now, she was in too deep. Though she is too young to be caught up in this lifestyle, she is.

Blood in, death out.

That has been the policy of the Marchetti mafia for longer than I've been alive.

"Nineteen years," Bille says, scoffing playfully. "That's nothing. Although, I think I see a few gray hairs starting to form."

I shake my head, the corner of my mouth twitching. "You're a brat."

"Why did you bid on me?" she asks, her tone a little softer.

The truth is that I don't know why I bid on her. Part of it was to keep her away from Paolo, but that was only part of my reason.

Maybe curiosity pushed me to do it, though that doesn't seem quite right either.

"I don't know," I say as I get up and climb the porch steps. "I'm going to grab some leftovers. Tomorrow's your night to make dinner. The chef is going to be taking a few days off."

Billie nods and opens her sketchbook, pulling the pencil out of her hair.

For a moment, I stand in the doorway, watching the way the tendrils of her blonde hair brush the back of her neck. I consider going to sit with her longer and talking about anything. It was nice to feel like I was a normal person for once and not the person that everyone feared.

Instead, I did the smart thing and left her alone before I fucked my life up even more.

13

——————

BILLIE

I sit cross-legged on the floor beside the sliding glass door, running through the list of ingredients I need to get for dinner for the next few days. With the cook off, there's going to be nobody around to act as a buffer between me and Alessio.

Things have been weird between us since he fucked me on my desk, but I thought that last night things were going to go back to normal.

Instead, he left me confused.

He doesn't know why he bid on me.

There is no denying that something in me sparks to life whenever he's around. It's a dangerous spark. One that starts off small and ignites to the point of a wildfire within seconds. The kind of spark that soon consumes you in a fiery inferno.

The way Alessio makes me feel is like diving headfirst in hell and hoping to dance in the flames instead of burning to a crisp.

I have to put some distance between us. As much as I hate the awkwardness, it's better this way. It's easier to avoid each other and not spend time together. If we do, I might beg him to bend me over a desk again.

It might not have been my finest moment, but it was fun.

"You know, we have a perfectly good couch to sit on," Alessio says as he walks through the kitchen. "You don't have to sit there like some orphan waiting for a nice lady to take pity on them and put money in their cup."

"You really are a stellar human being, aren't you?" I ask as I mentally debate between roast chicken or ham. "I look like an orphan. Great."

He shrugs and pours himself a cup of coffee. "I'll be staying on the compound today but I'll be at the office here. If you need anything, that's where you can find me. Take the day off from the casino. There's some things going on there that I would rather not have you around for."

"Like what?" I ask, curiosity getting the better of me.

"None of your fucking business," Alessio says as he takes the cup and heads back toward his room. "I mean it, Billie, stay away from the casino."

"Okay. I have some shopping to get done today anyway. Ham or chicken?"

"Chicken."

I nod and make a note of it on my grocery list. The door shuts down the hall as I finish the grocery list before getting off the floor. The pool is glistening outside and calling my name.

I could do with a swim before going to the store. I have a few hours to kill now that I don't have to work.

Though I want to know what's going on at the casino, I know better than to push my luck. Alessio has been more open with me than I would have expected.

It only makes me feel worse for deceiving him, but I have to keep reminding myself why I'm doing this.

I stretch and head outside to sit by the pool, watching the sun climb higher in the sky. As much as I want to get into the pool, I should get the shopping done. Life is easy right now, but it's only going to stay that way if I meet the terms of the contract.

Still, the sun is calling to me. I can't remember the last time I was able to fully relax.

My phone starts ringing the moment I close my eyes. With a groan, I pull the phone out of my pocket and glance at the screen. My heart plummets to my stomach as the hospital's phone number flashes up at me.

I take a deep breath before answering the call. "Hello?"

"Hello, is this Billie Carbone?"

"Yes." My stomach lurches, and the world feels like it's shrinking around me. "Is this about my dad?"

"It is," the woman says, her tone cheerful. "Doctor Michaels wanted me to call and let you know that your father is awake."

Tears spring to my eyes as I stand up and hurry back into the house. "Is he alright? Is there anything I need to bring with me? I should be able to be there in about an hour."

"Your father is still not doing well. While he is awake, he is going to need another week or two in the hospital. Doctor Michaels will be able to tell you more when you get here. There's nothing you need to bring, but you should prepare yourself. The news may not be what you want to hear, but he is awake."

"Thank you so much." I rush to the front door and toss the grocery list in my purse. "Have nice day."

I end the call and toss the phone into my purse before

pulling on my shoes. My heart is racing as I head outside to my car.

Papa is awake. Everything is going to be fine. He's going to get better and then we're going to be able to start our lives over.

"BILLIE," DOCTOR MICHAELS SAYS AS HE MEETS ME outside Papa's room an hour later. "Thank you for coming. We have a few things to discuss regarding your father's care. If you want to follow me this way, we can find a private room to speak."

I follow him down the hall, though all I want to do is run into Papa's room and hold him tight. I was so close to losing him.

"If you want to take a seat," Doctor Michaels says, gesturing into a small waiting room.

There is nobody else in the room. I almost wish there was. Other people would have given me something to focus on while Doctor Michaels speaks. It would have been a welcome relief to whatever it is I'm about to hear.

I enter the room and pick a seat near the open window, hoping the fresh air will keep me from throwing up. Everything about being back in the hospital feels like racing here to find him in a coma only a few weeks ago.

I'm going to take him home eventually. Being here today is a good thing. It means that Papa is getting better. I just need to keep my head up and focus on the good. Papa wouldn't want me to be upset.

"As you know, your father went through a traumatic experience." Doctor Michaels sits down in one of the chairs across from me and sets his tablet on his lap. "We have a lot to go over with his care, and I know that all of it is going to be a bit overwhelming. Especially once we start talking about his going home. However, we're not there yet."

"Do you know how long it will be before I can take him home?" I ask, my voice wavering slightly.

My hands clench into fists. I dig my nails into my palms, trying to remain calm. I count my breaths as Doctor Michaels gives me a sympathetic look.

"It's going to be a while yet. He is still not breathing on his own. And there is still massive trauma to his body. As you already know, he underwent several surgeries to fix the immediate problems within his body and we have monitored the healing. However, there are several issues that are not healing as well as they should."

"What does that mean for my father?" Tears blur my vision slightly, but I force them back.

No crying. Crying is for the weak. I have to be strong for Papa.

"He's going to need a couple revision surgeries. The healing period shouldn't be too long, but it's going to be a couple more weeks before he'll be able to go home."

"And what's his plan for going home?" I swallow hard, trying to force down the lump in my throat.

"We can talk about that when we get closer to the date, but he will likely need a caregiver for several weeks after we release him. There is going to be a lot of physical therapy and we will be going to administer constant tests to make sure that his brain is still alright."

I nod, trying to process all the information without freaking out. None of this is going to be easy, but I didn't lose Papa. That's what matters the most. He is alive and he's still with me.

I'm getting him out of this fucking life before it kills him.

Doctor Michaels emails me a more detailed document regarding Papa before taking me back to his room. I stand in the doorway for a moment, watching him stare blankly at the television on the wall.

After a few seconds, I take a deep breath and walk into the room. I plaster a bright smile on my face as I close the door behind me before turning to Papa. He blinks slowly at me, the breathing tube still in his throat.

I try to force back the tears as I sit beside his bed and take his frail hand. The bruises are fading to yellow beneath the tattoos, but they're still there as a reminder of the beating he took. I try to speak but I can't. If I open my mouth, I'm afraid that I might start bawling.

Papa squeezes my hand, running his thumb over the back of it. I smile at him and reach up to wipe away a tear before it has a chance to fall.

"Hey," I say, my voice soft as I squeeze his hand back. "You look like you've seen better days. What did I tell you about running around like you're a thug at your age?"

Papa rolls his eyes, the corners of his mouth twitching around his breathing tube. He tries to shrug but winces from the pain.

"You don't have to do anything other than rest." I smile and lean forward, my elbows resting on his bed. "We do have some things to talk about, though."

His blue eyes search mine as his eyebrow raises slightly. I can see the question in his eyes, and though I don't know how to bring up leaving the mafia with him again, I have to.

At least he can't argue with me if there's a tube down his throat.

As much as I hate seeing Papa like this, I know that he would want me to find the humor in the situation. There is nothing he loves more than a little dark humor.

"Papa, you know that we have to be done with this shit. I'm working on a way to get us out. I have some money coming in. Money that the mafia won't come after. We can finally move away. You can retire and I can start building the resort I've always dreamed of."

Papa shakes his head, his eyes narrowing. I glare at him and sigh. This is going to be yet another uphill battle with him.

"I know that you and Alessio have been best friends since you were kids, but you have to get over that now. Sure, he might be here nearly every day to visit you, but he's the one who put you here."

He shakes his head, dropping my hand and trying to sit up. Papa groans and falls back against the pillows, frustration in his eyes as the beeping machines start to speed up.

"You need to relax," I say as I stand up and fluff his pillows. "We have a lot to talk about, but I'm done arguing with you about this. I almost lost you, Papa. I'm not going to let it happen again. As soon as you're better, we're getting the hell out of here."

Papa's gaze is distant as he waves a hand at me. I sigh and run my hand through my hair, knowing that this is going to be more difficult than I hoped it would be.

With all the pain medication they're pumping through his body, I don't know how much of our conversation he's going to remember. Even if he remembers it, I'm willing to bet on him pretending not to.

It's the same argument that we've been having for years. I think that it's time to go and he insists on staying. His loyalty is to the mafia, not to me. When I try to call him out on it, he starts yelling.

It's the only time in my life that Papa ever yells at me.

I'm not backing down this time, though. One way or

another, we're getting out. I will tie him up and throw him in the back of my car if that's what it takes to get him to go with me.

As his eyes start to close, I sit back down and consider all my options. Whatever plan I come up with for the day of our departure has to be one that can be executed seamlessly.

I only get one chance to escape, and Papa is going to make it that much more difficult.

It's GETTING LATE WHEN I GET HOME WITH THE groceries, exhausted and frustrated. Papa has been weighing on my mind all day and sitting beside him while he slept did nothing to ease the worry. I didn't think that life was going to be this difficult when I got older, but I should have expected it.

Now, I have to walk through that front door, plaster on a fake smile, and pretend that my life isn't ripping apart at the seams because I have a damn contract to see through.

I take my time getting out of the car and grabbing my bags from the back. The longer I can delay going inside and talking to Alessio, the better. I'm sure that he's heard about my papa waking up, but I don't want to talk about it.

Not yet.

"What do you think you're doing?" a woman says as I walk through the front door with bags of groceries dangling from each arm. "You have that little whore living here. You think that I didn't notice her things when I went upstairs? You're supposed to be finding a wife, not sleeping around with a woman nearly twenty years younger than you."

"She's not a whore, first of all. Second, I love you, but

who do you think you are?" Alessio asks, his voice booming through the house.

It feels wrong to be standing in the entryway listening to them yell at each other, but I can't walk away. My blood is boiling as I slide off my shoes and put them on the rack.

"I'm your mother. If I want to come over and check on you, then that is what I'm going to do," Alessio's mother says, her voice shrill. "You have been living with a young woman who only wants you for your money. That makes her a whore. Don't even bother trying to lie to me, Alessio. I know what goes on here, even if you don't want me to."

"If you are going to keep calling her a whore, you can leave. I'm not going to tolerate the disrespect in my household."

"I'm your mother."

"And that does not give you free rein to insult and disrespect people who live in my home!"

I take a deep breath before walking into the main section of the house and heading straight for the kitchen. Alessio and his mother are standing in the living room looking murderous.

"Figures she would be listening in," his mother says, crossing her arms as I put the bags of groceries on the counter and start unpacking them.

"Billie, you can wait to do that later," Alessio says, his cheeks turning a bright shade of pink. He crosses his arms and glares at his mother. "You don't need to be around to hear this."

"Don't worry. I heard your mother calling me a whore already." I give his mother a polite smile before turning to put the carton of cream in the fridge. "And I have to get dinner going. Lemon gnocchi takes a long time to make."

His mother scoffs. "You think that prepackaged garbage will take a long time to make?"

I force myself to keep the smile on my face. "Actually, I make gnocchi from scratch, so it does take a fairly long time. If we want dinner before midnight, I need to start cooking now."

Even though I want to tell her where she can go, she is still Alessio's mother and the matriarch of the mafia until he takes a wife. Making an enemy out of her and disrespecting her would be a mistake.

It would put me in Alessio's bad books and his mother would be out for blood. She would try to ruin me.

I've heard countless stories about what she's done to other women she doesn't like. I'm not going to be one of them.

I have zero desire to end up in the bottom of a lake. His mother may look like a frail woman, but she was a criminal long before she ever met Alessio's father.

At least, that's how the stories go. I've never seen any proof, but if she was as good as everyone says she was at theft and murder, there wouldn't be a trace.

His mother turns up her nose at me before focusing on Alessio again. "You have to make her leave. Do you really think that a woman is going to want to be with you when you have her living here?"

"Billie is going through a tough time right now. Her father asked me to look after her and that is what I'm going to do. I don't know if the men who attacked her father are after her or not, which means that the safest place for Billie is here."

"I set you up on a date with my friend's daughter. Laura is a nice young woman, and she would make you a good wife. She has strong connections to the Irish."

A date?

Jealousy rolls over me.

I know I have no right to feel like this. I have no ownership over Alessio, but the thought of him being with another woman is enough to make me see red.

Alessio throws his hands up in the air as I put away the last of the groceries. "I already told you that I'm not interested in dating right now. I have more important things to deal with in my life. And if I was ready to date, it's certainly not going to be with someone who is tied to the Irish. Stop trying to insert yourself into my life and stop trying to shape my mafia in the way you want it run."

"I raised you. What I have to say should matter to you. I will not tolerate this person you are becoming. You may have a lot going on in your life, but you are still my son, and you will do as I say. In this matter, I know best. Laura is a good woman and will bring you even better connections if you marry her. You cannot continue relying on cartels for support."

Alessio looks like he's ready to blow as he grinds his teeth together. "You will not stand here and tell me what to do. I will not be marrying anyone, especially someone you pick for me. Marriage is just a fucking shit show of emotions and another person trying to tell you what to do. I already have you filling the position of bossy woman in my life, so what do I need a wife for?"

His mother steps closer to him, planting her finger in the middle of his chest. "You are going to regret speaking to me this way, Alessio. You are nothing but a child and you don't know what you're talking about. I will forgive you because I'm your mother, but if I did not love you, this would be the end for us."

"Mother, I love you too, but this is too much. You can't

walk into my house and force your opinions on me." Alessio gently pushes her hand away from him. "I will not be going out with Laura and Billie will live here for as long as she needs to. You will not have a say in the matter as it is not your home or your life."

His mother scowls before spinning on her heel and facing me. "You are the cause of this attitude."

I hold my hands up. "I did nothing. All I did was come back here to make dinner."

"Get out," Alessio says, his tone darker than anything I've ever heard from him before. "I told you that if you disrespected Billie, you would be out of here. Now leave."

His mother shakes her head and snatches her purse from a chair. "This is far from over. The sooner that little whore is out of here, the better. She's a disgusting filth that you've allowed into your home. Do you really think that she is going to do anything other than take advantage of you?"

"Alright, I'm fucking done," I say before heading for the loft.

I don't need to stand there and listen to it. Though I may need to tread carefully where Alessio's mother is concerned, I'm not about to stand around and be insulted for no reason. I did nothing to her, yet she is lashing out at me.

Just to piss her off more, I change into a bikini before striding back downstairs. I don't bother to listen to what the pair is arguing about as I make my way through the kitchen and straight out the sliding door to the backyard.

"That's enough!" Alessio's voice seems to shake the house as I turn to close the door behind me. 'Get out of my house now!"

I shut the door and take a deep breath. I walk to the edge of the pool, trying to leave everything his mother said about me in the past. My plate is already full. I don't need to waste precious time and energy worrying about what she thinks.

Whatever. It doesn't matter. I'll be out of here soon.

It shouldn't matter that she says horrible things about me to Alessio, but how will he see me after everything she's said?

I don't want him to think of me any differently, though I doubt his opinion is high in the first place.

Get yourself together, I think as I surface and float on my back. *Just try to enjoy what is left of your evening.*

Though it seems impossible at this point, I'm determined to pretend that I'm a normal woman living a normal life for a few hours.

14
____

ALESSIO

"You're really going to do this to your own mother?"

I take a deep breath, trying to keep calm as I walk my mother to the door. It's the same argument that it's been for years. While I may have been willing to tolerate her pressuring me to find a wife before, I'm done with that now.

Especially after the way she spoke about Billie.

"Yes, I am." I stuff my hands in my pockets and follow her to the front door. "You're not welcome here anymore. If you need to see me, you can book an appointment with Billie. She's my new assistant."

My mother stops and turns to scowl at me. "You think that is an appropriate way to treat your mother? Your father would be disappointed in you. He did not raise you to put some little hussy above your family."

"Until you learn to respect my boundaries, that is the way things are going to be. You want to see me, you make an appointment. I'm done with this argument."

She storms out the front door and slams it behind her. I twist the lock in place and pull out my phone, sending a message to Davide about getting a locksmith to my home immediately. I need the locks changed.

Coming home to find her rooting around in the loft and looking through Billie's things was the last straw. I love my mother, but this is too much. I'm a grown man and who lives with me is none of her business.

I run my hands down my face before turning and heading back into the kitchen. I watch Billie through the window as she swims from one end of the pool to the other. My cock stiffens as I take in the curves of her body and the fabric that does little to hide them from me.

Bad idea. Stay inside. Stay away from temptation. Your mother was right about her being too young for you. Keep your shit together and keep your dick in your fucking pants.

Except all I want to do is go outside, talk to her, and feel like someone other than who I am. Just for a little while.

And I need to apologize to her for the way my mother spoke.

As I walk outside, I try to convince myself that this is a good idea, though everything in me is screaming at me to go inside, make dinner, and pretend that nothing happened.

However, I'm learning that when it comes to Billie what I should do and what I actually do are two very different things.

Billie looks up at me as I approach the edge of the pool. There is fire burning in her eyes as she dips back beneath the water.

Clearly, she isn't going to make this easy on me.

I stuff my hands in my pockets and try to readjust my cock before she comes back up, but I'm too slow. She smirks as she pushes her wet hair back from her face, her gaze dropping to the bulge in my pants.

"So, that was something in there," she says, floating on

her back. I roll my eyes at her taunting, even though it excites me. Her nipples pebble against the thin blue fabric of her bikini top. "I don't want to be rude, but is it too much to say that your mother is a piece of work?"

"I'm sorry," I say, kicking off my shoes to the side. I'm debating whether to get in the pool with her or not. I've always liked swimming when life gets too hard to handle at times. "You can call her a piece of work. She is. She has her reasons, but that doesn't excuse the way she acted toward you."

"I've been called worse," Billie says, her eyes shutting as she floats in the middle of the pool. "You learn to not let things like that bother you when the single women around you are in competition for the men."

The corner of her mouth twitches upward and I want to know what's going on in her mind. I know that several of the young women are constantly fighting with each other over the capos. Most of the other young women tend to stay out of it, but I could see why Billie would be dragged into it.

Her beauty isn't a secret in the mafia. I've heard more than one of my men talking about braving Arturo to get a chance with Billie. Most of them only ever talk about who can sleep with her before Arturo kills them.

What those idiots don't realize is that Arturo is the least of their worries. Billie is more than capable of handling herself. Any woman who breaks a nose with a frying pan isn't going to be playing games with horny men.

"You keep looking at me like that, and I'm going to think that you're trying to read my mind," Billie says, her tone teasing as she opens her eyes and looks up at me. "You know, if you want to strip down and get in the pool with me, I wouldn't mind."

"That's a bad idea."

Billie laughs, her cheeks flushing. "I know what a terrible idea it is. You made that perfectly clear last time. It's your pool, though. If you want to swim, I'm not stopping you. Hell, I'll even get out if you want me to."

"Stay." I crouch to roll up the hem of my pants before sitting on the edge of the pool and dangling my legs in the water. "You don't have to go just because I'm here."

She starts treading water, her body distorted slightly by the ripples forming around her.

"Does she always come here and pull that shit? You don't deserve to be treated that way. You should be able to make your own choices in life without your mother pressuring you."

The corner of my mouth twitches. "You sound like you're more upset by what she said to me than what she said to you."

"I am. I've been dealing with mean girls my entire life. Your mother is just the adult version. You're her son, though. She shouldn't be bullying you into settling down when you've told her that you're not ready for it. That's not fair to you."

"Bille, you are something else, you know that?" I shake my head and kick some water at her. "I heard your dad woke up. I didn't have a chance to go see him today, but I'll be heading over there tomorrow."

"Can we talk about anything other than Papa? I've been having a hell of a day and talking about him right now is just going to make everything feel worse."

I nod and stare up at the setting sun. "You know, I think we should order a pizza for dinner. After that, I really don't feel like cooking."

Billie laughs and splashes water back at me. "We're

going to pretend that you were going to be the one cooking dinner tonight?"

I smile and shrug. "We could if you like."

She studies me, playfulness in her gaze despite the shit day she said she had. There is something always bright and sunny about her attitude, even when she is being dealt a shit hand at life. Billie's been that way for as long as I've known her.

There's something admirable about that.

"You know, when you smile, I would almost think that you're not the cold bastard everyone says you are." Billie smirks and dips beneath the water as the pool lights start to come on. I laugh as she swims around beneath the water before popping back up and spraying more water toward me.

"You should believe them when they tell you that I'm a cold bastard, Billie. There's a reason for it."

"I know. I do believe it and I've seen the reason behind it. I also happen to think that there are parts of you that you're hiding deep away and not allowing anyone else to see."

"Oh?" I ask, my tone amused. "And what would you know about hiding parts of yourself away from the rest of the world?"

Billie smoothes her hair back from her face. "I live in a man's world, Alessio. I don't pretend that I don't. I've killed people. I've done other shit that is going to sit with me for the rest of my life. There are days that I wake up disgusted with myself, but I have to hide that away because there is no room for perceived weakness in the mafia."

"And Arturo expects that of you."

She nods. "And Papa expects me to be able to hold my own. You know as well as I do that I cannot disappoint him.

If I look like I can't bear the weight of being the consigliere's daughter, then that will pass on to him. The capos will look for any reason to get rid of him."

"Well, maybe you do know a little about hiding yourself from the world, then."

"I just might." She sighs and floats on her back. "There has to be more to you, though. I'm not convinced that a ruthless killer is *all* that you are."

I stare at her, trying to figure out how much of me she already figured out. "It would be a mistake to think of me as anything other than what I am, Billie."

The corner of her mouth twitches. "Did you spend a long time coming up with that line?"

"No."

"People are not as simple as they seem," Billie says as she swims over. She rests her arms on the edge of the pool, pulling herself up out of the water slightly. "I'm sure that there's a part of you that's hiding deep down and just waiting to be let out."

I watch small droplets of water roll down between the valley of her breasts. "You're wrong about that too."

"I don't think I am." She combs her fingers through her hair, pushing the wet locks back from her face. "I know what this life is, though. Being who you are and going after the things you want will get you killed."

Billie slips beneath the water again and swims to the shallow end of the pool. I stand up and slide off my pants, leaving me in nothing but black boxer briefs. She surfaces, her gaze dragging down my body.

I don't care that she can see the bulge of my cock as it hardens under her gaze. Right now, I'm trying to convince myself why I shouldn't jump in that pool with her.

All it takes is her tongue darting out to swipe across her

bottom lip. That simple motion is enough to break the last of the restraint I have for the day.

I jump in the deep end of the pool, enjoying the feeling of the water rushing up around me. It's been too long since I just got in the pool and swam around to enjoy myself.

"Damn," Billie says, her tone teasing as she joins me back in the deep end. "I've seen children doing belly flops that looked more graceful than that."

"Alright," I say, smoothing my hair back from my face. "So, you're in a mood today. Either pissed off or making fun of me. Is there any happy medium in which you don't act like a brat?"

She laughs and shakes her head. "Only in your fantasy world."

"Trust me," I say, my voice husky as I swim closer to her. "That's not what's in my fantasy."

A pink tinge spreads across her cheeks as she swims backwards, trying to put more distance between us. Fire burns in her eyes and beneath the smooth ripples in the water, her nipples pebble against the thin material of her bikini.

"You know, strings have always been my favorite," I say as I back her up toward the wall.

I grab her leg and use it to pull her to me while I tread water. Billie's breath hitches as she hooks her legs around my waist to stay afloat. I run my hand up and down the back of her toned thigh before wrapping one of the strings at her hip around my finger.

"Are you sure this is a good idea?" she asks, her voice breathy as she moves her arms through the water, her back pressing against the wall.

"When it comes to you, I'm sure that everything is a bad idea." I pull on the string until the material falls away from her hip. "There is something about you that makes it impossible to stay away, though. It feels like a siren calling my name and luring me to my death."

She smiles as I pull the strings on her other hip. "You think I'm luring you to your death?"

I pull the fabric away from her body and throw it onto the deck. "I think that being with you in any capacity — even one like this — is something your father would kill me for. Especially if he saw us right now."

"Good thing that he's never going to find out about this, then."

"You're right. Nobody is ever going to find out about this." I pull on the bikini string around her neck and back, tossing the top out of the pool.

I move us into part of the pool that is shallow enough for me to stand. I groan as her body brushes against my cock with the movement of the water around us. I run my hands up and down her curves, feeling her body beneath my fingers.

I'm going to have to delete the security footage of this after.

Her back arches off the wall as I roll her nipples between my fingers. Her soft moans are music to my ears as I kiss my way up and down her neck. Her hips rock against mine as I graze my teeth along her collarbone.

"You know, it really is a shame that you're not going to get off today," I say, nipping at her earlobe. "I'm going to leave you aching and needy for me."

"That's cruel."

"So is taunting me." I move away from her slightly — just enough to run my fingers along her wet slit. "Consider this your punishment. Maybe next time if you want my cock inside you, you'll consider being a good girl."

She grips my shoulders as I circle her clit and suck on her neck. Billie's moans are breathy as I push my fingers into her. My thumb presses against her clit with every thrust of my fingers. Her pussy clenches around me, pulsating as I massage her inner walls.

"Please let me come," she says, her voice barely more than a whisper.

"No. You don't deserve to come today."

I loop one arm under her ass and lift her higher out of the water. Her back curves as I take a nipple into my mouth. I tease her nipple with my teeth and tongue — biting it and soothing away the sting — as she writhes against me.

Her pussy pulses around my fingers as I switch to the other nipple. I thrust harder and faster into her, loving the feeling of her pussy responding to my every touch.

Just when she is about to come, I pull away from her completely and get out of the pool. Her frustrated sigh follows me as I walk into the house, my cock hard as a rock and begging to be buried in her tight pussy.

Instead, I head for a nice cold shower to punish myself for being so stupid when it comes to Billie.

15
─────

BILLIE

I LEAN AGAINST THE WALL AND SIP MY COFFEE, watching as the ancient photocopier struggles to make copies of profit and loss statements. The machine groans and whines as copies spit out onto the tray.

I could go home and pack my things right now. I could leave the mafia right now and Alessio wouldn't have a clue.

Though it's a tempting thought, Papa is still in the hospital. It's only been a couple of days since he woke up and the doctor still says it will be weeks before he can come home. Since I can't leave without him, I'm stuck with Alessio.

Being around him is making me reckless and I know it. What happened in the pool the other day never should have happened.

And I certainly shouldn't have gone to my room and pulled out a vibrator after.

Getting myself off to the thought of him fucking me in the pool was reckless. There is a chance that he heard me and thinking about that while I came only turned me on more.

I'm losing my damn mind in that house.

What I should be focusing on is my escape. I've started hiding money around the compound, picking places that will be easy to access if my escape plan goes wrong. In reality, it should be as easy as driving out of the compound and never coming back.

I'd be stupid to not have several different contingency plans, though. This isn't a perfect world, and nothing is ever as simple as the easiest plan.

Although, I should be doing more to plan my way out. I don't even know where I'm going to take Papa once we leave. I could take him to another country, but I don't know anybody who would be able to smuggle us in. Between me and Papa, there is enough suspicion surrounding what crimes we may have committed that the authorities would tie us up for as long as they wanted.

The photocopier stops, giving a loud thud before it shoots out its final paper. A man walks into the room with a stack of papers in his hand.

"Is that thing acting up again?" he asks, shaking his head as he sets the stack of papers down on a counter that runs the length of the wall to my right. "I swear. You would think that with the money this place makes, they would replace a copier. Instead, they just keep calling in a repair man and supposedly fixing it."

He grins and walks over to the machine, pulling off a side panel. The man hums to himself as he reaches inside and twists something before standing up and putting the panel back on.

"Alright, you're going to have to show me what you did the next time this thing starts sounding like it's going to blow up," I say with a grin as I head for the door. "Nice to meet you, though. I'm Billie."

"Jefferson." He holds out his hand and I shake it quickly. "You're the new assistant, aren't you?"

"That I am."

His gaze moves down my body, landing for a moment longer than polite on the hem of my faux leather pencil skirt. When his gaze connects with mine again, he's got a smile on his face that I'm sure is meant to charm women.

It's nothing compared to the way Alessio looks at me when he wants me.

"Do you want to go out and get drinks sometime after work?" Jefferson asks. "I know that it can be hard to meet people around here since the job is so demanding."

"That's nice of you to offer, but I'm not much of a drinker," I say, hoping to get out of this conversation without letting Jefferson down too hard.

Though he isn't the kind of man I would normally go out with, I don't want things at work to become difficult either. I've worked in other places where my coworkers haven't taken too kindly to me rejecting their advances.

"We could go get coffee or lunch."

"I'm sorry," I say, giving him a polite smile as I back toward the door. "I'm seeing someone right now. It's still pretty new, but it's the kind of thing I don't want to mess up."

"That's alright," Jefferson says, his tone still cheery. "See you around, Billie. Let me know if you ever need help with anything."

"Will do. Have a good day, Jefferson."

I turn the corner, the papers clutched to my chest, and run straight into Alessio. He scowls down at me as the papers flutter to the ground.

"You should watch where you're going," he says, his tone cold as I stoop to pick up the papers. "And I would ask that you keep yourself from having personal relationships with the staff while on work time."

"What are you talking about?" I gather the papers and stand, already dreading having to put them back in order before the meeting.

"My office," he says, his hands balling into fists before he stuffs them into his pockets. "Now."

I sigh but follow him through the main office and into my own. He doesn't stop, just nods to my desk as he passes on the way to his own office. I drop the papers on the desk, trying to keep them in a neat pile, before following him.

Alessio stands to the side as I enter the room, waiting until I'm inside before closing the door. He strides to his desk with long steps, his shoulders tense beneath the gray suit that hugs his body. For a brief second, I consider begging him to bend me over the desk, just so I can relieve some of the tension from the other night.

He walked away and left me there, naked and needy like he said he would. It had been infuriating. I should have begged him to stay and have his way with me. To fuck me until I didn't even know my own name anymore.

Get it together. He is the man you're trying to get away from. He stands for everything I find wrong with the mafia. He is the representation of a life I no longer want to live.

Yet, I still can't get the image of him making me beg out of my head.

"You wanted to talk about my personal life in the office?"

Alessio nods and paces in front of me, crossing his arms over his chest. "I will not have you and other staff members discussing your dates or the dates you will be going on while you are at work. It is unprofessional. And I feel the need to remind you that you are under a contract that outlines you're doing whatever I tell you to."

I arch an eyebrow and cross my arms. "Are you trying to tell me who I can and can't talk to?"

"No. I'm telling you that while you are under *my* contract, you will not be going out with other men. For the duration of the contract, you're *mine*, Billie."

I nod, my mouth pressing into a thin line. There is not much that I can say to argue with him. I did sign a contract. Whether I like it or not, I am his for the next several weeks.

Sometimes I really regret signing that damn contract.

"I wasn't planning on going out with him," I say, my tone a little sharper than intended. "He asked me out and I told him I was seeing someone."

Alessio's eyes nearly bulge out of his head. It would almost be funny if he didn't look murderous right now. "Who the hell are you seeing?"

"Calm down." I smother the smile that threatens to escape me. "I'm not seeing anyone. I just wanted to let the guy down easy. He seemed nice enough and I don't really want to be known as the frigid bitch at The Fortuna. Do you know how well that reputation would serve me?"

"You shouldn't be worried about getting along with the other staff. You should be worried about making the most out of this job. You seemed interested in it. I'm paying you well on top of the contract money."

"Wow," I say, shaking my head. "You sound like you're jealous that another man might have even shown a little interest in me."

Alessio stops pacing and spins to face me. He closes the distance between us in two quick steps, looming so close to me that his chest brushes against mine.

"There is nothing to be jealous of. Whatever does or

does not happen between us is not my problem. You're alright, but it's only a bit of fun. Nothing that I truly have to commit to."

His tone is cold and cruel, as if he knows that the words may as well be a punch to the gut. I wipe all emotion from my face and shrug.

"Well, I'm not sure that I would call it fun for either of us. You tease me and then regret it the next day, or I let you fuck me and regret it the next day. Either way, there seems to be a lot of regret involved."

Alessio's frown deepens. "Billie, that's not what I meant."

"Sure sounds like it every time you tell me that I'm a mistake. Which isn't wrong. I'm a mistake who could ruin your carefully cultivated life and you're another complication that I don't need right now."

While the words may be true, it's not how I feel. Right now, I feel like he's saying what he can to try and hurt me. He seems like a scared child who doesn't know what to do with the situation.

I'm not about to stand around and inflate his ego. I won't tell him that he's the only man who has ever managed to keep my interest for more than a couple weeks. There is no way in hell that I could ever tell Alessio about the crush I've had on him since I was twenty.

Admitting the curiosity I have about him will only make all of this hurt more in the end.

"I need to go organize the profit and loss reports before the meeting," I say, sighing and heading for the door. "I assure you that I'll keep my personal life away from The Fortuna."

Even though I should wait for him to finish the conversation, right now he isn't the leader of the mafia. He is just a man who pissed me off and is unable to admit that he might be slightly jealous.

Instead, he pushes me away harder than ever before.

I'm going to let him keep pushing. I'm going to use that hurt as a reminder of all the ways that I shouldn't be getting caught up in whatever romantic fantasy my mind keeps coming up with.

I walk out of the office with my head held high. As I sit down at my desk, I keep my posture rigid even though I want to curl in on myself.

Alessio doesn't need to know the hold he has over me.

All I have to do is get through the next few hours and then I can go home for the evening.

If I'm lucky, tonight will be one of the nights where Alessio has mafia business to deal with that keeps him away from home.

I hum to myself as I sort through the papers, organizing them and trying to put myself in a better mood. No matter how many times I tell myself that today is going to be a good day, it's getting harder and harder to believe it.

As I finish sorting the paperwork, I see other people through the open door starting to head to the conference room. I glance over my shoulder at Alessio's closed door, wondering if I should go in and get him or not. He knows that we have this meeting, and I don't want to go back in there and argue with him again.

However, I have a job to do.

I stand up and smooth my skirt down, taking the time to pop open the top button of my cream blouse. It doesn't reveal a lot of skin, but just enough to remind him of what he is missing. It might be cruel to both of us, but I'm not going to make this easy on him. If he wants me to be his and only his for the remainder of the contract, then I'm going to have my fun.

Distracting him by teasing him might just allow me to leave the mafia easily. He's going to think that I'm going along with everything he wants while the reality is far different.

I knock on his door, waiting for an answer. Instead of the gruff *come in* that I normally get, the door opens. Alessio's hair is disheveled and his blue eyes are shining with anger. He doesn't look at me as he strides out of the office.

As I grab the reports, I watch him make his way to the conference room. In the past few days of working here, I've noticed him arriving early to every meeting. It's almost as if he wants to give himself the upper hand in every situation by making others believe that they've wasted his time before the meeting begins. I've already heard more than one person apologize for being late when they walk into the room and see him sitting there.

I follow him into the conference room and place copies of the reports at several of the seats. It's going to be a small meeting with the accountants and some of the upper management, but an important one. Alessio is constantly going over his numbers, making sure that the casino is turning over a profit every day.

Who wouldn't be concerned about turning a profit when they're using their business to launder money?

Alessio takes his seat at the head of the table as I finish passing out the reports. I make sure to stand a little too close to him, my arm brushing against his. Though he doesn't say anything, his jaw tightens.

I smile to myself, enjoying the new game for a moment before other people start to filter into the conference room.

They talk and laugh with each other, falling silent only when they see Alessio already sitting down and flipping through the reports.

"Well, thank you all for joining me today," Alessio says, looking around at the other employees as they take seats around the massive oak table. "I've been looking over our profit and loss statements for this month and I have to admit that I'm not pleased with what I'm seeing."

I make a note at the top of my copy of the reports. Alessio stands and grabs a remote, turning on a projector and the screen at the front of the room. The door to the conference room opens and Jefferson rushes in.

"Jefferson, the meeting started already. We will discuss your tardiness afterward." The glare Alessio gives Jefferson is one that could melt flesh from bone. He scowls and pulls up the reports on the projector, flipping to the first graph.

"While our overall numbers are up, the percentages are down. We have taken more losses this month than we have in the past several. This is not a trend I want to continue for the rest of the quarter."

His voice booms and the way he speaks while meeting the eyes of everyone in the room exudes control. He is in charge, and everyone knows it. Alessio commands their attention in a way that few people have the power to do. When he addresses the room, he is confident and at ease.

I clench my thighs together, thinking of the way his authoritative tone and confidence would pair together in the bedroom. Heat floods to my core as images of him telling me what to do to please him flash through my mind.

Get control of yourself. You're at work and you've both agreed more than once that this is a stupid idea. Get it together.

When he finally looks at me, I know there is no getting it together.

When it comes to Alessio, I've lost control.

As soon as this meeting is over, I'm ordering a new vibrator. One that might make me feel half as good as he does.

A new vibrator might be my only chance at resisting the attraction I feel for him.

16

———

ALESSIO

Another few days spent avoiding Billie mean another few days that I've fucked my hand while picturing her on her knees. By the time this contract is done, I'm not sure how I'm ever going to close my eyes and not see her begging for me to fuck her.

I drum my fingers on the steering wheel of my car and stare up at my house. For the first time ever, I'm dreading going home. This used to be the one place where I could fully relax. I didn't have to worry about saying the wrong thing to a woman I definitely shouldn't be interested in.

Instead, I'm sitting out in my car and considering getting a room at a hotel for a night. Seeing Billie at work today, in another one of her tight little skirts with a blouse that bordered on sheer, has me ready for a cold shower and another round of fucking my fist.

A cold shower that I would take at a hotel if I was a smart man. If I wanted to avoid temptation, I would go in there, tell her that she could move back to her own house for the duration of the contract, and be done with it.

Except if I told her that, I would be lying. There is no being done with Billie. That much I'm starting to realize.

If I tell her to go back home, then I know damn well my nights are going to consist of finding excuses to go over there just so I can be close to her.

Billie is the breath of fresh air after a forest fire, breathing a life back into me that I didn't know I had lost.

Sooner or later, I have to go in there.

My stomach growls as I consider going somewhere else once again. I could go to my office on the compound or I could spend a night in my office at The Fortuna. If I really don't want to see her, I can pay for a hotel room at any hotel in the city.

I want to see her, though, and that's the part that scares me. When I think about my days now, seeing her after work every night is part of that. The way she smiles and dances around the kitchen to music I hate on nights she has to cook. The way she sits at the kitchen island and learns from the chef on the nights she doesn't.

Then there are the mornings when I find her sitting out by the pool with her nose buried in one business book or another. Even though she's already graduated, she's always studying.

There're so many layers to Billie that I don't know and as the days pass, I find myself wanting to peel them back and discover her.

Arturo is going to kill me. There is no doubt about that.

I visited him in the hospital earlier, and though he can't properly speak yet due to his brain trauma during the attack, the message was clear. He had pointed to a picture of Billie.

Take care of her.

I groan and run my hand down my face. I'm clearly doing a great job of that. I have her trapped in my house after buying her at an auction. I put a clause in our contract that I'll only sleep with her if she begs me to. That clause is only in there to try and ease some of my guilt for the attraction I feel for her.

At first, it was only physical, but it's starting to turn into something more. Something I can't bring myself to put a name to, because if I do, something bad will happen to her. Paolo will find out how I feel about her and use that against me.

He'll kill her because I can't stay away from her.

I 'm going to have to try my best to stay away from her. If that means being cold and detached, then that's what I have to do.

Even though I hate being that person. I feel like a carbon copy of my father at times.

One foot in front of the other and go into the house. Your house. Stop stalling. She is just a woman, and you are only stuck with her for the next few weeks.

I wait for the song on the radio to finish — stalling for more time — before turning off the car and getting out. Each step I take feels like I have lead weights tied to my feet.

This is ridiculous.

I shouldn't be this worried about going home and facing Billie. Even with the way that she's been teasing me recently, I know that nothing is going to truly happen between the two of us. I can't drag her deeper into this life than she already is. Arturo wants me to take care of her.

Acting like she is a partner to me is only going to get her killed. It will piss off her father and their relationship could be damaged forever. I don't want to do that to her. She doesn't deserve it. Billie already lost her mother, she doesn't need to lose her father too.

I climb the front porch steps, stopping when I see a brown box sitting in front of the door.

Perfect. Just what I need. Another one of Paolo's fucking games.

I've been searching high and low for the people in my compound who are working with Paolo. While I've found a few and killed them for their treason, I'm sure there are more. There is no way that Paolo would be able to get past my guards and leave dead bodies on my doorstep without someone inside helping him.

I stoop to grab the box before heading inside and making my way to the kitchen. Thankfully, it's empty. I can put off having to see Billie for a little while longer.

My stomach growls as I drop the box on the counter. I dig through the fridge for something quick to eat, pulling out the leftovers from the night before. As the food warms up, I grab a knife and slice through the tape on the box.

However, instead of a head staring up at me — or whatever else Paolo could come up with — there is a purple vibrator. My face warms and my cock hardens as I close the box and check the label. Billie's name is there with my address listed.

So, she wants to get herself off and isn't willing to beg for it.

Though that is probably a good thing, it only turns me on more. The thought of her toying with her clit and teasing herself until she comes is something I can't get out of my head. Everything else I've been thinking about us has disappeared, giving way to every dirty thing I want to do to her.

The microwave beeps as I grab the vibrator out of the box. I open the door and slam it shut before kicking off my shoes and taking off my suit jacket. I sling the jacket over the counter before heading up to the loft with the vibrator.

Billie is sitting in her bed and reading a book when I reach the loft. She closes the book and looks at me, her gaze darting down to the vibrator box in my hand. Her cheeks turn pink as she smiles and gets up.

"Thanks for bringing that up here," she says, though her voice wavers slightly.

It's the only sign that she is nervous about the situation. She reaches out to take the vibrator, but I hold it out of her reach.

"Now, why would you need this?" I ask, my tone husky as I take the vibrator out of the box. Her blush darkens as she shrugs, still trying to act as if she's unbothered by my finding the vibrator. "I told you that if you wanted to come, all you had to do was beg for it."

"I'm not interested in begging you for anything." Billie crosses her arms. The silky camisole she wears dips lower, revealing more of her breasts to me. My cock strains against my pants, and I know I'm about to chase down yet another bad idea.

Fuck it. I want her and I have her for the next few weeks. I'm going to enjoy it while it lasts. This is just another casual hook up that will mean nothing when it ends.

At least, that's what I try to convince myself of as I turn the little rabbit vibrator on. Billie's eyes widen as the buzzing sound fills the room.

"You did not just do that," she says, shaking her head. "I don't want anything from you and I'm certainly not going to beg for it. Now, can I please have that? There is a hot bath and a spicy book that are calling my name."

I chuckle and shake my head. "Not going to happen, Billie. You want to get off, you're going to beg for it."

"There isn't a single line about me not using a vibrator

in the contract." Billie lunges toward me and tries to take the vibrator from me.

I move out of the way and catch her around the waist. She yelps as I lift her up and toss her over my shoulder. Her small fists hit my back half-heartedly.

"Put me down. What are you? A fucking caveman?"

"You want me to put you down?" I ask, crossing the room and standing at the foot of her bed. "Because I can put you down."

"Yes! Put me down!"

I toss her onto the bed, watching her bounce slightly against the mattress before leaning back into the cushions. She glares at me as she props herself up on her forearms.

"Was that necessary?" she asks, her tone sharp.

I turn off the vibrator and toss it to the bed beside her. "Don't fucking touch it or you won't get to come tonight."

"What happened to begging?"

If I'm not imagining things, she almost looks disappointed. I chuckle and shake my head as I start to unbutton my shirt. "Don't worry, Billie. You will be begging by the time I'm done with you."

Her tongue darts out to lick her bottom lip as I slide off my shirt and toss it onto her couch. She watches me, her thighs clenching together as I take off my pants and socks, leaving me in nothing but a pair of boxer briefs.

When her gaze drops to my hardened cock, all I can think about is the wetness I know is hiding beneath the silky shorts she wears. Billie looks at me with fire in her eyes as I grab her ankles. She yelps as I drag her down to the foot of the bed and spread her thighs.

As I sink down to my knees in front of her, she runs her fingers through my hair. It's a casual touch — one that is far too familiar for the relationship we have with each other. I don't know how to feel about it, but I'll deal with that later.

Right now, I want to taste Billie.

I hook my fingers in her shorts, pulling them down her long legs slowly. I kiss and nip at her thighs as I pull the shorts off her body. She gives a soft sigh and leans back against the mattress. Her fingers keep running through my hair as I suck on her inner thigh, leaving a dark mark.

"Did you just give me a hickey?" she asks, laughing as I pull away from her.

"I told you that you were mine until the contract ends, didn't I?" I switch to her other thigh, licking and nipping at the flesh until there is a matching mark. "I think that means that I can mark you if I want to. Just in case you need a reminder of who you belong to."

She lets out a breathy moan as I slide my tongue along her wet slit and circle her clit. Billie is already soaking wet for me. As I flatten my tongue against her clit, her grip tightens on my hair. I groan and continue to tease her with my tongue, flicking it against the little bundle of nerves until her legs are shaking.

I pull away from her, staring up at her. "You didn't want to come, did you?"

"Fucking hell," she says, glaring playfully at me. "You're really going to leave me horny and unsatisfied twice?"

"All you have to do is beg for it, Billie. Tell me how much you want me to make you come. Hell, your soaking wet pussy is already doing half the work for you. You just need to say the words."

She bites her bottom lip and shakes her head, defiance shining in her eyes. Even though we both know she wants it, she enjoys the teasing just as much. I can see it in her eyes.

She likes working for it. She likes giving up control and letting me set the pace.

I stand up and grip my cock, stroking it as I look down at her. I run my thumb over the head as she reaches for the vibrator. The soft buzzing sound fills the room and she starts to tease herself.

Seeing her playing with herself only makes me harder. She swirls the vibrator around her clit, pressing a button on the end to change the vibration pattern. With her free hand, she rolls her nipple between her fingers. When her back arches off the bed, I take the vibrator from her and turn it off.

"Do you really think that I'm going to let you come?" I grab her by the hand and pull her to the edge of the bed. "I want you to suck my cock. If you don't want to beg for me to fill your pussy, I'll fill your throat instead."

"So, you get off but I don't?" She raises an eyebrow as she takes my cock in her hand, sliding up and down the length at a torturously slow speed. "Doesn't seem very fair to me."

"You want to act like a brat, then you don't get to come. You want to come, you beg for my cock in that tight little pussy of yours."

I wrap her hair around my fist, pulling her head back so she's looking at me. Billie glares at me, but there is still fire in her eyes. She wants this. That much is clear by the way she keeps pushing me.

If she wants to play that game, I have no problem finishing in her throat.

Billie licks her lips as she looks back down at my cock. Her grip tightens on my cock as I guide it to her mouth. Her full lips part and her tongue darts out to lick the head. I groan as she opens her mouth wider and hollows her cheeks, taking me deeper.

She licks and sucks faster, swirling her tongue around me before swallowing me deeper. When I hit the back of her throat, she moans. My cock throbs in her mouth as she pulls back and looks up at me.

"Please fuck me," she says, her voice husky. "I need to feel your cock in me. I want to come all over your cock."

I groan and let go of her hair. "Move up the bed and get on your knees. Ass in the air."

She moves slowly, trying to tease me as she goes. Billie gets on her knees, her chest pressing into the bed. Her round ass is in the air as I kneel on the bed behind her. I run my fingers along her wet core, before grabbing the vibrator.

I turn the vibrator on and reach around her, pressing it against her clit as I enter her from behind. Her pussy clenches around me as she moans. I grab her hip with my free hand, dragging her back against me with every thrust.

My cock throbs inside her as I rock my hips harder and faster. Her wetness coats my cock and her back arches as I bury myself to the hilt inside her.

"Fuck, you feel so good wrapped around my cock."

I press the button on the vibrator, changing the pattern. Billie grips the sheets in front of her as she comes, her pussy pulsating around me.

"Good girl," I say, my tone low as I slow my pace, drawing out her orgasm until her body is done shaking. "Now, I'm going to fuck you until I come. Your body is mine to do with as I please."

"Yes," she says, her voice breathy as she looks over her shoulder at me.

I toss the vibrator to the side and gather her hair into one hand. I pull her head back, making her back arch deeper as I thrust harder and faster into her. Billie meets me thrust for thrust, her core clenching around me hard as she comes again.

Feeling her pussy milking my cock is all it takes to make me finish. I come hard and fast, keeping myself buried in her as she moans.

We fall to the bed together. She leans back into the pillows beside me, one arm draped over her face as her chest rises and falls rapidly.

I look at her for a moment, rolling onto my side to face her. Every thought running through my mind right now is at war with another. On one hand, I know that this is all that can exist between us — and it's more than what I should allow. On the other, I want her more than I've ever wanted anyone else.

"How do you feel about casual sex?" I ask, my tone low as I try to figure out what the hell I'm doing.

I'm complicating things between us. That's what I'm doing. I saw a situation that was complicated, but better than nothing, and then I thought that I would make it worse.

Billie moves her arm slightly to look at me. "What are you talking about?"

"There's something between us and don't bother arguing with me. We both know it. There is something happening between us and we can't let it go any further than casual sex. However, if that's something you want, then I could do that for you."

"Wow," Billie says, drawing out the word in disbelief. "You really know how to make that sound like you're doing me a favor, don't you? I don't want casual sex if all this is going to be is a pity fuck."

"It's not a pity fuck." I sigh and run my hand down my face. "That isn't what I meant. I enjoy what's going on between us and I want to continue it — without the begging every time you want to fuck — but that's all I can offer right now."

She bites her bottom lip and stares up at the ceiling. After what seems like an eternity, she nods. "I could use some sex without strings attached. It ends when the contract ends, though. I don't want either of us to start thinking that it could turn into something it's not when this is all over."

"This ends when the contract ends," I say, moving to hover over her body. She looks up at me, reaching up to slide her hands over my shoulders.

I push whatever feelings I'm starting to have for Billie to the side as I kiss my way down her body, losing myself in the heaven I've found between her legs.

I'm too broken to be anything more than casual sex to her, but I'm not going to let her know that. This is just a bit of fun before we have to go our separate ways.

Even if, in an entirely different world, I might be able to see something more between us.

17

———

BILLIE

I roll over and see Alessio still clutching the pillow in the bed beside me. My heart pounds against my chest as I slide out from beneath the covers, trying not to disturb him. There's something so innocent-looking about him when he sleeps.

Knowing that he is a cold and dangerous killer is very at odds with the version of him currently in my bed.

Last night was the best sleep I've had in a long time. I don't know how I'm going to go to bed tonight without him beside me, but that's a problem for later. Right now, I have to get ready for work and try to ignore the feelings at war within me.

I still want to leave the mafia. It's why I've done everything that I have so far this summer. That desire to leave the mafia is why I auctioned my body off to the highest bidder.

But there is a part of me that doesn't want to leave Alessio.

Though we both agree that all that can be between us is casual sex, my dreams still ran wild last night. I dreamt about a life that would never exist. One where I'm settled down with Alessio, happy. Our children ran around us and dogs played in the yard.

It's the kind of life I know I'm never going to get if I stay here.

I make my way to the closet, grabbing out a pair of black plaid slacks, a white blazer, and a white bodysuit. As I head into the bathroom to get dressed, I grab my phone from the couch and check the time. It's still too early to go to work, but getting a coffee from my favorite café on the way there sounds good.

With that in mind, I hurry to get dressed and head out. I decide against saying goodbye to Alessio. That's the kind of thing that people do when they're in a relationship.

How the hell do I act around him now that we're having casual sex?

I sigh and run my hands through my hair, trying to tame the wild waves as I head outside into the cool morning air. As soon as I get in the car, I start scrolling through my playlist for the perfect song to start the morning.

For the first time in a long time, I feel good about what I'm doing with my life. I'm not wasting time in the mafia. I have a plan to get out and half a dozen back-up plans. I'm working toward the life I want, even if that means doing something I wouldn't normally do.

However, there's a little voice in the back of my brain that says heartbreak is headed my way.

Casual sex with the man I've been attracted to for years — the leader of a mafia — is a recipe for disaster.

Casual sex with my father's best friend seems like a recipe for a nuclear disaster.

I hum to myself, trying not to freak out. Soon, I'll have a coffee in hand and I'll be able to focus on work instead of the mind-blowing sex I had last night.

The coffee shop is nearly empty when I park the car in their lot and head inside. There are a few people in suits, already talking on their phones about their plans for the day. A couple people are working on their laptops in dark corners of the café while soft acoustic music flows through the room.

I order my coffee, waiting for it by the counter as the bell above the door chimes. I glance across the room to see Paolo walk in, a bright smile on his face as he makes his way toward me.

In all the years that I've known him, he's only ever smiled at me at the auction. It sent a chill down my spine then and it sends another chill down my spine now.

It's a smile that I know better than to trust. It's the one that men give to women when they want them to be comfortable, even when they shouldn't be.

Every alarm bell is going off in my head as the barista hands me my coffee.

"Well, Billie, it's nice to see you again," Paolo says as he leans against the counter beside me. My heart races. I didn't think he would realize who I was. Not after the auction. "You know, it took me longer than I care to admit to find out you're Arturo's daughter. Just another thing to add to my list of disappointments, I suppose. I really thought that we were going to be spending the summer together. Such a shame that we aren't."

"It really is, isn't it?" I ask, trying not to make whatever is about to happen worse. "You know, I really can't talk this morning. I have an important meeting I need to be getting to."

He lifts the hem of his shirt slightly. It's enough for me to see the gun he has holstered at his hip. "If I were you, I would want to hear me out before you go scurrying away."

"Well, since you put it so nicely. What can I do for you, Paolo?"

He chuckles and loops his arm around my waist, pulling me toward the door. "Not where so many people can hear us."

His arm is a tight vice around me as he leads me out of the café and into the parking lot. As he starts to turn me toward a black car, I stop in my tracks and turn to him.

"I don't want to be disrespectful, but I really do have a meeting I need to get to soon. What is it that I can do for you?"

"Life in the Marchetti mafia can't be good for you. Especially not with who your father is. You would think that would gain you some respect, but I remember my days there. The men used to have a bet going. Whoever was the first one to sleep with you would win a lot of money."

My blood boils at the mention of the bet. It's not the first time I've heard about it, and I doubt it will be the last.

Is Alessio part of the bet?

It's a dark little thought, but it's one I can't shake. The longer I stare at Paolo, hoping that this will be over soon, the more I wonder if Alessio is in on the bet.

I bite back the urge to tell him to fuck off, knowing that it will only get me hurt. "It's certainly not an easy life."

"If you were to marry me, you could escape that."

"Excuse me?" Has he gone mad? What is he even talking about?

Knowing Paolo, I don't think I even want to know.

I shake my head and give him a polite smile. "I'm sorry. Unfortunately, I'm not really looking to get married anytime soon."

"Billie, you should really see things my way. Think of how powerful we would be together. We could draw away support from the Marchetti mafia. We could take down an organization who doesn't respect you."

"With all due respect, Paolo," I say, reaching around to the small of my back and pulling out a gun. I keep it down at my side and hidden from the other people in the parking lot. "I'm not going to be marrying you. Not now. Not ever. The life I have may not be perfect, but I was raised better than you. I do not betray the people who protect me. Now, if there is nothing else, I *will* be going."

Paolo laughs and shakes his head. "You don't know what you're doing, Billie, but one day you'll understand."

He gets in the black car without another word. I slide the gun back into my waistband beneath the blazer, my heart racing. Normally, I leave the gun in the car. It stays in a hidden compartment unless I know I'm going to be walking into danger.

I don't know what compelled me to grab it before I went into the café, but I'm glad I did.

I might not be standing here if I didn't.

Yet another reminder of why I hate this fucking life.

Paolo's car peels out of the parking lot as I head back to my own. I take a deep breath as I get in the car and put my coffee into the cupholder. My stomach is tossing and turning. If he knows that I frequent this café nearly every morning, I'm going to have to start going somewhere else.

It was foolish to think that I could have a routine anyway. Papa always taught me that it was better to keep my schedule varied. To switch it up often in case anyone was watching me.

I should have listened to him.

After taking a few more deep breaths and checking my mirrors to make sure Paolo is gone, I head to the office. It's only a short drive, but I look over my shoulder the entire time. If he is bold enough to approach me in public about joining him, then I suspect he is willing to try just about anything.

I wouldn't put it past him to kidnap me to get to my father.

The interaction with Paolo is all that circles through my mind as I park the car before heading to my office. What-ifs keep popping up, each one of them making me question how safe me and Papa truly are.

The sooner he gets out of the hospital, the better.

There's nothing that I can do for him there, though Alessio does have men guarding him day and night. It's a peace of mind that I wouldn't otherwise have, but the worry still seeps in.

Alessio stands in my office when I get there, glancing at the calendar on my computer. He pulls out his phone and checks something before turning to me. He's about to say something but his mouth snaps shut and he steps around me to shut the door.

"Is everything alright?" he asks, his tone low in case anyone is on the other side of the door. "Come into my office and we can talk."

I sigh but follow him with my coffee in hand. I take a long sip and try to think of a way to get out of talking to him. Sooner or later, he will need to know that Paolo is trying to recruit me, but it's a lot to think about right now.

"You look like something's bothering you," Alessio says, shutting his office door behind me. He gestures to the couches near the window. "Does this have anything to do with last night?"

I cross the room and sit down on the plush couch. He sits in one of the armchairs across from me. His stare is unnerving, like he already knows what happened and is waiting for me to own up to it.

Though what he thinks happened and what actually happened are likely two different things. If he is asking about last night, then he has no clue that Paolo cornered me.

"No, this has nothing to do with last night." I take another sip of the coffee, hoping it will settle the storm in my stomach. "Although, I do want to know something."

"What is it?" He leans forward and rests his forearms on his legs, his hands clasping together. "If it's something that I can talk about, I'll tell you."

"Do you know about the bet running within the *famiglia* on who will sleep with me?"

He frowns but he won't look me in the eye. "I do know about it."

I swallow the lump that rises in my throat. "Are you a part of it?"

If he says yes, I'm walking out of his office and never looking back. I don't know what I'll do without being able to move Papa, but I'll break the contract.

Betting on whether or not he could sleep with me is a line I'm not going to let him cross.

"No." He looks up at me. "I would never, Billie. It's a disgusting bet and I've shut it down several times, but it always comes back up."

"And don't you think that's part of the problem with the way you run things?" I ask before I truly realize what I'm saying.

To question his leadership is a sign of treason. We both know it.

"Billie, it's not as simple as just putting an end to the way things are. Look at what happened when I've tried.

Paolo is trying to take us down and he has support because I'm trying to change things."

"So, does that mean that you stop trying? You want women to feel like property in your mafia? You want us to allow men to treat us how they please? To make bets on who will be the first to get their fucking dick wet? Is that really the way you want things to run?"

Alessio glares at me. "You're toeing a dangerous line, Billie."

"I don't give a fuck right now — pardon the language. You said that I could speak freely with you, so that is what I'm doing. Do you really want a mafia where half the people in it mean nothing?"

"No. I don't want that. And you need to believe that I'm trying to change that."

"I don't need to believe anything." I put my cup of coffee on the table. "You need to prove that you want things to change. That you're trying to make a difference. You're a better man than your father and your brother, but you still follow in their footsteps. You wear their shoes like they should fit you."

"And how the hell would you know anything about it? You were a child when I took over."

"I was fifteen. I was far from a child at that point in my life. Plenty old enough to remember what your father and brother were like." I shake my head and cross my arms. "You want to know what's really bothering me? Beyond the way you're content to sit back and allow things like a sex bet to carry on for years?"

His eyes flash with anger and his jaw tenses. "What?"

"Paolo came to me today. He cornered me at a café. He said that if I were to marry him, I would be an equal in the mafia he is starting. He wouldn't allow things like the bet to form."

"And you believe that?" Alessio shakes his head. "You're an idiot if you did."

"No, I don't fucking believe that. But you know what, he's at least willing to say something like that out loud."

"Where did he go after he cornered you? Did he put his hands on you?" Alessio asks, the conversation shifting gears.

I allow the topic to drop for now, but I'm not going to stop pressuring him to do better. If there's one good thing I can do for the people still in the mafia before I leave, it's going to be that. I have his ear, I may as well use it to make lives better.

"He left. And not really. Just an arm around me to force me out the door so we could talk. It was nothing serious."

I grab my coffee from the table and finish it off. I want to be done with this conversation as soon as possible and back to work.

"I'm going to kill him," Alessio says, standing up and pacing back and forth. "I'm going to murder him for putting his fucking hands on you."

"It's fine. He didn't hurt me and he backed off once I pulled a gun on him."

"You keep a gun on you?" he asks, stopping his pacing to stare at me.

The way his gaze drags down my body, trying to figure out where with the fitted clothing I could hide a gun, lights all my nerves on fire. Heat pools in my core but I remind myself that I'm angry with him right now. He may not have been part of the bet, but he's known about it and never put a true end to it.

All it will take to end it is making an example of someone.

He doesn't want to do that, though. He doesn't want to cause more trouble in a mafia that is already filled with turmoil.

While a part of me can understand that, the other part is pissed.

"In my car. I don't go anywhere without one." I get up and turn to the door. "I have work that I need to get done before the day starts. There's a few different reports on employee satisfaction that I have to comb through before the management meeting."

"I'm going to handle this, Billie. He won't bother you again."

"Don't bother, Alessio. If you can't put an end to a bet, how can you deal with a man who wants to marry me for his own advancement?" I shake my head and open the door to his office. "Don't worry about dealing with Paolo. He is nothing that I can't handle on my own."

"Billie."

I stride out of the office and open my own door before taking a seat at my desk. Within a few minutes, I've successfully buried myself in paperwork.

But I know it won't be enough to distract me from everything that happened in Alessio's office. Those thoughts are going to race through my mind all day.

The sooner I get away from the mafia, the better.

18

ALESSIO

Ever since yesterday, I've been thinking about what Billie said. I know that I should have put a complete stop to the bet about her sooner. I don't want the women who look to me for safety to feel like their *famiglia* isn't going to protect them. I've allowed it to go on for too long.

Which is why I storm into the main house where several of the younger capos and most of the soldiers live. Davide tags along behind me, already dialing the number for the cleaning crew.

"Get me Antonio," I say to one of the soldiers as he passes. The man nods and takes off racing up the stairs.

A few minutes later, the soldier reappears with one of my capos trailing behind him. Antonio wears an easy smile, as if he thinks that this is just another meeting. Other people start to gather around, watching as Antonio joins me in the center of the main hall.

"Boss, what can I do for you?" Antonio asks, tucking his hands into his pockets.

"You're the one who started the bet about several of the

young women in the *famiglia,* are you not?" I ask, my tone cold.

Though I already know the answer, I want to see if he is going to admit to it. Antonio stutters and stares at me, the smile dropping from his face. His shoulders slump as he looks at the ground.

"Yes."

"Great, now that we have that settled, I would like to remind everyone here that women are not objects and I will not allow you to treat them as such if you wish to remain a member of this *famiglia.*"

I pull out my gun and shoot Antonio between the eyes. His body crumples to the ground as a few people start to whisper. I tuck the gun into my holster before turning and walking out of the main house.

My stomach lurches with the thought of what I've just done. Killing someone never gets any easier, but the men in my mafia needed a reminder of who is in charge.

I look down at my shirt, taking in the blood splatters on the pale gray. *Yet another shirt that I'm going to have to burn.*

People rush toward the main house, glancing at me as I pass. I have no doubt that the story is already making its way through the compound and will soon be to the members of the mafia who don't live here. It's only going to be a matter of time before the old capos — the ones who have been around since my father was in charge — start to question my leadership.

I'm doing this for Billie.

And that's the most dangerous thought of all. One woman is enough to make me change the way the mafia has run for the last several decades.

Except that she isn't just one woman. She is far more than that to me, even though she shouldn't be.

I make my way to my office building. Thankfully, Davide is still dealing with the scene at the main house, so I have a little time alone. I take a seat on the couch in the main lobby and pull out my phone.

The phone rings several times, the sound never-ending as I wait for Christian Herrera to pick up. It's time that I deal with Paolo, and I'm going to need all the help I can get.

"Hello," Christian says, his voice gruff as screams sound in the background of his call. "I thought you would be calling soon, but you sure do have shit timing."

"Well, we need to talk about this now. I'm assuming that Jovan filled you in after I spoke to him?"

"He did." Christian chuckles and a low thud echoes through the phone. A groan follows it. "Alright, I've finished up with what I was doing. What can I do for you?"

"Jovan has agreed to allow us to meet in Florida. It's neutral territory for me and you. We need to discuss how we are going to deal with this Paolo situation without either one of us having the upper hand."

"When do you want to meet? I have some things going on this evening that I need to be in Nashville for, but I could meet you in Miami in a few hours."

I sigh and kick my feet up on the coffee table. "That works. I have to tie up some loose ends here today before flying out tonight. I've had to dispose of one of my capos who decided he didn't need to stay in line. There is going to be tension in the next few days that I won't be able to escape but getting away to Miami will save me a headache that my consigliere can deal with."

Though I normally wouldn't discuss business with a cartel

leader who wasn't already a solid ally, I want to build trust between us. Speaking with him about business that doesn't matter that much is a way to build that trust with Christian.

"Oh yeah? What did this capo do? I have to admit, I heard of the brutality of your *famiglia*, though I have yet to believe it. You would think that someone so brutal would have already taken care of Paolo."

"Yes, well, this capo was targeting someone important to me. Killing him sent a message to the others."

"In that case, I hope your message works. If we both want to survive, we're going to have to make an example of Paolo. I know that you have history with him, but I'm not going to allow others to think they can follow the same path that he did once he is dead."

I swallow hard. Even after all that he has done, it's still hard to stomach the idea of killing my brother's best friend. I promised Enzo that I would look after him and now I have to go against that promise.

"I can do what needs to be done."

"Good," Christian says, an engine roaring to life on his end of the call. "I hope that proves to be true. For your sake."

The call ends, leaving me with an unsettling feeling deep in the pit of my stomach. Christian is a dangerous man. He is not the kind to hesitate if he thinks that I can't get the job done.

There is a good chance that I could end up dead alongside Paolo.

I'm not going to let that happen, though. Paolo has been plaguing my family for too long. He has been testing his limits and he's crossing lines left and right. All I do to retaliate against him — to force him into backing down without killing him — isn't working.

I'm sorry, Enzo. I'm going to kill your best friend.

Maybe that will teach Paolo a lesson about putting his hands on Billie.

If for no other reason, I'm doing this for her.

When I get home that night, Billie is singing to herself in the kitchen while she prepares two pizzas to go in the pizza oven outside. Her back is to me as she shakes her ass and sprinkles cheese on top.

She spins around mid-ass shake and grins at me. For a moment, I think that the fight from yesterday is forgotten and all is water under the bridge. That is until the smile falls away and she grabs her phone to turn off the music.

"I heard you killed Antonio this morning," Billie says, grabbing a pack of pepperoni from the other counter and starting to lay slices on the pizzas. "What was that about?"

"He was the one who started those fucking bets in the first place. Now he's dead. I doubt you'll have any more problems with bets being made about you or other women here."

Her mouth drops open slightly before it snaps shut. She nods and grabs some slices of bell pepper. "Do you like pepper on your pizza? I have some mushrooms cut up too. And slices of fresh mozzarella ready to go."

"It all sounds good. It's going to need to go in the oven soon. We have to be on a private jet headed to Miami in two hours."

She looks at me over her shoulder, her eyes wide. "Why are we going to Miami?"

"I don't want to leave you alone to deal with the fallout of what I did, but I have business in Miami tonight. And likely for the next few days. Which means that you need to pack and get ready for at least a week there. I don't know if it will be that long, but I doubt it will be any shorter. There is much that I need to discuss with some allies regarding how we will deal with Paolo."

I walk over to the sink and wash my hands before helping her finish topping the pizzas. She says nothing, her mouth set in a thin line. I want to ask her what's going through her head, but I know sooner or later she won't be able to resist telling me off. I can tell by the twitch in the corner of her eye that she's not happy about being ordered around.

"I have work to do,'" she says, her tone stiff. "And I have to check in on Papa. I was at the hospital today and he isn't doing much better yet. What if they need me there?"

"Then I will put you on a plane right away, but this is not up for debate. You will be coming with me whether you like it or not."

"And what if I don't like it?" She glares at me as I load the pizzas onto trays to take them outside. "You don't need me there to do business."

"I'm going to make this very clear. I put up with your arguing because I think it's entertaining. It's been a long time since anyone other than your father tried to argue with me. However, I'm not going to budge on this. You can either get your ass upstairs while I cook these and pack a bag or you can go to Miami, kicking, screaming, and naked. I really don't give a shit but I'm giving you a choice."

"How kind of you," she says, her tone dripping with sarcasm. "Maybe I will go naked, just to prove a point."

"And what would that point be?" I ask, trying to stuff down the waves of jealousy that roll through me at even the thought of other men seeing her naked.

She's mine.

There is no way in hell that I'm going to allow anyone else to see her naked. If I'm being honest, I don't want anyone to see her the way she already dresses. It would be better for the jealous streak I have if she wore the largest quilt I could find.

"The point that you may control me for now, but you won't control me forever."

"Are we really going to start a fight over this right now?"

She stares at me, her eyes narrowing. Her shoulders relax and she shakes her head. "There really is no point in arguing, is there? It's not like I have a choice."

"You made your choice when you entered that auction. The fact that you regret it now is quite frankly not my problem. Go upstairs and get ready. We'll eat dinner and then we'll go."

Billie gives a sharp nod before spinning on her heel and walking up the stairs. I sigh, feeling like somehow I've lost the battle even though she's doing what I want.

As much as I want us to be friendly with each other — for the duration of the contract — it's a bad idea.

Paolo is a dangerous man, and he is looking for her. He knows who she is and sooner or later, he will figure out what she means to me. He'll kill her first and then he'll come for my *famiglia.*

We're both in danger until I kill him.

19

———

BILLIE

Nearly two hours later, the plane lands and I take off my headphones. While I may have gotten on the flight with my bags packed, I'm still not happy about being in Miami. I was hoping that Alessio would leave me behind and I could work on plotting my escape route.

Although, the more I think about escaping now, the more guilt starts to creep in. I try to tell myself that it's only because sleeping with Alessio has my mind messed up.

That has to be all it is.

Leaving is still the best option for me and Papa. I have to keep that in mind, even when Alessio is giving me that smile that sends my clothes flying to the floor.

"I've booked a beach house for us. My friend Jovan has been getting it set up." Alessio leads the way off the jet and to a waiting car. "Do you want to drive?"

I look at the sleek little black sports car, wondering if I would ever get a chance to drive something like that again. I know he is just offering the keys to me as a way to try and make me less pissed off with him.

"Come on," he says as he opens the driver's door while

someone loads our bags into the trunk. "The keys are already in the ignition. I'll even let you pick the playlist."

There isn't going to be another chance like this one. Once I'm gone, I'll be driving shitty cars for a while so I can funnel most of my money into building my resort business.

With that in mind, I stride past him and slide into the driver's seat. Alessio's chuckle sends butterflies erupting in my stomach.

Down, girl, he might have put casual sex on the table, but it would be a mistake to take him up on that. You're trying to get out of here, not get closer to him.

I turn the key in the ignition and the engine roars to life. For a second, I consider driving away and leaving Alessio there. I would probably loop back, just to see the look on his face.

There is no way I could disrespect him like that, though. Especially not when there are other people watching and we are in cartel territory. It would make him seem weak and he would have no choice but to punish me.

"You know, you get this devilish look in your eyes that I really don't like sometimes," Alessio says as he shuts my door. He rounds the front of the car and slides into the passenger's seat.

"Good." I smile over at him before pulling out my phone and connecting it to the stereo system. "Now, do you want country or pop?"

He groans and shuts his eyes, leaning his head back against the seat. "Neither. Don't you have something saved on that phone with some bass?"

"For this drive? No. If you keep letting me drive while we're here, then maybe."

Alessio opens his eyes and smiles, shaking his head. "I'll

let you drive when I can, but if we're going to any meetings, that's not happening."

"Have to look like the big man in charge," I say as I pick a song and turn up the volume. "I get it."

"Sure you do." He reaches out and taps the display screen, pulling up the map. "GPS will tell you where we're going. It's about a half an hour drive."

I nod and glance at the screen before putting the car into drive and pushing down on the accelerator. The car takes off like a dream, speeding up as I steer us toward the highway that leads away from the private airport.

The music pounds through the car as I roll the windows down and let the warm breeze stream through the car. Everything smells like the ocean and sunshine.

Maybe I should move somewhere on the coast. I've always loved visiting the beach.

I weave in and out of traffic, loving the way the car handles. Alessio hums along with the music as it blares, looking like he is genuinely enjoying himself.

Despite why we are in Miami, he actually seems relaxed for once. Oddly enough, I can't think of many other times when I've seen him relaxed and enjoying himself. Alessio's hand hangs out the window and his fingers spread as they slice through the air.

The drive is shorter than expected, and soon I'm pulling into a long driveway lined with hedges. I stop in front of an iron gate and lean out the window to punch in the code Alessio gives me.

The iron gates open with a loud creak, revealing the rest of the driveway. I take it slow, trying to soak up the gorgeous landscaping that surrounds us. It feels like I've stepped into a lush jungle with bright flowers and tropical bushes growing everywhere.

"Like it?" Alessio asks as a white Spanish-style house comes into view. "There is a private dock and two pools out back. Several bedrooms inside, so pick which one you like the best. I've hired a private chef for the week, so there is no need to worry about cooking."

I shrug, parking the car beside the cascading waterfall fountain in the middle of the driveway. "It's alright. I've seen better."

Alessio laughs and shakes his head. "You're so full of shit. I saw how big your eyes got when you saw the house. You love this place."

"Alright, fine. It's stunning. I love the charm that Spanish-style homes have to them. All those massive windows and the stucco walls. The architecture alone is beautiful."

"This particular house dates back to nineteen thirty-six. There have been a few renovations since, but the family who has owned it since then have tried to maintain the charm of the original construction."

We get out of the car and Alessio grabs the bags. When I try to take mine from him, he holds it out of my reach.

"I can carry my own bag, Alessio."

"Yeah, sure. Get moving. You look like you want to go take a look at the house. I can deal with this. The key should be in a lockbox beside the door. The code is the same one it was for the gate."

I leave him with the bags and head for the house. Excitement is racing through me as I get out the key and step inside. Dark wood floors run the length of the hallway and the living room to my right. I glance around at the arched doorways and the high ceilings, picturing myself living in a home like this.

The stucco walls are painted a pale cream, adding more warmth to the space around me. Large mirrors and beautiful depictions of Spain hang on the walls. I stop to look at one of the watercolor paintings, taking in the warm tones and the light reflecting off the water.

"This house really is something else, isn't it?" Alessio says as he appears behind me. "I left the bags in the hall. Once you pick which bedroom you want, let me know. There's one on the main floor with a courtyard and its own private pool."

"Do you mean I get some time away from you if I pick that one?" I ask, my tone teasing as I look over my shoulder at him. "This is a really nice place. Thank you for bringing me with you."

Even though I still don't want to be here, it is nice to get away from everything for a little while.

While we're here, I know that Alessio has assigned an extra protection detail to my father. People are with Papa day and night making sure nothing happens to him.

As much as I may hate the mafia, Alessio is the kind of man who will protect his people with everything he has when he knows there's a threat.

Yet another reason why leaving the mafia is a hard decision. Me and Papa will gain our freedom, but there will no longer be protection in place.

At least for now, I have to let go of those worries and try to enjoy this trip for what it is.

Papa is in safe hands which means that I may be able to relax a little.

"Is there anything we have to do tonight?" I ask as Alessio pulls out his phone.

"No. The security detail have arrived. They will be watching over the house and wandering around the property grounds. If you want to leave the property and I'm not with you, you need to find and notify one of them."

"I thought you trust the man who runs Miami?"

Alessio nods and tucks his phone back in his pocket. "I trust Jovan as much as any person in power can trust another. He is a good ally and a great friend, but that doesn't mean that there aren't others here who wouldn't want to hurt me. Do you honestly think that Paolo wouldn't have us followed down here?"

"I know he would." I sigh and make my way back into the hall to start exploring the bedrooms. "I just thought that there wouldn't be a bunch of people following us around."

Alessio chuckles. "Why? Were you hoping to get some alone time with me? Because that can still be arranged."

I scoff and open the wood door to the first bedroom. My mouth drops open when I glance up and see the exposed beams. "You know what, I'm definitely taking this bedroom. Not for the courtyard or the pool — those are bonuses, though — but for this architecture alone.

"If I knew that this house was going to get you that excited, I would have brought you here a long time ago."

"This is my dream house." I look around at the wooden furniture, all stained dark while still allowing the natural texture to show through. "The earth tones and the way one room is cohesive with the next really makes a statement."

"If you want to see a statement, head into the ensuite and take a look at the shower." Alessio leans in the doorway with his arms crossed over his chest. There is an easy smile on his face as he dips his head toward a wooden door to my right.

Behind the door is the most amazing bathroom I've ever seen. The floor is made out of terracotta tiles, but the shower has stunning hand-painted tiles in various shades of blue. I pull out my phone and take a picture, my cheeks aching from smiling.

"This house is amazing. You should have gotten to Miami first. Made this your home," I say as I walk back out into the bedroom.

I glance over at the glass doors and see a courtyard paved with the same terracotta. A fountain with blue and yellow tiling sits in the middle of a mini forest. Comfortable-looking chairs line the small area, making it seem like the perfect little oasis.

"The pool is just through those trees.

There's a gate beyond that which will take you to the backyard."

"This is all amazing." I look around, trying to take it all in. Our time in this house is limited and I want to remember as much of it as possible.

"Want to go for a walk on the beach and get some dinner? There's a great place to get some burgers down by the boardwalk."

"Can I drive the car again?" I ask, dangling the keys from my finger.

Alessio laughs and shrugs. "Why not? You didn't kill us the first time. You might not kill us this time either. Jovan and Hadley are going to meet us there, though."

"Hadley?"

Alessio nods and leads the way out of the room and back through the house. "Yeah. His wife. They've got a baby on the way in a couple months."

"This week won't just be a sausage fest, then." I grin as we head outside. The stars are hanging high in the sky as we make our way to the car. "Good. I could use a little girl time instead of putting up with you."

Alessio rolls his eyes and gets in the car. "We'll see if you're still saying that after you've spent time with Hadley."

"THERE IS NO WAY!" I GRIN, GLANCING BETWEEN Hadley and Jovan. He glares at his wife, shaking his head. "I can't believe you got him to put on a dress. How the hell did you manage that?"

"Fucking pregnancy hormones," Jovan says, glancing at Alessio. "The tears come out and I'm the bad guy if I don't do what she wants."

"Still doesn't explain why you put on the dress," I say, propping one foot up on the bench and wrapping my arms around my shin. "You could have said no."

"And risk pissing off the pregnant woman?" Jovan shakes his head. "Like fuck that's going to happen. She's hell on wheels when she isn't pregnant."

Hadley laughs and reaches out to pat her husband on the shoulder. "Don't worry. You'll survive. The baby will be here soon."

"And then I'll really be outnumbered." Jovan looks at her like she is the most important person in his world.

Even just in the couple hours that we've been with Hadley and Jovan, I've seen the love between the two of them. At first glance, they seem like an unlikely pair. The way they look at each other is magic, though. It's the kind of love I want for myself one day.

The kind of love that would walk to the ends of the world for each other.

"We should get going," Alessio says, smiling like he's having the time of his life. He is fully relaxed, though every now and then he does glance around the beach for any sign of danger. "It's been a good night. Christian landed tonight too. He wants to meet in the morning. Does that work with you?"

Jovan nods. "I've cleared my schedule for the week the two of you are here. Whatever you need, just let me know."

Alessio nods and gets up, holding out his hand to me. It's a casual gesture, but one Hadley doesn't miss. Her eyebrows raise as she looks at me, mischief sparkling in her eyes.

'You know, I was looking at the courtyard attached to that master bedroom. There's some lights that are strung above it. Turn them on, slip in the pool, and it's a pretty romantic little spot."

"Hadley," Jovan says, his tone a soft warning.

She holds her hands up, her grin stretching from ear to ear. "I didn't say anything."

"Yeah, sure." Jovan shakes his head and gets up, helping put Hadley to her feet.

I put my hand in Alessio's, allowing him to pull me up. His cheeks are red and he avoids looking at me as he reaches into my pocket to pull out the car keys.

"We'll see you tomorrow." Alessio nods before pulling me toward the car.

His calloused palm is rough against mine, sending a shiver down my spine. All I can think about is the way it felt to have his hands on my body. The way he makes me beg for him.

Heat floods to my core. I try to shove the thoughts away as we get back in the car, but I can't. The way he makes me feel is something entirely new to me. It's as if my body is on fire and instead of quenching the inferno, all he does is feed the flames.

I want him and he's offered himself to me. It's not an ideal situation to be in, but it isn't the worst either. He is a confident and attractive man.

He is a killer.

I'm a killer too.

I lean back in my seat as he drives down the road to the rental house. Rock music is playing softly in the background, a song I barely recognize from a band I don't know. It doesn't seem like the kind of music Alessio would like. I would have expected more of a taste for metal or classical. Something that seems more fitting for a man like him.

"What's going through your mind right now?" he asks as he drums his fingers on the wheel. The wind whips in the window, tousling his dark hair.

My heart skips a beat as he looks over at me. The look in his eyes tells me that he actually cares. That he wants to know more about me.

That's dangerous territory. I've known him for years, but I've done a good job at keeping myself guarded. Papa taught me not to trust others — even the man who ruled the *famiglia* we were a part of. Although, he had only ever mentioned Alessio's brother and father.

Maybe I was wrong about not trusting Alessio.

Although, I have a hard time believing that. I think that Alessio can be trusted to a point, but I don't think that point would ever include my heart.

Not that I would be sticking around long enough for us to get to that point. Casual sex would be the most we could ever have.

Casual, mind-blowing sex that leaves me struggling to remember my own name.

'Billie, you look like you're spiraling. What's wrong?"

"If you had one chance to do whatever you wanted with the mafia and nobody would try to fight you on it, what would you do?" I don't want to tell him what's really on my mind. He would get too close. See too much of me.

"I don't know," he says as he pulls up to the iron gates

and punches in the code. "I have a lot of things that I would want to do, but we don't live in a world where nobody would fight me on those things. I have people waiting for me to slip up every way I turn."

"Alright," I say as he parks the car in front of the house. "Think about it. Pretend that just for tonight, the world is a perfect place and you could change anything you wanted in the *famiglia*. Nobody would ever come for you. Nobody would try to fight you. What would you do?"

He sighs as we walk into the house. "I don't know. I'm tired of everyone thinking that they are better than everyone else. People will do and say what they need to if they want to get ahead. My father and brother were great at creating a toxic environment for everyone around them."

"How would you be different, then?" I ask as we walk to my room. I want to go sit beneath the stars and the pretty lights as we talk, surrounded by tropical plants in a place that feels like our own little paradise.

"Everybody would have to earn what they have. Women would have equal places among the men. If you don't earn what you have, then you start over again. There is no blaming others when you are passed over on a promotion or an opportunity. I want them to see me as the bad guy, instead of seeing everyone else that way."

"Why do you have to be the bad guy?" I lead him out to the far side of the courtyard where an outdoor sofa bed sits. There is a curved canopy hanging over it, soft white curtains cascading down either side.

Alessio reaches for a light switch on the wall to turn on the string lights overhead. "Someone has to be the bad guy. Right now, I'm still seen as weak. I know I am. It's been ten years of being in control, but the men who came to their positions under my father and brother still see me as weaker than they were."

"So," I say as I climb onto the sofa bed and lean back into the cushions. "In a perfect world — one where you could turn the Marchetti mafia into anything you wanted — you would still be the bad guy."

"It's the only option there is." He climbs onto the bed beside me, looping an arm over the back. "Someone has to be the bad guy."

"I fail to see why it has to be you. Why couldn't you be a leader who was respected instead of one who was feared?"

"Marchettis are men who earn respect through being feared."

"Do you think that is true respect?" I shuffle a little closer to him. "I think that you are more capable than you realize, but you keep using your dead brother and father as an excuse to not step up and take full control. You let men who were alive when the dinosaurs roamed the earth whisper in your ear and tell you the way that things should be."

"The same way that you're telling me the way things should be?" The corner of his mouth twitches as he stares at me.

"I haven't told you what I thought you should do with the mafia once tonight, though I've had plenty of opportunities to. I'm questioning why you seem to allow others to run the mafia for you."

"It's easier than creating waves."

"No great empire was built by a man who was too afraid to make waves."

Alessio sighs and leans back, closing his eyes. "Maybe I don't want to build a great empire. Maybe, in another world where everything is perfect, I would be working a normal job with a wife and kids. I wouldn't have killed anyone. I wouldn't have flown us to another state over a war that is on the horizon."

"You have chance after chance to walk away and leave the mafia to another. You could pick up tomorrow and leave if you really wanted to."

"Blood in, Billie, but death to get out. You know that as well as I do."

I nod and close my eyes, pushing away the guilt that rises at those words. He doesn't know that I'm planning to leave. It won't be death out for me. I will get to have the life I want.

I wish he could have the life he wants.

When I open my eyes, Alessio is looking at me. There are a thousand different questions lingering in his eyes, but he doesn't voice any of them. Instead, he sighs and looks away.

"So," I say, sensing the need for a change in topic. "How about that casual sex trend the kids are all about these days?"

Alessio bursts out laughing, the tension in the air fading away. I laugh with him, staring up at the gauzy white canopy above me.

He takes my hand and kisses the back of it, driving the butterflies in my stomach wild. There are more and more moments like these where I see the person beneath all the shit going on in his life. There are glimpses of a man who is terrified of who he is.

It's that man that interests me the most. The one who hides away from the world while being able to take control of everyone around him. The man who is calm in a crisis, even though his own life is falling apart.

I move to straddle his lap, my heart racing in my chest. I

may not know what I'm doing when it comes to Alessio, but if I have a few more weeks left with him, I may as well make the most of them.

"And what do you think you're doing?" he asks, his tone surprisingly playful as his hands land on my hips.

I roll my hips, feeling his cock harden beneath me. "I told you that I heard about this new casual sex thing. I was thinking of trying it."

Even though it's only going to get me hurt in one way or another.

He laughs and his hands slide beneath my shirt, his thumbs brushing against my skin just beneath my bra. "Oh, really?"

"Well, unless you don't want to," I say, pretending to get off him.

Alessio flips us over and pins me beneath him. There is fire burning in his eyes as he looks down at me and shakes his head. "I don't remember saying that I didn't want to."

I prop myself up on my forearms and kiss him. He groans into the kiss as I nip at his bottom lip. He takes control quickly, pressing his hardened cock against me while hovering over me. His tongue slips into my mouth, tangling with mine as he nudges me back down against the bed.

Alessio makes his way down my body, his hands running along my curves until he comes to the button on my shorts. He flicks it open before dragging my shorts down my legs. I sit up long enough to haul off my shirt and toss my bra to the side before relaxing back into the pillows.

He pulls my shorts off and carefully removes one sandal and then the other. His tongue flicks against the curve of my ankle before he steps away. My core aches as he unbuttons his shirt slowly, taking his time to reveal himself.

My nipples pebble against the cold summer night as he stands naked in front of me, his hand wrapped around his cock. He strokes it while staring at me. The look on his face makes me feel like every layer of who I am has been stripped away.

"Your pretty pussy is wet for me already," he says, his voice raspy as he kneels on the sofa bed between my legs. "I'm going to bury myself into that tight little pussy and you're going to take it for me like a good girl, aren't you?"

"Maybe." I grin as his fingers brush against my wet slit, circling my clit once before he pulls away.

"Well now, that sounds like you don't want me to fuck you. I have no problem going inside and fucking my fist, Billie."

The image of him jerking himself off has my pussy pulsating. I bite my bottom lip, my gaze dropping to his cock. He arches an eyebrow and kneels between my legs.

"That's what you want, isn't it? You want to watch me play with my cock. Don't think I haven't seen the way you look at me when I do." He chuckles and grips his cock, running his hand down the length. "Any other day, I would be happy to play out your little fantasy but right now, I need to be inside you."

"Then fuck me," I say, my voice breathy as I part my legs a little wider.

My gaze connects with his as I run my hands up and down my torso. I take my time playing with my breasts, massaging them until they're aching while he watches me. My pussy is dripping as I roll my nipples between my fingers, an orgasm already building.

Alessio lowers himself over me, his cock brushing against my core. I moan as he slips inside me, stretching my inner walls. He rolls his hips, thrusting slowly as I hook a leg over his hip.

"Fuck, you feel good," he groans and drops his head to my shoulder, sucking and nipping my skin as he thrusts faster.

I arch my back, allowing him to push deeper into me. Alessio kisses his way down to my breasts, taking a nipple in his mouth. I moan and grip his shoulders, my nails digging into his flesh as he drives harder into me.

My pussy squeezes around him, my wetness coating his cock as I come. Alessio thrusts faster and harder, his cock throbbing. He rolls his hips before pulling back to kneel between my legs.

He grabs my thighs and pulls me hard against him, my legs wrapped around his waist as he slams into me. I grip the cushion as another orgasm washes over me. My pussy clamps down on his cock as he comes, thrusting slowly until he is satiated.

Alessio pulls out and falls to the bed beside me, his chest heaving. When he rolls onto his side and gives me that smile, my heart melts.

There is no way that I'm getting out of this with my heart intact.

20

———

ALESSIO

BILLIE SMOOTHES DOWN HER GREEN SUNDRESS AS SHE steps out of the car. Her eyes dart around the parking lot, looking for danger that isn't there. Both my men and Jovan's swept the area before we arrived.

Jovan had suggested meeting in the little boathouse by the water. He said that few people were ever here beyond some of his men. It was where he housed the small boat he used for quick runs up and down the coast.

"Are you sure that this is safe?" Billie asks as she looks up at the gulls circling overhead. "Christian Herrera isn't exactly the kind of man who works well with others."

"Jovan recommended him. If I didn't trust Jovan, I wouldn't be here. He is close to Christian and he knows what kind of man he is." I run my hand through my hair and watch as the waves crash against the shore. "But now, I'm not sure that this is safe."

Billie takes a deep breath and nods. "Do you think Paolo followed us out here?"

"I'm sure that he did. Or had someone follow us. He would be stupid not to. He wants to kill me and he's not all that fond of you. Someone is watching us, it just might not be him."

"Alright. What do you want me to do when we get in there?" she asks as we head down the wooden boardwalk that leads from the parking lot to the boathouse.

"Just be quiet and watch. If something feels off to you, tell me immediately. We'll call the meeting off and get out of here."

I don't want to have to walk away from this meeting. It's the best chance that I have at being able to put an end to Paolo and his little mafia. I need Christian and Jovan's help. While I already know Jovan is on my side, Christian is a wildcard.

"You think I'm going to know when things are going sideways?" Bille scoffs and shakes her head as I reach around her to knock on the door. "I don't know these men."

"You have a strong intuition. I trust you on this matter. If you think something is wrong with the meeting, you let me know and we'll leave. I'm not going to risk both of our lives for this."

"Alright. If there's anything weird, I'll let you know."

"Do you have a gun with you?" I ask, though I know Jovan is going to take them and secure them in a safe.

Billie hikes her dress a little higher, showing off the thigh holster and the small gun in it. My cock hardens as I look at her, straining against my jeans.

I could skip this meeting and drag her back to bed with me. Or I could fuck her on the hood of my car with that holster still wrapped around her thigh.

There is something about seeing her armed and ready to kill that turns me on. She gives me a small smile and lets go of her dress. The door opens and Jovan stands there with a basket in his hands.

"Weapons." He smiles and nods to Billie. "Nice to see you again. Hadley is already waiting in there to ask you a million questions."

Billie smiles and takes out her gun. She tosses it into the basket before reaching up into her loose bun and pulling out a sheathed knife. Jovan arches an eyebrow, looking impressed as she tosses the knife into the basket.

"Anything else hiding?" he asks as I drop my guns into the basket.

Billie places one hand on my shoulder to steady herself while she lifts a foot. I watch as she pulls a knife out of the sole of the wedge and drops it in the basket.

"Is that all?" Jovan laughs and shakes his head. "I swear, if you pull out any more weapons, I'm going to have to wonder where you stash them all. Hell, I'll have you teach my people how to hide them."

Billie grins. "That was the last one."

"Well then, come inside and make yourselves at home. There's two bedrooms and a washroom up the stairs to your right. The kitchen and living room are just down the hall." Jovan steps to the side to let us in. "Alessio, we're going to be meeting with Christian in the living room. I've got some lunch going on the grill outside if you're hungry."

"No, but I do need to make a call first."

The call isn't something I thought about before today. Listening to Billie talk on the phone with Arturo while she got ready this morning had brought it to mind. He was barely able to speak still, but he tried.

"We'll all be in there when you're ready. Christian should be here soon too. My study is that room. Feel free to use it while you make the call."

I nod and disappear into the room he nods toward. As

the door shuts behind me, my heart pounds. I should have thought about Arturo sooner.

I pull out my phone and dial Davide's number, listening to the phone ring until the call connects. There is shouting in the background that makes me think maybe I shouldn't have left.

"Davide, how are things going there?" I ask, my tone stern. "What the fuck is all the commotion in the background? You told me that you would be able to handle this while I was gone."

"I'm handling it. Some of the men are pissed that you killed Antonio. More are pissed that I killed Zade yesterday for trying to start a new bet about one of the girls who just turned eighteen."

I sigh and pinch the bridge of my nose. I can't afford to lose more men, but I did tell him to make an example of anyone who tried to follow in Antonio's footsteps. It doesn't surprise me that the men are trying this shit while I'm out of town.

"If anyone else tries to start something while I'm gone, lock them up. I will deal with them when I get back. Beat them every day until I do get back, though. We don't need these men thinking that they're on vacation while I'm away."

"Will do, boss." Davide groans and something shatters in the background.

"Do I even want to know what that was?"

"I doubt it. I'll deal with it. Some of the capos are on their way and this place should settle down shortly."

"Well, checking in on you isn't why I called." I lean against the wall and cross my legs at the ankles. "I need you to arrange for Arturo and his security detail to be moved into my house. The guest suite in the basement will do."

"When do you want it done?"

"As soon as possible. If Paolo is going to try and take out another hit on Arturo, he is going to do it while I'm out of town. If Arturo is safe in my home, that leaves Paolo with no options to personally hurt me."

"I'll see to it personally as soon as the capos arrive to deal with the soldiers."

"Good." I'm about to hang up when I think of my conversation with Billie. She thinks that I'm capable of being a better leader than my father and brother. "Thank you, Davide."

There is a long pause before he clears his throat. "You're welcome, sir."

"Good luck." I hang up and slide the phone back into my pocket.

That little thank you may not have been a lot, but it was more than my father and brother would have given anyone they deemed beneath them in the hierarchy.

I rake my fingers through my short beard before opening the door and stepping out. Billie's sweet laugh echoes through the boathouse. I smile and take a moment to just listen to it. It's little moments when death isn't surrounding us on every side that I enjoy the most. Billie laughing and smiling as she teases me are my favorite parts of any day.

Billie looks up from her conversation with Hadley as I walk into the room. She has her legs pulled up beneath her, tendrils of her blonde hair falling around her face. I take a seat across from them in one of the beige leather armchairs.

The sky outside the massive windows is dark and gray. It looks like a storm is rolling in. The waves rock the boat tied to the dock.

Jovan bangs around some pots and pans in the kitchen,

the scent of garlic and onion filling the room. He puts a plate draped with a towel on the kitchen island.

"Did you make carnitas tacos?" Hadley asks, her eyes lighting up as she gets up from the couch. "Please tell me that you made carnitas."

Jovan laughs and nods, putting a tray of shredded meat on the counter beside the tortillas. 'Yes. There's some cheese, pico de gallo, and lime wedges ready too. Didn't bother with the rice this time, but everything else is ready."

"You guys are going to die when you taste this," Hadley says, grabbing Billie's hand and pulling her up from the couch.

There is a knock at the door as I go to stand. Jovan looks at me and nods before abandoning lunch and heading for the door. His voice is too low to make out the words he says, but I'm sure he is giving Christian the speech he gave me about where everything is.

Jovan leads Christian into the room a few minutes later. Billie stops in the middle of stuffing a taco in her mouth to look at him. Her gaze flicks over to me before she returns to eating.

I stand and hold out my hand. "Good to see you."

Christian nods and shakes my hand. "It's good to see you as well, though I wish it was under different circumstances."

"Well," Jovan says as he claims a black recliner by the fireplace. "Why don't the two of you grab some food and take a seat. We can get to business right away."

Billie nods to a plate loaded with tacos sitting beside her. I wink at her before grabbing the plate and sitting back down in the leather chair. Christian makes himself a plate of food before taking the seat beside Jovan.

"So, I know Hadley, but who is that?" Christian asks, his tone sharp as he cuts his gaze toward Billie.

"Billie Carbone. She's the daughter of my consigliere. He is unfortunately unable to be here, so she is with me until he heals."

Christian nods and digs into the food. "Alright. So, this Paolo problem. He needs to die."

Jovan chuckles. "Nobody is going to argue with you there."

"How did this fucker even get to power? He should have been put down the moment an uprising began."

I grit my teeth.

"You're not wrong about that either. I allowed him to live after I made a promise to my dying brother. For years, Paolo fell in line and acted the way he was supposed to. It has only been within the last several months that he has decided to try to take control."

"He is doing a decent job," Christian says, putting his plate on the wooden coffee table. "You would think that you would have been able to take him out on your own."

"You would think that *you* would have been able to take him out on your own," I say, my tone sharp as I lean back in my chair, my plate of food balanced on my lap. "He is stealing your people as well. Last I heard, there were two different attacks in Nashville at a couple of the bars you own."

"You've been doing your research."

I shrug. "I may allow him to live, but that doesn't mean that I'm not watching his every move and attacking where I can. I've been working on cutting off his drug supply, but I can't track down his latest supplier."

"I have a lead on that," Jovan says, pulling out his phone and opening up a message. "One of my informants saw

Paolo in Miami last week. We think that he is trying to create a deal with one of my suppliers."

"That's three states that he is now trying to take control of. If we don't work together, he is going to start turning us against each other. Paolo has been in the mafia since he was born. He knows how to play the game and he's determined." I eat one of the tacos and glance over at Billie. "He is going to destroy the people you care about the most before moving on to everything else."

Hadley catches me looking at Billie and raises an eyebrow. I focus my attention on Jovan, pretending that I didn't see the look she gave me. Billie laughs at something Hadley says to her. Both of them get up and head outside onto the deck.

I watch as Billie sits in one of the lounge chairs and tilts her face to the sky.

"Great." Christian sighs and shakes his head. "I have a security detail on my baby sister already, but I suspect Paolo is trying to get to her. She's my heir. If anything happens to her, my people may turn against me. My sister is beloved among our people."

"It sounds like we all have a reason to work together," I say as I look at the other two men. "Paolo is ruthless. My father raised him like a son and taught him everything he knows. He will stop at nothing to get what he wants."

"Well, we will have to make sure that doesn't happen."

"So, it's agreed, then," Jovan says, his voice solemn. "We will work together to take down Paolo Marino."

Christian nods. "We will work together. We first need to pool the information we have on him. Alessio, as you are the one who knows him the best, you should take point."

I finish my tacos and put my plate on the table. "This is true. I don't know him well anymore, it would seem. There was a time when he was due to be my new consigliere when Arturo was ready to step down. He had begun training about a year before this mess started."

"What prompted this, then?" Christian looked out the window at Billie. "Does it have anything to do with her? You watch her like she is important to you."

"Arturo is my closest friend. I've known Billie since she was born. I would never be able to forgive myself if something happened to her." I try to subtly swallow the lump in my throat, not wanting to dive into the relationship I have with Billie. Christian will read more into it than there is.

He nods while Jovan smirks and shakes his head. "So, she is nothing more to you than that."

"Correct." I cross my arms and glance over at Jovan. He drops the smirk and takes a big bite of his last taco. "Now, Paolo is going to be looking for more low-level people to join him. I've been burning his hideouts in Georgia as I find them, but I can't do much about the ones in Florida or Tennessee."

"I've been taking care of what I can find, but he is building more support. There are people who aren't happy with me, and I have a suspicion that the FBI are starting to sniff around my operation." Christian crosses his arms. "We need to deal with this quickly and quietly."

"We need to gather more information about Paolo's operation first. We have to figure out what is going on and how to prevent his next moves. If we launch an attack too soon after meeting, he is going to see it coming." I get up to grab a beer from the fridge. "We have to be smart about this. We're only going to get one chance to take him down."

Jovan nods. "We have to keep attacking him on our individual fronts. We keep in communication, but we do what we can on our own to take him down."

"When the opportunity presents itself, we take him down together," Christian says. "If this turns into a war, we're going to have to be prepared to die."

"He will escalate it to a war if he gets the chance." I pop the top off the beer and take a sip. "I'll do what I can to find out how big his organization really is. Most of his people are in Georgia, from my limited understanding. I'll have my men look into it further."

"With that settled," Jovan says, getting up and grabbing a beer of his own. "Why don't I run to the store for dinner ingredients, and we can all celebrate here. There is a storm coming in, but there is nothing quite like watching the waves crash against the dock."

"Let's do it," I say, glancing out the window at Billie. It will do her good to spend some time with Hadley. To see how women in other cartels and mafias are treated.

Or it might only make her hate me for the way things work back home.

21

BILLIE

The sun is climbing above the horizon as the waves crash against the shore. Bright oranges and pinks streak across the sky as I walk along the cold sand. I pull my hair back from my face in a messy bun and glance over my shoulder at the men trailing behind me.

It's been a good week, though I've spent the last two days trapped alone at the rental house while Alessio goes about his business. Hadley has been too busy to come over, and exploring Miami with a couple meatheads following me around isn't my idea of fun.

This morning, I just need a walk. I need some time on my own to wrap my head around everything happening.

Alessio is a different man away from the mafia. He is more relaxed and enjoying himself. He smiles more and jokes around with me in the morning. At night, he sits down to whatever meal the private chef has made and talks about his day. He avoids anything that has to do with Paolo, but he makes an effort to seem like a normal person.

It's at odds with the Alessio I've always known. The

cold man is fading away and he's transforming into someone different.

The person he would have become if he had never been forced into this life.

Sometimes I wonder why he took the mafia over when his father and brother died. It could have been his mother's pushing. She seems like a delight — though I haven't had to deal with her since Alessio kicked her out.

Did she tell him that he had to do something he hates? Or was he raised to believe that the mafia is all he would ever be able to do?

Laughter sounds on the boardwalk to my left. I look over and see a young couple running together, their towels slung over their shoulders. The man tosses the woman over his shoulder when he catches her, spinning her around.

Someday, I'm going to have something like that.

I just have to figure out the rest of my life first. I need to leave the mafia and start building my resort. There is a life that I want and I'm not going to get it by falling for Alessio.

The worst part is that I know it's a risk. When he smiles at me or plays around with me, I feel like things could be different between us. It's easy to believe that there could be something more than just casual sex.

But there can't be. We have an expiration date.

As soon as the contract is up, I have the rest of the money, and Papa is able to move, I'm leaving.

Even as I wish I could stay...

I glance around the rest of the beach, trying to distract myself from thoughts of the future. I'm not going to ruin my last day in Miami by thinking about all the things that could be. For the rest of the day, I'm going to try and enjoy myself.

My heart skips a beat when I see a familiar face

standing in the parking lot. I rub my eyes, glancing at the same spot again, but Paolo is no longer there.

Maybe he wasn't there to begin with. Maybe I'm seeing things.

I take a deep breath and try to slow my racing pulse. As I try to calm down, I count the waves crashing against the shore.

"Something wrong?" one of the men asks as he appears beside me.

"Just thought I saw someone but they're not there." I shrug and sit down in the sand.

"Alright. We're going to go get a coffee from the stand right behind you. We'll be able to see you if anything happens. Just wait here. Got it?"

I nod and pull my knees to my chest, wrapping my arms around them. "No worries about me going anywhere. If I finally get some time without the two of you following me around, I'm going to take it."

He chuckles and shakes his head. "You sure are Arturo's daughter. I hope that he gets better soon."

"I'm sorry," I say, looking at him over my shoulder. "I don't recognize you."

The man shrugs and stuffs his hands in his pockets. "Shane. Used to go to school with your dad before he dropped out. Knew your mom too. Hell, I remember when they found out they were pregnant with you. I got locked away after that. I'm sure that you are his pride and joy, though. He was so excited to be a father."

"Well, thank you for saying that." I smile and nod to him, watching as he and his partner walk to the coffee hut.

It's close enough that I can see them as they stand in line. Shane nods to me before looking around. The other man says something to him as they step forward in line.

I turn and focus back on the ocean, trying to soothe the nerves running through my body. Everything about my life right now is twisting out of control. Papa is doing a bit better. Being in Alessio's home and watched over is pissing him off, but that anger is fueling him to work harder to speak properly again.

"You know, I was waiting until the two of them would be stupid enough to leave you alone," Paolo says as he sits down beside them. His shoulder brushes against mine and cool metal presses into my bare ribcage. "If you alert them or reach for your gun, I'll shoot you right here and now."

"Good to know that this is going to be that kind of conversation," I say as I glance at him. "What are you doing here? You're really stupid enough to follow Alessio to Miami?"

"Thought that it might be time to add a little more tension to the game we've been playing, don't you think? I mean, I tried to get to your father, but Alessio already had him moved. Smart, on his end. I thought that he would have forgotten about him now that he has you."

"I don't know what that's supposed to mean." My stomach lurches. For a second, I consider throwing sand in his eyes. It might give me enough time to pull my gun and shoot him.

There isn't enough time, though. If Paolo was new to wielding a weapon, it would work. He's been using a gun for years. Fighting for even longer. He would shoot me before I ever got a hand on my gun.

"I can tell by the look in your eyes that you're trying to figure out a way out of this, but it's not going to happen. You don't have to worry, though. I'm not going to kill you right now. I just want to leave Alessio a little message."

Hands wrap around my biceps at the same time Paolo

grabs my hair and yanks my head back. He grins as he looms over me, swapping his gun for a knife. The scent of cheap cologne invades my senses as someone else holds a gun to my head.

"I know that this looks bad," Paolo says, his tone sympathetic despite his grin. "It really is sad to see you caught in the middle of this, but the other two over there aren't worth my time. I want to rile Alessio up. Show him what happens if he continues to underestimate me."

I glare at him, imagining ripping his head from the body and drop-kicking it into the ocean. Paolo smirks as he drags the blade lightly along my neck, breaking the skin.

"I thought about my name, but that would be taking it too far, don't you think?" Paolo asks, tucking his knife back in his pocket as he steps back from me. "Have a good afternoon, Billie. From what I hear, Alessio is in meetings all day and won't be able to see you until tonight."

"As if I'm going to tell him about this," I say, getting to my feet and holding a hand to the cut. "If this is the best you can do, I think he's right to underestimate you."

Paolo glances over my shoulder, his eyes narrowing. "If your little friends weren't coming back, I would stay to teach you a lesson. Unfortunately, I don't feel like dying today."

He winks at me before taking off down the beach, disappearing between the crowds starting to make their way onto the beach. I turn and make my way to the coffee stand, still holding a hand to my throat. Warm blood coats my skin as I approach Shane and the other man.

"I need some napkins and to go spend the rest of the day out until this closes over." I pull my hand away from my throat long enough to show Shane what's been done. "We both know Alessio will kill you if he finds out you left me alone for even a few minutes. Help me spend the day away from the house and I'll make sure he won't come after you."

Shane nods and grabs napkins from the counter, passing them to me. "We should take you to see a doctor. You might need stitches."

"It isn't that deep." I take the napkins and hold them against my neck. "I need some things to wear. Let's go to the mall and kill some time there."

"You want to go to the mall with a bloody neck?" Shane shakes his head and stuffs more napkins in his pocket. "Billie, that's not a good idea. Who did this to you?"

"I need one of those damn crop tops with a turtleneck, unless you don't want me to hide this?" I ignore his question, looking at him expectantly. I don't like holding this over his head — it was nothing he did wrong — but I'm not ready for Alessio to find out about this yet.

I just want to enjoy my last day in Miami.

Shane sighs and leads the way back to the car. He looks at the other man and jerks his chin toward the beach. "Sweep the area for whoever might have done this."

The other man takes off as we get in the car. I lean back in the seat, pulling away the napkins and looking in the mirror to check the damage. It isn't a deep cut, but it's going to take some time to heal.

I better buy a lot of turtlenecks.

"Did you have a good day out?" Alessio asks when I walk into the kitchen later that evening. He looks up from the document he's reading, his eyes narrowing. "What the hell are you wearing? That's not what you wore when you left this morning."

"You pay attention to what I'm wearing?" I ask, my tone teasing as I open the fridge and grab a bottle of white wine. "I didn't know you cared that much, Alessio."

He scoffs. "And now I know you're trying to hide something from me. Are you going to tell me or do I have to beat it out of Shane."

I glare at him as I grab a glass down and pour myself some wine. "You're seriously going to beat a man because I might not tell you about my day?"

"I have never seen you wear a turtleneck before today, Billie. Either you have one hell of a hickey that I didn't give you, which violates our contract, or you got into some trouble."

Knowing that there is no other choice, I sigh and pull down the collar of my shirt. Alessio's hands clench into fists as he gets up and comes over to me. He swallows hard before gently taking my chin in his hand and tilting my head up.

"Who the fuck did this to you?" he asks, his tone deadly as he takes a step back. "I'm going to fucking kill whoever it was."

"Well, funnily enough, killing him is what you've been meeting with Jovan and Christian about all week," I say, though my tone is dry. "Alessio, it's nothing. Paolo did this as a game to piss you off. He wants you to be angry and make stupid decisions."

"Killing him is the best decision I'm ever going to make," Alessio says as he walks out of the kitchen.

The front door slams a few seconds later, leaving me alone with my glass of wine. I sigh and take it to the courtyard outside my room, needing some time to relax.

This day has been more than I bargained for.

The stars are hanging high in the sky, glittering above

the courtyard by the time I finish the bottle of wine and head inside. I drop my book on my bed before taking my glass to the sink. My stomach growls as I open the fridge and look for the leftovers the cook put in there earlier.

Alessio walks into the room as I shovel cold chicken parmesan into my mouth. Blood trickles down the side of his face from a cut on his forehead.

"What the hell did you do?" I ask, abandoning my food to grab a clean cloth from the drawer. I soak it and wring it out while Alessio sits down in the living room. "Damn it, Alessio."

I look down at the blood stains on his shirt, wondering whether they are his or not. My heart jumps in my chest as a lump in my throat threatens to choke me. I sit on the arm of the couch beside him, pressing the cloth against his cut.

"I found the men who were with Paolo. They won't be giving you any problems." Alessio grabs my hand and stops me from cleaning the blood from his face. "Billie, you should have told me the moment that happened this morning. I would have dealt with it then."

"I can appreciate that, but he didn't hurt me. He tried to scare me, and it didn't work."

"Cutting you is hurting you." Alessio shakes his head and lets go of my hand. "I didn't find Paolo. He's long gone. Shane has been looking for him for the last several hours, but we're sure that he's on a flight out of Florida."

"You should have just left it alone. You did exactly what he wanted you to."

"It doesn't matter if I left it alone or not. Paolo came after you. I'm not going to allow that to happen."

"He came after me because he's watching us. I'm sure that he thinks there is something between us. We haven't been careful enough while we've been in Miami. I don't know what he's seen and what he hasn't."

Alessio sighs and nods. "When we get back to Atlanta, this has to cool off. Arturo is living with us, and Paolo is watching."

"Once we get back, we have to keep our distance from each other." I put the bloody cloth on the table and flick the collar of his gray dress shirt. "Is this your blood?"

He looks down at the stains and shakes his head. "It's not. I'm going to go get cleaned up. You should get some rest. We have to leave early in the morning."

Alessio gets up and leaves the room, heading for his own bedroom. I watch him go before grabbing the cloth and taking it to the sink.

This is where things have to come to an end between us.

22

———

ALESSIO

It's been a week since the plane landed back in Atlanta and I keep thinking about that week in Miami. It felt good to spend time with Billie, enjoying each other's company and not worrying about other people seeing us together.

Since we've been back, I've been avoiding her as much as possible. Not that it's hard to do. When I'm not at the casino or checking on things at the compound, I'm running around the city and digging up any lead I can find about Paolo.

Since last week, he's gone into hiding. Him and all his men. There is no sign of them anywhere, even when we light his businesses on fire. We've been destroying every business and operation of Paolo's that we can find, but he still doesn't come out of hiding.

I'm getting tired of looking for a ghost. I want this to be over as soon as possible.

These games are getting old, especially with Billie getting hurt.

I'm doing everything I can to protect her, but it still

doesn't seem like it's enough. I doubled her security detail, but I still worry about her constantly when she's not with me.

Paolo has gotten to her twice already. The next time he gets to her — and I'm sure that he's going to try — could be the last.

I sigh and push myself away from my desk. I've been trying to do paperwork at the casino for the last hour, but I can't focus. The only thing I can think about is everything else going on in my life. Thankfully, I have a good team at the casino who is capable of keeping things running if I need to take some time off.

Billie knocks on my door frame, a stack of binders in her arms. My gaze drags down her body, taking in the faux leather skirt and the dark blue shirt with billowing sleeves that cinch at her wrists.

If there is one thing I've realized about Billie since giving her a job at the casino, it's that she's going to dress up for work every day.

She's beautiful.

Her heels click against the floor as she walks into the office and drops the binders on the corner of my desk. "You know, you could have less reports to go over. Year end isn't until December. Why do you want to go over all these numbers now? The quarter isn't even over yet."

There is curiosity in her voice as she comes to stand beside me while I grab the top binder and open it up. Sometimes I forget that she is here to learn.

Though I want to kick her out of the office before I make yet another bad decision, I don't. She leans a little closer to me, the vanilla scent of her perfume wafting around us.

"Alright, well, this is the book of vendors that we use for

the hotel portion of the casino and the three restaurants that are on the property, as well as the club. The other binders are filled with vendor information for the clubs I own downtown. I think the last one in that pile should be for the real estate company I've just recently purchased."

"Diverse portfolio," she says, pulling over a chair to sit beside me. "Why do you review the vendor books?"

"I like to take a look at them every month to keep up with costs and trends in the markets, depending on which business we are talking about. I don't want to be buying the wrong things and essentially lighting my money on fire."

Billie nods, her eyes shining as she pulls out her phone and makes a note. "Do you work with national vendors or local ones?"

"I try to work with locals whenever possible. It helps with the other, less than legal sides to the business as well. You would be amazed at how many people are willing to look the other way when you spend tens of thousands of dollars at their business every year."

Billie nods, though her frown deepens. "I'm not going to be doing anything illegal when I start my own business. I want to keep everything above board. Risking it all is not for me."

I shrug and flip to another page in the book, showing an overview of the monthly expenses for the casino. "That's fine. Some of my businesses aren't fronts, but owning a casino is an easy way to clean money. There is so much moving through here every day that nobody thinks to look a little deeper."

She bites her bottom lip, looking torn between asking me something and keeping her mouth shut.

"Billie, if there's something on your mind, just say it. I thought we had agreed that you could talk to me?"

The corner of her mouth twitches. "How much do you pay the cops every month to look the other way?"

I chuckle and flip to another page, pointing at a number. The company listed beside the amount is a front, one used by the police to accept bribes. "You would be amazed by the things a little money can do in this city."

"That's a lot of money." Her leg shakes as she looks over the other numbers on the rest of the page. "Was all of this in place before you took over or after?"

"Some of it was before but most of it was after."

She nods. "Is it safe to be talking about this here? The cops don't have your office bugged or anything, do they?"

I shake my head. "No. It's fine. I would have stopped you if it wasn't. The office isn't bugged. None of the casino is. Shane sweeps through it every morning and then another man does a second pass. If they're listening, it's not here."

"How many times have you been to prison?" she asks as she leans back in her chair and crosses one leg over the other. Her skirt rides a little higher on her leg.

I could bend her over the desk right now and nobody would know.

"Why do you want to know?" I ask, pushing the binder away from me. "I don't mind talking about it, but this seems like a lot of questions. Normally you don't seem that interested in the illegal parts of life."

Billie shrugs and looks down at her nails, picking at something that isn't there. "I don't know. It just seems like we still have a lot of time to spend together, and I don't know what happened in the years I was away."

"I didn't go to jail while you were away. I think the last time I did any time was ten years ago. Right before I took over, I got out. It was on a minor drug charge. Before that, I'd been in and out of jail since I was sixteen."

She presses her lips together in a thin line. "I had to sit in a cell overnight once."

I grin as I look at her. Though I know that she's killed people before, she's never gone to jail. Billie has a natural talent for covering up her crimes.

"What were you in a cell for?"

Billie smiles, her cheeks turning pink. "I might have punched a cop in the face. I was out at a bar with some of my friends once. I don't know how I ended up on the table dancing, but I did. Anyway, the cop tried to pull me off the table. I didn't like that too much, so I punched him in the face."

"Did you break his nose? Or do we only break noses when we have a frying pan?"

Billie laughs and rolls her eyes. "You think you're funny, don't you?"

"You didn't answer my question."

"I broke his nose." She bursts out laughing, shaking her head. "I still can't believe I did that. I should have known that it was going to get me in trouble, but I was too drunk to care."

"That's amazing."

She nods. "It was. You know, I haven't seen much of you in the last week. I know we're staying away from each other, but it feels weird. I guess I got used to talking to you. Or you pissing me off."

"It's better this way," I say, even though I don't believe it.

If I'm being honest with myself, I've missed her too. I miss coming home and having someone dancing around the kitchen and making me feel better about my day.

"I know it is." Billie gets up and moves the chair back

where she got it from. "I have some other things that I need to get done. Have a good day."

Her tone is cold, and her shoulders are stiff as she walks out of the room. I don't know what just happened between us. One minute it felt like we were having a good time and the next we acknowledged the reality of our situation. I didn't think that would make her this cold to me, though.

She is the one who has been wanting this to end since the beginning.

There's something going on in her head that she isn't sharing with me.

Maybe she's starting to fall for me the same way I'm falling for her.

It's a wild thought and one that has no place in my life right now. I need to focus on finding Paolo and putting an end to the shit he's doing.

BILLIE IS IN THE POOL WHEN I GET HOME LATE THAT night. She swims beneath the stars, the pool lights set to a dark purple tone. I should go inside and continue putting distance between us, but after the day I've had, I need someone to talk to.

"Hey," Billie says as I kick off my shoes and take off my clothing. I leave the clothing heaped in a pile before jumping into the cool water. As I surface and push my hair back from my face, she climbs into one of the floating loungers.

"Hey." I climb onto the other lounger and cross one leg over the other. "How was the rest of your day?"

"It was alright. Got some of that filing done. Reworked your schedule."

I nodded and sighed. "Thank you for that. The last thing I was expecting was a call from Christian."

"Why would Christian be calling again? I thought the two of you got everything sorted out when we were in Miami."

"We did. And then we didn't." I sigh and tilt my head back, trying to find a constellation in the sky above me to distract my mind from the thousands of racing thoughts. "Paolo has pulled out of Tennessee completely. I spoke to Jovan after speaking with Christian and there is no sign of him in Florida anymore either. He's coming to Georgia and he's planning something."

"So, Christian called to warn you?" Billie asks, braiding her hair back from her face.

"Sort of. He called to warn me that he would be coming out here. He's at a bunker right now, but he's going to be moving into the house later today. I don't want anyone else to know he's here."

"Won't people see him coming and going from the compound?"

I shake my head. "I'm going to go pick him up personally. Turn off the cameras when I approach the house and pull into the garage. He'll come and go using the tunnels that run beneath the house and out into the rest of the city."

"You have tunnels beneath the house?" Billie's eyes widen. "You're going to have to take me walking down there one day. I only knew about the escape tunnels from the main house."

I laugh and shrug. "It's not that exciting, but one day, maybe."

Billie gets a strange look on her face before nodding and closing her eyes. "So, with Christian in town, do you think that the Paolo situation is going to be dealt with faster?"

"I don't know. Paolo is clever and he knows how we operate. He's been a member since he was born. He was raised alongside me and my brother. But he's also losing control."

"What makes you think that? Didn't he just pull everyone back here?"

I skim my fingers through the water. "Yes. But if he was playing the long game, he would have gone farther underground. He would keep his moves hidden until he was ready to attack. He wouldn't make it known that he had pulled out of both Florida and Tennessee. That makes me think that he's getting desperate."

"Or that's what he wants you to think." Billie glances over at me and gives me a soft smile. "I should get to bed. It's getting late and it's been a long day."

She slides off the lounger and into the water, swimming to the edge of the pool. I watch as she hauls herself out of the pool, water dripping down her sun-kissed skin.

I should be going to bed with her. I should be showing her how much she means to me.

I should be keeping my distance because chasing after my best friend's daughter — especially while he is living in my home — is a recipe for trouble.

As I relax in the pool, the cool breeze blowing, I know that this is going to be the last chance I have to relax for a long time. It's the last chance I have to prepare myself for dealing with Christian Herrera.

The sooner Christian goes back to Tennessee, the better.

23

———

BILLIE

"What are you working on?"

I nearly jump a mile, spinning to face the stairs to the loft. Christian stands there with his arms folded on the banister, looking at me. Something about the way he looks makes me want to reach out and hug him. There's a deep sadness in his eyes that I want to uncover.

It's a sadness I recognize well. I used to see it in my own reflection when I was trying to get out of this life.

He might be the leader of a cartel, but there is a scared little boy in there. I can see it now, when he's let his guard down enough to talk to me. From the limited interactions I've had with him, he seems to keep to himself, preferring to listen instead of speaking.

Who does he speak to when he needs to vent about all that sadness?

I wonder if there is someone back home waiting to give him that big hug when this is all over.

"Nothing much," I say, glancing down at the notebook in front of me. "Future business plans."

Christian nods and continues his way up the stairs,

coming to stand beside my desk. He crosses his arms, his tattoos prominent as his muscles flex. "What future business would this be?"

There is suspicion in his tone, though there is curiosity as well.

This man is a study case in contradiction, and as a part of me wants to cuddle him, the other part wants to get as far away from this man as possible.

"I want to open a resort and eventually build that into a national chain. I've been working on the plan since high school, but don't have anything concrete nailed down yet."

Though I hope that the answer bores Christian, he only seems more intrigued. As if a veil is lifted, I can see the suspicion fading away. He pulls up a chair and sits down beside me, glancing at the sprawling notes across the page.

"Do you mind if I take a closer look at this?" he asks, nodding to the notebook. "I've opened a couple different resorts overseas if you want some advice."

I let out a short laugh, my nerves getting the better of me. He shoots me a questioning look as I hand the notebook over to him.

"Sorry," I say, heat rushing to my cheeks. "I'm normally more composed. I just wasn't expecting you to ask that after everything I've heard about you. Especially your time spent in Colombia."

Christian shrugs, reading my notes. "People can surprise you, Billie. You shouldn't allow your initial thoughts of someone — especially those based on rumors — to cloud your judgment. It may be true that I have my enemies and I've killed more people than most, but I have other interests."

I bite back another nervous laugh. "Well, what do you think of the plans?"

"Where do you want to build the first resort?" he asks, handing the notebook back to me. 'You said that you've been thinking about this since high school, but you don't have a starting location? That's the first thing you need to figure out. Location is important."

"California sounds nice," I say, though I have no intention of starting the resort business in California. I would like to expand out there one day, but it isn't where I plan on escaping to with Papa.

"California has a lot of resorts. Hell, you'd be competing with a giant mouse out there." Christian grabs my pen and writes down a list of cities. "These are some places I would consider if I were you. They have a high yearly tourist number, but most of them only have smaller hotels and inns."

I'm surprised by his willingness to share information with me. From everything I've heard, Christian Herrera is the kind of man who keeps to himself outside of business and murder. He's relatively young, in terms of cartel leaders, but he is powerful.

Not only that, but his heartbreaker reputation precedes him. I know more than one woman who has fallen for the combination of light brown hair and dark blue eyes, thinking that they would be the one to get the Colombian heartbreaker to finally settle down.

"Thank you for this," I say, gesturing to the list. "I'm kind of lost when it comes to location. I've done my research, but actually sitting down to figure out the best place always seems like one of those impossible tasks."

Christian smiles, though it doesn't meet his eyes. "In the coming weeks, you are going to be a weak point if these dreams are distracting you. I need your head to be in the game. Is Alessio going to have to come running to your rescue every five minutes?"

I scowl at him. "I can take care of myself."

He laughs and gets up. "Sure. If you insist. I know that the Marchettis have a long list of not utilizing their assets. I'm willing to bet most of the women in the compound aren't trained to fight. What do you know about that?"

"Did you only come up here to try and get information out of me?"

He tucks his hands in the pockets of his dark jeans. "I prefer to think of it as a trade of information. I gave you some good locations to consider building a resort, you are going to give me information on the Marchetti mafia."

"If you want information, ask Alessio," I say, my tone sharp as I stand and my hands curl into my fists. "You have me mistaken if you think I'm the kind of woman who is going to betray her *famiglia*."

The words are bitter on my tongue. Though I know they're a lie — after all, I'm planning an escape — I have to make Christian believe that I am loyal to the Marchetti mafia.

He studies me for a minute before his shoulders stiffen slightly. "That was almost convincing. I think that you're hiding something. Not that I'm questioning your loyalty, but you're on edge."

'I have a lot going on in my life. And did you ever think that perhaps the personal relationship I have with Alessio complicates my loyalty to the *famiglia*?"

I'm scrambling for excuses and I know it. I'm just hoping that Christian doesn't. If he doesn't believe me, then I'm sure he will go to Alessio and tell him of his suspicions.

"So, there *is* a personal relationship that I should be concerned about." Christian nods and grins. "That's all the information I was looking for, Billie. Keep your secrets, as long as they do not put me or my business in danger."

"My secrets have no effect on your life or my *famiglia*."

Christian shrugs and takes the first few steps down the stairs. "I believe you. For now."

As he walks back downstairs, my heart is racing. Though Christian gave me some valuable advice, it was all in the name of digging for information. He is trying to see if I will put the mafia first when the time comes.

Does that mean that Alessio has his doubts about me?

The thought doesn't sit well with me. Though I still plan on leaving, I'm starting to waver. I know that walking away from him is going to be one of the hardest things I ever have to do. Our situation isn't ideal and after our conversation in his office yesterday, I doubt it's ever going to improve.

Still, there is something between us whether we act on it or not. I want him. If there was a way to make this work between us and improve life as part of the Marchetti mafia, then maybe I would stay.

I take a deep breath and run my hand through my hair. I don't know what I'm thinking. Leaving is all I've wanted for so long but in the last couple of weeks, I've been rethinking that more than ever.

Christian is just trying to get in my head and cause doubt. I just need to stick to my plan.

With that in mind, I grab some sketches of the resort I did last night and head to Papa's room.

Papa is sitting up in bed when I enter the in-law suite with a smile. His smile is more lopsided than it used to be, but his health has only been improving. Eventually, I should be able to take him away from this place.

Especially now that I know there are other sets of tunnels that run beneath the house.

"Kiddo," Papa says as I sit down in the chair beside his bed. I tuck my legs up beneath me and lean over to hand him the sketches. "What are these?"

"Some designs for the first resort. I wanted to see what you thought."

His hands shake as he flips through the designs. I watch his mouth press into a thin line before the corners turn up slightly. He smiles and nods at everything he sees, though his hands are shaking. He still looks frail, especially with the big bed surrounding him. He doesn't look like the man who used to toss me up on top of his shoulders and run with me through the main house. The man who taught me how to fight or shoot a gun.

The mafia is sapping all the life out of him and turning him into a shell of who he once was. He has tried to keep up with the younger capos and soldiers, despite his position of consigliere.

And now look at where it's gotten him.

"You look worried," Papa says, his voice wavering slightly. He hands the sketches back to me. "These are good."

"It's still going to be a while before I ever get to designing the actual rooms of the resort, but I think these will be a good starting point."

Even just sitting beside Papa is enough to make me feel better after the conversation with Christian. It makes me feel better about all the lies I've been trying to keep straight. I'm doing this for Papa. I'm willing to betray the only life I've ever known for Papa.

"I was thinking of building it somewhere other than Georgia, though. Maybe somewhere that gets a lot of snow.

You would be able to finally retire," I say, as if this is a normal conversation and not a suggestion of treason.

Papa's face goes red and his hands shake harder. "No. We do not leave."

"Papa, this life isn't good for you anymore," I say, keeping my voice soft in case someone is outside his room and listening to me. "You need to think about this. You almost died on a run that you never should have been on. This mafia is nothing but brutality until death. There is more to life than working for a man who doesn't value you."

"You don't know him," Papa says, spitting his words out as if they are venom. "We will stay. That is final."

I sigh but let it go for now. Papa is in no state to be moved and I don't want to get him worked up for nothing. We will talk about this later when he is in a better frame of mind. One of these days, Papa is going to see things my way.

"How have you been feeling? The nurse says that you're doing good with your physical therapy." I reach out and take his hand, giving it a squeeze. "I'm glad that you're alright. I was really worried about you."

"I'm fine." He looks away from me, reaching for the remote and turning down the volume on the television. "Have you started seeing anyone? How is Emilia?"

"I'm still not dating," I say, though I feel awful for lying to my father. Telling him the truth about Alessio isn't going to happen. "Emilia hasn't been around a lot, though. She's been seeing someone new recently."

"Good for her. You should find a good man too."

My cheeks warm as my mind immediately goes to Alessio. I try to distract myself, looking at the movie that is playing on the television. There is nothing there. We are having casual sex, but nothing is happening between us. It can't happen between us. He is Papa's best friend and I'm planning on leaving.

"Papa, I'm happy with the way my life is right now. I don't need a man. I have a business to build and focus on."

He shakes his head. "No. You avoid falling for someone because you saw how miserable I was without your mother."

A lump threatens to choke me as I shrug. "That could be part of it."

"Don't lie to your Papa, Billie. I know what that did to you."

"I'm alright, Papa. Believe me. I just don't want to find anyone to settle down with right now. Not when I'm looking at the next chapter of my life and seeing it away from here."

Papa presses his lips into a thin line. He grabs the remote and turns the volume back up, cutting off our conversation. I sigh and lean back in the chair, pulling one knee to my chest and looping my arms around it.

I don't know how I'm going to navigate an escape when Papa is so unwilling to even talk about it. Though I know that this has been his way of life since he was born, it doesn't have to be that way until he dies.

If I ultimately decide to leave, I might have to drag him out of the compound kicking and screaming.

Papa glances over at me, disappointment shining in his eyes. I hate when he gives me that look, but I'm an adult now. I'm trying to make the best decision for us, I just have to make him see that. If things don't change, staying in the compound is going to get him killed.

There is nothing that I can say right now to get him to listen, though.

And then there is the thought of staying and convincing Alessio to be the man I know he has hidden deep inside him.

I learned a long time ago that you can't make people change if they don't want to change. Alessio will do what he wants as he always has done. I can't change that, even though I wish I could. I see the potential in him, but he doesn't see it in himself.

The mafia is not my problem. I have to convince Papa that we have to leave and then I have to get us out.

Except, I don't know how to walk away with a clean cut anymore. No matter what I do, I'm going to leave with jagged edges, wondering if things could have gone differently.

I leave and I break my own heart.

I stay and I risk getting my heart broken.

Either way, I'll always be risking death.

"Enjoy the movie," Papa says, his voice gravelly. "Stop thinking about all the things you want to do right now."

He's right, but I can't shake the feeling that whatever I decide, it's going to be the wrong decision. My stomach tosses and turns even thinking about it.

For a little while, I try to turn off my brain and enjoy my time with my father. I watch the movie, laughing at all the right parts and making jokes with him. It's only when Alessio walks into the suite and helps Papa in the wheelchair that everything comes rushing back.

Alessio winks at me before wheeling my father out of the room. "Dinner is ready."

I swallow down the nauseous feeling and follow them down the hall to the kitchen. Christian is standing in front of the stove, stirring a pot that smells like chorizo and cumin.

"It smells amazing in here," I say as I wander over to the stove. "What are you making?"

"Sopa de lentejas." Christian grabs a small spoon and scoops up some of the soup, holding it out to me. "Lentil soup. It's my mama's recipe. I thought that I should make some dinner since Alessio has extended his home to me."

My mouth waters as I taste the soup, nearly moaning at the mix of flavors together. "You have to give me the recipe for this, if you don't mind. This is amazing."

"As long as you promise not to serve it once you have a wildly successful resort, I would be happy to," Christian says as he grabs a few bowls from one of the cupboards. He grins and starts to ladle the soup into the bowls. "It may be the middle of summer, but I don't think there is a wrong season for sopa de lentejas."

"You're right about that," Papa says as his stomach growls. Alessio makes room for Papa at the table before bringing a bowl of soup over. "Thank you."

Christian hands out the remaining bowls of soup before we all take a seat at the table. For a few minutes, the only sound is spoons scraping against bowls. I clean my bowl, going back for another bowl when it's empty.

"Glad you like it," Christian says, glancing over at me. "I'll write that recipe down for you after I've finished cleaning up tonight."

Alessio scoffs. "You cooked. I'll get the kitchen clean while everybody else relaxes."

"I'm not going to argue with that." Christian gets another bowl of soup and sits back down. "I spent the day going around town, but I have not seen Paolo. I checked that list of locations you gave me, but he isn't at any of them."

Alessio nods. "That doesn't surprise me. If he is starting to build up to a war, then he would stay underground. His normal places wouldn't do him any good since I know where they are. He either has somewhere I don't know about, or he is hiding in plain sight."

Christian hums for a moment, leaning back in his chair and pushing his hair back from his eyes. "Have you had anyone you trust check the property for him? I know you said he had been able to get a dead body on the property, what if he has been here the entire time?"

"I've searched the grounds personally a few times. My acting consigliere is also doing his own search each morning. We would have found him by now if he was on the grounds. We did find three people who have allowed him into the compound and they've since been disposed of."

"His club." I look over at Alessio. He arches an eyebrow, waiting for an explanation. "If he's hiding in any one of the properties you know about, it's his club. There are already hidden rooms you know about. He's likely got more hidden rooms that you don't."

Alessio considers that for a moment before nodding. "I can't go in there and search the place. We will station men as close as we can to the building to watch if he's coming and going."

Christian looks at me, his eyes narrowing. He gives me that searching look that makes my skin crawl, as if he is trying to sort his way through my thoughts. I stare back at him, not wanting to look scared in the face of a man who could get rid of me without a second thought.

"Christian, we have much to talk about. Do you mind meeting with me in the pool house to talk about this further?" Alessio looks at me and Papa, giving a sharp nod before walking away.

"Billie, will you take me back to my room?" Papa says,

his voice raspy. His eyes are shining, and he looks like he's been stabbed in the back.

Although, I'm sure that I would feel the same way if I was in Papa's shoes. He has been Alessio's consigliere for years, and now Alessio is talking business without him.

"Sure, Papa. Do you want to bring some of this soup with you?"

"No. I've had enough for one night."

After I take him back to his room and help him into the bed, I make my way back to the kitchen. My stomach is tossing and turning as I clean up the dishes and wipe down the kitchen. I busy myself with figuring out what to make for breakfast the next morning while glancing outside at the pool house every now and then.

It's going on midnight by the time Alessio comes back inside alone. There's a thin outline of smoke climbing toward the sky outside the pool house. Christian's silhouette sits in the dark, as if he would rather be alone than spend time with more people.

"Is everything alright?" I ask as Alessio leans against the counter and looks at me. He crosses his arms over his chest, his eyebrows furrowing.

"Having Christian here is good for the *famiglia*, even if he is a tough pill to swallow," Alessio says as he glances out the sliding glass doors. "That's what I keep trying to convince myself of. I don't like the way he looks at you, though."

I roll my eyes and walk over to him, cupping his face in both my hands and gently tilting his head down until he's looking at me. "Christian looks at me like a predator getting ready to tear apart its prey. He's looking for weaknesses and that's it. Trust me. There is something unsettling about that man."

Alessio chuckles, his shoulders relaxing slightly. "If that was supposed to make me feel better about the way he's looking at you, then you should probably know that it didn't work."

"He doesn't trust easily. In his line of work, that doesn't surprise me. Besides, I'm far more interested in the way you look at me."

Alessio spins us around and pins me against the counter. His arms bracket me as he leans forward, his nose nearly touching mine. "And how do I look at you?"

The room feels as if it is burning hot as my hands slide up his shirt, flicking the buttons open one by one. "Like I'm a figment of your imagination. Something you can't quite believe is in front of you."

He takes a deep breath and looks like he's torn between stepping away from me or getting impossibly closer. "That is the problem with us, isn't it? We keep doing this dance around each other like anything that happens is going to actually become reality."

One of his hands slips beneath my shirt. His fingers trace patterns along my hip as his gaze drops to my mouth. I tilt my head back, giving him the invitation he so clearly needs.

Alessio groans low in his throat and shakes his head. "This is a bad idea and we both know that it's going to end terribly."

"I like bad ideas," I say, my voice barely more than a whisper. "Hell, you might even be the best bad idea. But if you don't want to take me to bed, I can go upstairs and use that vibrator I got. Make myself come while thinking about the way you feel inside me."

The last of his restraint snaps and his mouth collides with mine. I moan into the kiss as his hands sink into my hair, pulling me closer to him. His hardened cock strains against his pants, pressing against my body and igniting a fire in my core.

Wetness pools between my legs as his tongue slips into my mouth. I moan and slide my hands up his bare chest, trying to memorize the feeling of every inch of his body. If the present is all I get with him, then I'm going to do my best to burn every touch and swipe of his tongue into my memory.

"My room," he says, pulling away from me and taking my hand.

He leads me through the house like we're a couple of teenagers sneaking around and trying not to get caught. As we race by Papa's door and down another hall, I bite back the nervous laughter that threatens to escape.

Alessio tosses open a door at the end of the hall and pulls me inside. The spicy scent of his cologne greets me as he spins me around and pushes me up against a dark green wall. Everything in his room is dark green or pale wood. It feels like walking into a forest and finding peace.

I don't know what I pictured when it came to Alessio's bedroom, but it wasn't that.

"Are you sure we shouldn't go up to the loft?" I ask as Alessio pulls my shirt over my head and tosses it to the side. He reaches around me to close the door before flicking open the button of my denim shorts. "Someone could hear us here."

He chuckles and cups my breasts, massaging them through the thin fabric of my bra. "Nobody is going to hear us. Don't worry about that. Just relax and enjoy the feeling of my hands on your body."

I moan as his head dips and he kisses my neck. He squeezes my nipples through the bra, rolling them between his fingers until they're aching. I arch my back and tilt my head back, giving him better access to my neck as his hands work their way down my body.

He pulls my shorts down my legs before kneeling on the ground in front of me. His fingers hook into the silky fabric of my underwear, pulling them down and tossing them to the side.

At the first swipe of his tongue along my wet slit, I see stars. Alessio nips and sucks at my inner thigh, teasing me as he lifts one of my legs over his shoulder. He kisses his way back to my clit, sucking it into his mouth while his fingers press inside me.

My pussy pulsates around him as he thrusts his fingers slowly, teasing me to the edge of an orgasm while his tongue flicks against my clit. I run my fingers through his hair, my upper back pressing against the cold wall behind me.

"Come on my face," he says before he thrusts his fingers faster and deeper. "Fucking do it, Billie. I want to taste you."

Shivers run down my spine as he toys with my clit while plunging his fingers deeper into me. My pussy clenches around him as I come, my legs shaking. My grip on his hair tightens, keeping his mouth on my clit as I come down from my high.

He stands and grabs me by the hair, pulling my head back. His tongue darts out to lick his bottom lip before he kisses me. Alessio bites my lip, groaning as his free hand grips my hip.

"I want you to get on your knees and suck my cock," he says, his voice raspy.

Alessio uses his grip on my hair to guide me to my knees. I run my hands up his thighs, digging my nails gently into his skin. He grips his cock and presses it against my mouth. I lick the head, swirling my tongue around the tip before sliding it down the length of his cock.

I moan as I take him into my mouth, hollowing my cheeks. My head bobs up and down as I toy with his balls, squeezing them as his grip on my hair tightens. His hips rock faster as I suck his cock, taking him to the back of my throat. I run my other hand up and down the length of him, tears gathering in my eyes as I pull back.

"Get on your hands and knees on the bed." Alessio pulls fully out of my mouth, stroking his cock from base to tip. "Put that pretty ass in the air."

He takes my hand and helps me to my feet before nodding to the bed. I take a wobbling step before crossing the room to the bed. I get on the silk sheets, facing the headboard with my ass in the air.

Alessio runs his hands over my ass before bringing one down. A sharp sting sends more wetness dripping down my thighs.

"I need you," I say, my voice breathy as his fingers slide through my wet slit. "Please fuck me. Please."

He chuckles and runs his fingers down my spine, setting my nerves on fire. "Is that what you want? You want me to fuck you until you come all over my cock? You want to feel it stretching that tight pussy of yours?"

"Yes, please," I say, looking over my shoulder at him. "I want to come on your cock. I need to feel it inside me."

He groans and presses the head of his cock against my core before sliding inside me. My pussy squeezes his cock as he pushes deeper into me. Alessio grabs my hips and drags me back against his body, burying himself to the hilt.

"Fuck yes," he says as he rocks his hips.

I grip the sheets, pushing back to meet him thrust for thrust. Alessio grabs my hair in one fist, pulling my head back. My back arches, deepening the angle as the world around me starts to disappear. My senses are overloaded with the scent of his cologne and the feeling of his cock slamming into me.

My orgasm comes hard and fast, my pussy clenching around his throbbing cock. Alessio groans and holds me against him as his come spills inside me. We slump together on the bed, wrapped in each other, breathing heavily.

As I start to drift off to sleep, I wonder how casual sex can feel that good and not be something more between two people.

There is no question about it. When I leave, there will be an Alessio-shaped hole in my heart and nothing I can do about it.

24

ALESSIO

CHRISTIAN SITS BESIDE THE POOL WITH A CIGARETTE dangling from his lips when I walk outside a few days after his arrival. I've barely seen him over the course of the last two days, but I know he's still looking into Paolo.

"How's the morning treating you?" I ask as I take a seat on one of the chairs beside the pool. "Missing home yet?"

"I'm here until we get this dealt with." He looks over his shoulder at me with a smirk. "If you're here to try and get rid of me, you might want to think again."

"That almost sounds like a man who is trying to avoid something at home," I say, crossing one leg over the other. "Trouble in paradise?"

"There would have to be a paradise for there to be trouble. I just don't trust you to handle this job fully with Billie around. And before you try to argue with me and say that there is nothing there, I saw the two of you in the pool together around midnight."

I shrug and tuck my arms behind my head. "Look, Billie and I are having a bit of fun. You can't tell anyone about it, though. Her father would kill me if he knew that I was sneaking around with his daughter."

Christian takes a long drag of his cigarette before flicking the ashes from the end. "I'm not going to run in there and tell her father, but you know this looks bad, right? On top of that, she is a distraction that you don't need right now."

"You know, my father used to say the same thing when I brought a woman home. She was always a distraction I didn't need. My mother was sure that I was bringing the wrong woman home. We're not speaking right now."

Christian chuckles. "That doesn't surprise me at all. I'm sure most mothers would be pissed that their son is sleeping around with someone who has to be nearly twenty years younger than them."

I sigh and look up at the clouds drifting across the sky. "Billie is a lot of things, but she isn't a distraction. Some time spent together after a long day, but nothing more. My focus is on Paolo and hers is on building her business."

"If I were you, I wouldn't be so sure of that either. She has the same look in her eyes that my mother and ex used to get right before they lied to me."

Though I know that Billie is keeping something from me, I don't like that Christian sees it too. Maybe what she is hiding from me is bigger than I initially thought.

"She has a lot going on in her life right now, but I have no doubts about her loyalty to the *famiglia*." I move to sit on the edge of the chair. "Have you found what Paolo has been up to yet? I have to go on a run later and I want to know if he is going to be a problem or not."

Christian looks interested as he gets up and crushes his cigarette in an ashtray. "I think that I should go out on this ride with you."

"The point of you being here is to stay hidden and get information that I couldn't otherwise get. I fail to see why you should go on a run with me when that would put you out where everyone can see you."

"Not if you let me drive that fancy black car of yours. The windows are tinted so dark that nobody will see me."

I scowl and weigh my options. Leaving Christian here is just as risky as bringing him with me. I don't know who else might be working for Paolo and who is watching what. If I bring him with me, I might be able to make him more willing to work together in the future.

Christian is an important ally to have. He has the strongest connections to some of the best drug suppliers in the world. He knows what he's doing and the fact that he has moved back to the States after years away has put another major player back on the board.

When he decides to start expanding his kingdom again, I don't want to be someone he sees as an enemy.

"Alright," I say, pulling the keys to the garage out of my pocket and tossing them to him. "Get the car ready, then. The three of us will be heading out shortly."

"Three of us?"

I nod and get up, smirking at him. "Your favorite person in the entire world is going to be coming with us."

Christian groans and runs his hand down his face. "Billie seems like a nice woman, but you're not going to convince me that having her this involved in your business is a good idea."

I shrug. "She already works for me at the casino. There's not much that she doesn't already know about. Arturo has taught her how things work, and to be honest, she's a great shot. If we're about to head into a trap, she's who I want at my back."

Christian shakes his head and twirls the keys around his finger. "I've got to make a call before we leave. I should be ready in twenty."

"Good, it's a long drive."

With Christian coming and driving the car, I get the chance to take my motorcycle out. It's been a long time since I was able to ride. Excitement rolls through me at the thought of riding with Billie behind me.

I walk into the house and head up to the loft. She's sitting at the desk with one knee pulled to her chest and her long hair cascading over her shoulder. I stop at the top of the stairs, watching her for a moment.

"Hey," she says without looking at me. "What's up? I thought I had the day off today."

"You do," I say as I lean against the banister. "But I'm going out on a run with Christian today. He's going to be driving the car which means I get to take the bike out. Do you want to ride with me?"

Billie spins to face me, a smile spreading across her face. "You have a motorcycle? Papa never let me get one. I had one while I was away at college, but I had to sell it before I moved back here. He would have killed me if he saw me riding around on it."

I chuckle. "Is that a yes or were you planning on staying here?"

"Papa's nurse is here for the day. I could use a trip out of the house. One minute while I get changed."

She doesn't bother to leave the room as she pulls off her short dress. I bite down on a groan as I take in the matching emerald lace set against her skin. For a moment, I consider canceling the run completely and staying with her.

If an old business partner hadn't asked me to deliver the guns personally, I would cancel it.

Billie grabs a pair of tight leather pants and a black crop top. She shimmies into the pants, hopping around until they're fully up her legs. As she slides the crop top over her head, I adjust the growing erection in my jeans.

"See something you like?" she asks as she grabs a leather jacket and pulls it on. There is a mischievous smirk curving the corner of her mouth.

I make a point of allowing my gaze to run up and down her body. "Yes, but unfortunately, we don't have time for that today. An arms dealer needs some guns and he asked to meet him for the drop. It's a four-hour ride to Bainbridge."

"Bainbridge?" She pulls on a pair of black motorcycle boots before scrapping her hair back from her face in a low messy bun. "And you're personally meeting with this guy?"

Fuck, she's gorgeous.

"Yeah. He's new to the area but a friend in Oregon told me that he was reliable. I want to meet him myself, though. It's going to be a long ride. Are you sure you're good?"

"I used to spend the summers riding around the country when I was in college. Four hours there and another four back is nothing. Trust me."

"Alright, let's get going, then."

I lead the way down the stairs and to the garage. Billie gasps as I pull the cover off my sleek black bike. Christian is sitting in the car with the windows down, frowning as he looks over at us. When Billie notices him staring and wiggles her fingers in his direction, he rolls his eyes.

Well, at least they are getting along right now.

I don't know what is going on between the two of them. One minute they're friendly enough and the next they are avoiding each other. I don't know who said what, but the house is growing tense.

If he told her that he doesn't trust her, that would probably piss her off.

I grab a helmet and hand it to Billie before grabbing my own. She is practically bouncing with excitement as she pulls on the helmet and waits for me to get on the bike.

When Billie gets on behind me, her arms wrapping around my waist, I can picture a thousand more days spent like this.

It scares the hell out of me. Maybe my mother is right and this is a horrible decision. Maybe I should have given mote thought to the implications of any sort of relationship with Billie.

Christian gives me a look like he knows what I'm thinking before pressing a button to open the garage door and driving off. I flip down my visor and kick the bike to life, roaring out of the garage after Christian.

Billie squeezes a little closer to me, her hand dropping down to the front of my pants. My cock stiffens again, even as she pulls her hand away and starts giggling.

It's going to be a very long ride if she keeps this up.

"THIS SEEMS TOO QUIET," CHRISTIAN SAYS, SITTING IN the car beside me outside the warehouse. He pulls back into the shadows of the car as someone in a truck drives by.

I look around at the empty warehouse parking lot. Garbage litters the place and the windows are boarded up. It's the kind of place I would expect an arms deal to take place.

"I'm going to go inside," I say as I slip off my helmet and grab the bag of guns from the trunk. "You two should stay out here."

Billie scoffs and crosses her arms. "Not happening. You want to go into a suspicious warehouse alone without any backup when there is some deranged man running around trying to take down the *famiglia*?"

"Stay out here, Billie."

She rolls her eyes and pulls a gun out of her boot. "Yeah. Not happening. Colombian cowboy over there might not be able to come in with you, but I can."

"I knew bringing her along was a bad idea. You should have left her at home. She's nothing but bad luck." Christian glowers at Billie as she takes off her helmet and puts it on the seat of the motorcycle.

Billie shrugs. "I could say the same about you."

"Behave, both of you. I do not have the patience to deal with children today. Billie, wait out here with Christian and make sure that nobody tries to sneak up on me."

She nods once and flicks the safety off the gun. "Okay."

I heft the bag higher on my shoulder and head toward the building. As I get closer, I pull my gun out of my holster. Something about this drop does feel wrong, even though I was assured that I could trust the man I'm meeting with.

As I walk into the warehouse, gunshots ring out. I drop to the ground and hurry to get behind a stack of crates. Another gunshot cracks through the warehouse. I peer out from around the corner of the crate and see a man in all black moving along the opposite wall.

I stand up quickly and aim before pulling the trigger. The man drops to the ground. Footsteps echo through the warehouse as I spin and shoot two more men running toward me.

The door to the warehouse bursts open and Billie comes racing in like an avenging angel. She points the gun at me and for a moment, time seems to stand still. My blood rushes in my ears and my heart pounds against my chest.

She squeezes the trigger and there is a thud behind me. I turn to see a man lying a pool of his own blood, a hole in his forehead.

"I told you that you shouldn't go in alone," Billie says as she looks around at the bodies.

"Stay here," I say, pointing to a spot behind the crates. As she gets closer, I hand her the bag of guns. "Keep these close. If anything happens to me, get out of here."

"Drama queen," she says, her tone teasing as she does what I ask.

The corner of my mouth twitches even though I'm less than amused. This is the last thing that I want to be dealing with right now, but her teasing eases the mood a little. I pull out my phone and send a message to Davide.

"The cleaning crew will be here in a couple hours. Until then, we need to camp out here and make sure nobody finds the bodies. I'm going to make sure that there's nobody else in here and then open the doors for Christian to drive in."

"You know he doesn't like me much," she says, though there is amusement in her voice. "I don't think he likes most women, though, so I'm trying not to take it personally."

"He's had a lot happen in his life." While I may not know the whole story, I do know that Christian has been betrayed by nearly everyone he's ever trusted. "I didn't like him much when we first met years ago either. Some days I still don't know how to feel about him, but he grows on you. At least, that's what Jovan likes to say."

Billie nods and shrugs. "It is what it is."

I take off into the warehouse as she settles in behind the crates. Though I haven't heard or seen anyone else since she walked into the warehouse, that doesn't mean that they aren't lying low.

I shouldn't have gotten distracted by talking to her. Maybe Christian is right and she is going to be a problem for me.

Once I make sure that we're alone in the warehouse, I open the doors and head out to grab the motorcycle. Christian follows me inside and we shut the doors again. Nobody needs to know that we're here.

"Paolo is likely watching us right now," I say as I take the guns from Billie and put them back in the car. "This was all an elaborate set up. I'm going to have to get in contact with the man who recommended this buyer and see what he knows."

"And by get in contact, I hope you mean kill," Christian says, arching an eyebrow as he gets out of the car and lights a cigarette.

"Yes. I'm going to kill him. He's an old business partner that I've had on the west coast for years, but it seems as if Paolo got to him too. There is no room for treason among the Marchettis." I look over at Billie as she pulls herself up to sit on the hood of the car.

"So, Christian," Billie says, a mischievous look in her eyes. "Do you want to sit here and talk about the problem you clearly have with women? I've been told that I give good advice. And I am a woman. I could help."

"Billie," I say, a warning in my tone as I look at her. I don't need her prying into Christian's love life, even if I'm curious myself. "Now is not the time or place to start shit."

Christian shrugs and takes a long drag of his cigarette. "She's not starting shit. She's prying, yes. But it's entertaining. I'm not going to be talking about whatever may or may not be happening in my love life with you."

Billie shrugs and leans back, bracing herself on her forearms as she looks back up at the ceiling. "I could tell you about my emotional damage. We could turn this into sharing hour while we wait for the cleaners."

I sigh, already seeing that the two of them are going to go back and forth with each other regardless of what I think. On one hand, I think it's attractive that Billie is confident enough to poke and prod at Christian. He is an intimidating man and if she crosses a line with him, I'll do everything I can to save her, but I don't know if it would be enough.

If it came down to it, I would give my life for her, though. Hell, I would ruin an alliance just to protect her.

I can't imagine life without her.

"Billie, has anyone ever told you that you talk too much?" Christian asks, though the corner of his mouth tips up.

"Christian, has anyone ever told you that you're as moody as a teenager?" Billie sticks her tongue out at him like they are just two friends trying to get under each other's skin.

Even if he sounds annoyed with her, he finds her amusing. I look over at Billie and she is smiling with her eyes closed. Christian starts talking to her about some Colombian food while I listen for anyone approaching the warehouse.

She could be the woman I spend the rest of my life with. I could sit Arturo down and try to make him understand how much I'm falling for his daughter. I could give her the world.

The thought comes out of nowhere and it hits me like a runaway train. I haven't considered a life with anyone, yet here I am, looking at a woman on the hood of my car, joking around with the leader of a cartel, and thinking that I could spend the rest of my life with her.

As I watch her, I can see our entire lives laid out together. I can see the children racing around the yard with Billie. I can see her cutting the red ribbon at her resort before I take her out to dinner to celebrate all that she's accomplished.

This is so much more than casual for me.

"You've got to be kidding!" Billie says, breaking me away from my thoughts as she leans in the window. "There is no way that you did that on a plane."

Christian chuckles and shrugs. "There was nothing else to do and it was a long flight."

"How is that even possible?" She shakes her head, and I feel like I've missed something completely. Billie grins and fully reclines on the car. "You're going to have to tell me how that works, sometime."

"Tell you what," Christian says as he points the glowing end of the cigarette at Billie. "If we survive whatever this shit is with Paolo, I'll tell you that story one day."

I look between the two of them and note their matching grins. "Do I even want to know what's going on?"

Christian chuckles and shakes his head. "Don't worry about it. When are your cleaners going to be here? I could use some food and a nap."

"Should be here soon. Davide was sending them in a helicopter." I glance at my phone and hop down from the crates. "If you want to head out, me and Billie can wait."

Christian nods and pulls out his own phone. His smile drops as he sees something on the screen he doesn't like. He tosses the phone onto the seat beside him. "I'm going to take you up on that. It seems like I have a few calls to make."

"To the woman you're seeing?" Billie says, still teasing

him as she slides down from the car. "It's okay, Christian. You can keep your secrets for now. Sooner or later, you're going to spill your guts about the girl you like."

"And then maybe we can braid our hair," he says, his tone dry as he shakes his head. Christian glances over at me. "Good luck with that one."

Billie opens the doors for him, waiting until he disappears before shutting them. I lean back against the crates as she makes her way back over to me.

"The two of you have some weird relationship going on. One day you're at each other's throats and then next you're going to braid each other's hair. What's up with that?"

Billie shrugs and leans beside me, crossing her arms. "He thinks that I'm hiding things. He's not wrong, in a sense. I do keep a lot to myself. Nothing important that anyone else needs to know about, but it makes him suspicious of me."

I don't know what to say for a moment. I had been expecting her to play it off as a joke. "Oh? I didn't know about this."

She shrugs. "I didn't see any reason to tell you. Having him here is important to the *famiglia*. He may drive me insane, but there is an entertaining side to him."

I hum, not knowing what to feel about the entire situation. Christian told me that he has his doubts about her, but he didn't tell me that he had spoken to her. Hell, I didn't think that was something he would do without speaking to me first.

"You've got that *I'm going to kill someone* look on your face." Billie reaches up to smooth her finger along the wrinkles on my forehead. "I'm not upset by it. The man clearly has trust issues."

"I guess." I look down at her, still seeing that future in

front of me. "I've been thinking a lot lately."

Billie smiles. "That sounds dangerous. Should I be scared?"

"I was thinking about us." I clear my throat, my pulse pounding. I don't know how to start this conversation or what I'm going to say to her. Technically, she is still under contract with me, but I don't want her to think that my only interest in her is due to a piece of paper.

"There's an us, is there?" The corner of her mouth tips upward and her eyes shine. "I thought that this was just something casual and that's all that it could be."

"Yeah, well, I think I was wrong about that. About a lot of things when it comes to you, actually. I want to try to be something more."

Her smile wavers slightly. "I like you, Alessio, I really do. Hell, it could be more than that in the future, but right now I don't know if I can dive into something that deep."

I nod. I know where she is coming from, and I have my own reservations about diving in headfirst right now. There is too much going on in both our lives to race into anything.

"How about we take it day by day, then?" I ask as the doors to the warehouse open and the cleaning crew walks in.

Billie moves away from me to keep up appearances, but the bright smile on her face sends warmth spreading through me. "Taking it day by day sounds nice to me."

As she walks out of the warehouse, I finally feel some of the weight lifting from my shoulders.

Even though the logical side of my brain thinks that this is going to blow up in my face, I don't care.

Billie has me thinking it's better to take the risk and to find out than to spend the rest of my life regretting not loving her.

25
———

BILLIE

"Are you ready to tell me the story about the woman who you're clearly pining for?" I ask as I follow the scent of steak and scallops.

Christian scoffs and hands me a plate of food. "I have never met a more annoying human being. You'd think that you would stop bothering me about this and move on with your life. There's nothing interesting going on in mine."

"Alessio has been at work all day and Papa is sleeping. I have nobody else to bother." I take a seat at the kitchen island and dig into the food. "You know, you're never going to be able to go back to Nashville. I'm going to miss your cooking."

Christian laughs. "I have people waiting for me back home and a cartel to run. My second in command is a good man, but he has a lot on his plate right now. It wasn't exactly fair of me to get up and leave him the way that I did."

I swirl my fork in his direction. "I knew you were avoiding a woman. You have to tell me all about her. I need something to take my mind off the painfully boring day I've had."

"I thought you worked with Alessio." Christian brought his plate over to sit beside me.

"Not today. Alessio had things to do outside of the casino and I needed some time to work on the plans for the resort."

"Still thinking about California?"

Though I know he is trying to fully change the subject, I'm not going to call him out on it. I may want to know his story, but he clearly doesn't want to talk about it.

"I've thought about it, but you were right about that damn mouse. I don't know how I would ever be able to compete with that. Maybe I could open it in Nashville, though. I've heard that the leader of the local cartel is very accommodating."

Christian snorts. "I better not see you in Nashville. You amuse me, Billie, but if I had to spend every day with you, I would lose my mind. I don't know how Alessio does it."

I shrug as guilt washes over me. My conversation with Alessio the other day about starting something more than casual sex left me riding a high. I was in a good mood until I got home and started thinking about the way I would soon be leaving.

The truth is that I don't want to leave anymore. It's taken some time to wrap my head around the idea, but I know what I want. It isn't a life outside of the mafia. Not truly. Though I would like to be less involved with it.

No, what — or who — I want is Alessio. Whatever way I can have him. I don't have to give up my dreams to do that, even though I thought I would for the longest time.

Being with him is what I want. I want to be with him more than anything else and I'm willing to make those other dreams I have work with Alessio in them.

I don't even see those dreams coming true without him by my side now.

"You see, it's that look on your face right now that makes me think you're hiding something," Christian says, snatching a scallop off my plate. "Whatever it is, you should be honest with him."

"If only life were that simple." I smile and take another bite of steak. "My problems have nothing to do with Alessio."

As soon as the words leave my lips, a crash comes from my father's room. Christian leaps up from his stool and races down the hall faster than I can. I follow behind him, my heart pounding in my chest.

Please let Papa be okay. Please let him be okay.

I step into the room as a picture frame flies at Alessio's head. Papa is sitting up in bed, his face bright red. The vein on his forehead is popping as Alessio stands on the other side of the room with his arms crossed.

"You know what?" Christian says as he looks at me. He shakes his head and points a finger. "This is a you problem. I have more calls to make."

"Great. Leave me with the two angry men while you call the woman you're avoiding."

Christian chuckles as another frame goes flying. "There is no world in which I'm going to be staying for this show. Have fun. Scream if you need me."

He hurries out of the room as Papa struggles to get out of bed. I rush across the room toward him as he starts to stumble.

"Papa, you're not supposed to get out of bed without your nurse here. What do you think you're doing?"

He recoils from my touch before trying to lunge at

Alessio. Tears gather in my eyes as Papa falls to the ground with a shout.

"What the fuck is going on here?" I ask, turning to face Alessio. "What the fuck did you do?"

Though I want to help Papa get to his feet, I know I won't be able to lift him. He's too proud to let me help him up. Whatever is happening between the two of them right now is between the two of them.

"I told him that I care about you and want to be with you," Alessio says, not taking his eyes off Papa. "As you can imagine, he didn't take to that too well."

"You've known her since she was a baby! We've been friends since we were kids, and this is what you do to me? You decide that you want to date my daughter? My beautiful and brilliant daughter who is nineteen years younger than you and far out of your fucking league?"

Papa gets to his feet and shuffles to the chair in the corner. He sits down with his arms crossed. The expression on his face is deadly as he looks at Alessio. Alessio doesn't seem to care, standing tall with his shoulders pulled back and his hands in his pockets.

"This is what you two are fighting about? You have got to be kidding me. The only person who gets to decide who I'm with is me. Papa, I love you and this is not the way I wanted you to find out, but I am seeing Alessio."

Not only am I seeing him, but I'm seeing a life with him. I'm seeing a world in which I don't run away from the mafia, and it's scary as hell.

"Alessio, please leave so I can talk to Papa about this?"

He looks at me and raises an eyebrow. There is a stubborn set to his jaw that makes me think this isn't going to go over without a fight. I put my hands on my hips and stand in front of him. It's a silent challenge and we both know it.

After the longest staring competition of my life, Alessio turns and walks out of the room. He closes the door, leaving me alone with my father.

I sigh, some of the anger leaving my body as I cross the room and take a seat beside Papa. He looks over at me, his frown lines deep and fury in his eyes.

"I raised you better than this, Billie. I raised you to want more for your life than a man who is only going to treat you like a trophy. He may be my best friend, but he is not the kind of man to settle down."

Papa's words cut deep, but it's time to finally stand up to him. I'm an adult, and while he only wants the best for me, this is a part of my life that he doesn't get a say in.

"With all due respect, Papa, that is not something you get to say to me right now. Not even a little bit. I do still want all the same things I've always wanted. I have dreams and I fully intend to chase them, but I also see a version of the future where Alessio is at my side."

He shakes his head. "You're not the daughter I raised. You had plans to get out of this life, Billie. Does that mean that you're going to throw all that away for a man who won't even say that he is in a relationship with you?"

"We're *not* in a relationship," I say, though I make a mental note to talk to Alessio about that. I want more with him and I think he wants more with me. If he didn't, why would he tell my father about us?

"Great, So, you are giving up everything you've ever wanted for a man you aren't even dating."

"Enough!" I stand up and pace across the room. "Papa, you are going to listen to me this time because this is the first and last time I'm going to talk about it."

He presses his lips together but says nothing. I continue to pace across the room, sorting through all my thoughts. I know that I can't tell him about the auction and the contract — he would kill Alessio for that — but he needs to know that this isn't a joke to me.

It's been more than just a contract for me for a few weeks now. At night, I dream of the life I could have. I've been thinking more and more about helping Alessio change the state of the mafia even though I keep telling myself that I have to leave.

"I've been seeing Alessio for a couple of weeks. We haven't put a label on it because there is a lot going on with Paolo and neither of us has been ready to commit that much to each other yet. On top of that, I'm still on the fence about leaving. I want to go and spread my wings, but I want to stay. Papa, instead of you telling me that I'm not the daughter you raised, I need your support."

"And what if I can't support this?" Papa's voice wavers. It's the first emotion other than anger I've seen from him in a long time. "Billie, he is older than you. At a completely different point in his life. He is a brutal man."

"He wants to change the mafia and make it a better place for everyone. He doesn't want to be like his brother and father anymore." I come to a stop in front of him. "I can see a future with that version of Alessio. I can see myself with the version of him that wants more for his life than just killing people."

"And how do you know that's the version of him that's going to be around for the next however many years?"

I run my hand through my hair. "Did you ever think that might be the problem? That everyone in his life has had so little faith in him that they think he can't be anything more than who he was raised to be?"

Papa sighs. "Billie, you don't understand."

"No, Papa. *You* don't understand. That's fine, though. I

still love you and I'm going to continue to live my life the way I want. You didn't want to leave with me the other dozen times I asked. Now, I've found someone and something worth staying for."

I have nothing else to say to him, especially when I see the hard set of his jaw and the way he won't meet my eyes. He might need more time to come around to the new person in our lives, but I'm not going to let it hold me back.

I'm falling for Alessio, and I've been trying to convince myself that I'm not. I keep telling myself that I'm going to leave, even though that stopped being an option when I saw a different side of him.

After taking a moment to myself in the hallway, I head into the kitchen. Alessio is sitting down and eating dinner while Christian paces around outside, his phone pressed to his ear. Alessio looks up as I approach, hesitation in his gaze.

"How did that go?" Alessio asks, his voice soft. "I'm sorry to force you into dealing with that. I thought that if I talked to him first and tried to explain my side of the situation that he would be pissed with me and not you."

I shrug and wrap my arms around him. The hug is new territory for us, but right now I just need to be held. I need to have something holding me to the earth while my mind starts to spiral.

He sets his plate to the side before turning to face me and looping his arms around my waist. He pulls me close, kissing my temple.

"This is weird," I say as I pull away slightly to look at him.

"It is." He smiles and kisses my temple again. "If I'm being honest, I like it. I can't remember the last time that somebody hugged me."

"Do you really want to change the mafia?" I ask, my

heart hammering in my chest. "You meant what you said about wanting to change the way things work, didn't you?"

"Yes." Alessio cups my face in his hands. His thumb drifts across my cheek, wiping away a tear I didn't know was there. "I mean it. I want to change the way the mafia operates. I want to make the Marchetti mafia a place where people feel safe. Where they know that there is a *famiglia* who is there for them. Why?"

"I just want to make sure that I make the right choice."

I stand on my toes and kiss him, my tongue tangling with his. He groans and presses me against the counter, his cock pressing against my lower stomach. His hands slip into my hair, holding me in place as his tongue explores my mouth.

Heat pools in my core and I feel wetness between my thighs as Alessio pulls away from me. The smile he gives me is enough to send my heart soaring.

There is no way that I'm ever going to leave this.

I'm falling for him and falling hard. I know it, but there is a part of me that doesn't want to tell him yet. Not while the contract is in place. I want something real with him.

"What do you say we go to your bedroom before my father finds you bending me over the counter?" I ask, looping my arms over his shoulders and playing with the ends of his hair.

Alessio grins and stoops to toss me over his shoulder. I laugh as he hurries to his bedroom, slamming the door shut and locking it behind him.

He sets me down and pins me against the wall, his knee between my legs. His hands slide beneath my shirt, cupping my breasts through the lace bra while he kisses me. I moan, grinding my core against his thigh while we kiss.

As he kisses his way down my neck, I tilt my head and

arch my back trying to give him better access. Alessio grabs my shirt and pulls it over my head, tossing it to the side before continuing his path down my neck and to my breasts.

He grazes my nipple through the thin lace of my bra, sending shivers down my spine. I work my way down the buttons of his shirt, needing him naked and inside me now.

"Someone isn't feeling very patient today," he says, his tone husky and teasing as he steps back from me and sheds the rest of his clothing.

"Why should I be patient when what I want is right in front of me?" I ask, taking off my clothes before dropping to my knees in front of him.

I grip the base of his cock while I lick the head, swirling my tongue around it. He groans, his fingers sinking into my hair. I slip one hand between my legs, toying with my clit while I take him into my mouth.

"Fuck yes, swallow my cock."

I circle my clit with a finger while working my mouth and hand in time on his cock. I hollow my cheeks, taking him deeper. As I graze my teeth along the sensitive flesh, I moan. He rocks his hips, driving his cock deeper into my mouth. My orgasm starts to build as I suck him harder, his cock pulsing in my mouth.

"Fucking hell, Billie. I'm going to come if you keep doing that. Fuck your fingers like a good girl and stop trying to make me come fast."

I move my fingers faster, still teasing him with my tongue as my orgasm rocks through me. His hips rock faster, shoving his cock harder into my mouth until he pulls out completely. He uses his grip on my hair to guide me to my feet before nodding to the bed.

"Bend over the bed and put your ass in the air."

I do as he says, my pussy pulsating as he stands behind

me. Alessio's hands roam over my ass, massaging the flesh before his hand comes down hard. Wetness coats my thighs as he does it again to the other side before rubbing away the sting.

When he slowly sinks his cock into me, I'm already on the edge of another orgasm. He groans as he rolls his hips, pulling out before slamming back into me.

I arch my back as one of his hands sinks into my hair and pulls my head back. I push back onto his cock, meeting him thrust for thrust. His cock throbs as he comes, his grip on my hip bruising as he continues to slam into me.

"Sit on the edge of the bed and spread your legs for me," he says, pulling out of me. I spin around and sit down, spreading my legs and aching for him.

At the first swipe of his tongue along my slit, my hips buck forward. I drape one leg over his shoulder while his fingers push into me, massaging my inner walls while his tongue swirls around my clit.

I come as he sucks on my clit, his fingers moving faster. My legs shake as the orgasm crashes through me.

When I fall back to the bed, he climbs onto the mattress beside me. His arms wrap around me, pulling me closer to him. My heart skips a beat as I put my head on his chest and take a deep breath.

This is the moment. It's the moment when I should tell him how I feel.

I know that it's now or never, while we're relaxing in bed without the pressures of the outside world threatening to crush us.

"Alessio?" My stomach flips and flops as I look up at him. "I'm tired of casual sex. I want something real."

"Why, Billie," he says, his tone teasing as he nips at my jawline. "Are you asking me to go steady?"

"One of us has to have the balls to make this official."

Even as I say it, I feel like I'm at the edge of a cliff and waiting to tip over it. A small voice in the back of my mind says that this could be a colossal failure. I could be putting my heart on the line only to have him destroy it.

That little voice is the one that thinks a future with him could be troublesome.

However, my heart is overpowering my head. Even as I wait for him to answer me, my heart soars with the possibilities for our lives moving forward.

He smirks and reaches up to pinch my nipple. I gasp as he chuckles, my pussy pulsating. "Don't get sassy with me or there will be punishments."

"Oh?" I smile and run my fingers up his chest. "That sounds fun. If you answer my questions first."

"I want something more than just casual sex with you too."

Alessio rolls over, hovering above me as his mouth captures mine in a searing kiss.

For once, I feel like I'm on the right path to getting everything I want out of life.

26

ALESSIO

Arturo glares at me as I walk into his room a few days after telling him that I'm seeing Billie. I arch an eyebrow at him before making my way across the room and dropping into a chair. Arturo sighs and mutes the television.

"I don't want to talk about this right now with you," he says, getting out of bed and moving to sit in the chair across from mine. "I need time to wrap my head around this. I respect you, but I think you and Billie are making a mistake."

The words cut like a knife, but I keep my face blank. I need to be calm and collected if I'm going to get Arturo to see things from my point of view. I know that he is never going to accept me as a part of his family if he doesn't see the way I care about his daughter.

"I know that this is going to take time," I say, choosing my words carefully. "But I don't think that you're going to be able to wrap your mind around this without knowing all the facts. I know that Billie has spoken to you, but I want you to hear my side too."

"You're both putting me in an impossible position."

I nod. "I can understand that, and I can only imagine what you're feeling right now. We've been friends for too long to allow this to tear us apart without speaking about it first, though."

"And you think that I should listen to you because you're my boss and that is what I have done for as long as you've known me? Not when it comes to my daughter, Alessio. Never when it comes to Billie. She is more important to me than working for you will ever be."

There is a haunted look in his eyes as he glances out the window. I want to ask him what's going through his head, but I doubt that he would tell me even if I asked.

The rift that I've created between us is so big that I don't know if it's ever going to be fixed.

"I want you to listen to me as a friend. Not as your boss. I want you to know that I didn't enter into a relationship lightly with Billie. I've spent more time thinking about this than I've spent thinking about most things in my life."

"And you're ready to risk our friendship over this?" Arturo asks, his voice tense. "She is nineteen years younger than you. Billie should be out living her life and having experiences that you've already had, not considering settling down with you."

"I would risk everything for her. Hell, I would throw it all away for her. Everything. I would give up everything that my family has worked to build for generations for her."

Arturo presses his lips together and looks away from me. He stares out the window for a few minutes, the tension stretching between us. When he looks back at me, I can't get a read on what is going through his head.

"You think that Billie is worth giving up everything for?"

I cross one leg over the other, settling back in the chair.

"I do. And I want to make sure that she has the chance to pursue her dreams too. I will do everything I can to help her."

"And what you can do for her financially is supposed to make me feel better about this entire thing?" Arturo scoffs and shakes his head. "That isn't the way this is going to work, Alessio. She is her own woman."

"You think I don't know that? She's given me hell since day one. She is strong and capable. She doesn't need or want my help, but I want to give it to her. I want to be around to support her in whatever dream she chooses to follow. I think about the future with her, Arturo. A lot. She challenges me. She pushes me to be a better man. I want to be that better man for her."

Arturo gets up and paces from one side of the room to the other. He winces as his body protests, but he doesn't stop.

"If she comes to me and tells me that she doesn't want a life with me, then I'll let her go. You know that, Arturo. It's not my intention to hold Billie back. I want to grow with her. I want both of us to become better people because we are together."

He stops and looks at me. His frown deepens and he shakes his head. "You're nothing like your father."

My eyebrows furrow. "I don't think I know what that has to do with Billie."

"You've always thought that you were going to become a replica of your father. Your father never would have sat there and told me that he was willing to give up everything for a woman. You're a good man, Alessio, and Billie is free to make her own choices, but you have a habit of holding your-self back because of your fears surrounding your father."

I can already see where this is going even though I don't

want to. He is worried about what will happen to Billie if I keep getting in my own way.

I don't know how to convince him that it won't be a problem.

Arturo sits back down, stretching his leg out in front of him and massaging his thigh. "Like I said, right now, I can't be your friend about this. I can't sit here and talk to you about the woman you met. Not when it's Billie."

"I'm going to continue seeing her for as long as she wants to be with me, even if you don't approve of the situation. I want your support in this, but I don't need it."

"One day, you can have my support. Right now, I need to be upset about this. You're a good man and I'm sure that you'll make her happy and she'll make you happy. But for now, I need space to wrap my head around this."

"I'll give you the space you need. I would like you to stay here for the time being, though. I don't know what Paolo is planning and I don't want to see you get hurt again. I will keep my relationship with Billie respectful in front of you, but I'm not going to hide my relationship in my own home."

Arturo nods. "Billie would skin me alive if I even thought about leaving."

I laugh and stand, heading for the door. "Yes, she would. And then she would come after me for letting you leave. I don't want that to happen to either of us, so it looks like you're going to have to stay here."

"I'll come around eventually," Arturo says as I reach for the door. "I just need a little more time and a lot more liquor."

I nod and shut the door, standing in the hallway for a minute while I collect myself. The conversation went better than I expected. When I went in there, I thought he was going to throw things at me. Maybe try to punch me.

He just needs time to get through how he feels about this. I'm not going to lose my best friend even though I fell for his daughter.

BILLIE WALKS INTO THE CASINO BRIGHT AND EARLY THE next morning with a tray of coffees in her hand. She smiles at several of the staff standing around before joining me by the elevators. I take the tray from her as she presses the button.

"Morning," she says, running her hand through her hair. "I don't know how you slept last night, but I was kept awake by this incessant banging."

I chuckle and shake my head. "It's your fault."

The elevator doors open, and we step inside. She rolls her eyes but the corner of her mouth tips up with amusement.

"I'm pretty sure I'm not the problem."

"That's where you're wrong," I say, my voice husky as I lean closer to her. "That sheer dress you put on last night was entirely the problem. And then you got naked and that's even more of a problem."

A bright pink blush spreads across her cheeks as the doors open to the office floor. I wink at her before heading to our office with her beside me. It feels good to walk through the business with her, knowing that she is just as ambitious as I am. That we can build a successful future together where neither of us has to worry about the other not wanting the same things.

"Do you need me to do anything before I start to run

reports?" Billie asks as she takes her coffee from the tray and puts it on her desk. She pulls her laptop out of her purse before hiding the purse in the small closet.

"Actually, I wanted to talk to you about the resort you want to build."

She raises an eyebrow, curiosity shining in her eyes. She follows me into my office and shuts the door. I take a seat on the couch, setting my coffee on the table. Billie sits beside me, her knee brushing against mine as I open the folder I left in the middle of the table yesterday.

"I've been looking at the plans you have for a resort, and before you get mad at me, Christian brought them to me. He thought that it was something I should see."

Her eyes widen slightly as she looks down at her sketches. "I don't know why he would do that. I told you about everything I planned on doing."

"Yeah, but you never showed me these. Billie, these are amazing. You're ready to do this now. I know that I've already paid you a fair amount of money through our contract, but if you want me to, I'd love to be a silent investor in your resort business."

Her mouth drops open and she immediately starts shaking her head. "Thank you, Alessio. I really do appreciate the offer, but this is something I have to do on my own. I want to know that I accomplished it without the mafia backing me. I just want something independent. Something that can really be my own, you know?"

I smile and nod. "I do know. But this could give you an easy foot in the door. I have more money than I know what to do with and I want to support you in your dreams. Let me help you."

"Then support me by respecting my wishes," she says, her tone sharp. "I appreciate the offer, I really do, but I don't want to use your money to prop up my business. I want to build this on my own. I've been working since high school to make my dream a reality. Every single dollar I have has gone into saving for my future. I *need* to know that I worked hard for this."

"Billie, you're being unreasonable. This money wouldn't be to prop you up. It would be to help you make your dream a reality faster."

She crosses one leg over the other and takes my hand. "Thank you for being as generous as you are, but to me, this feels like propping me up. I need you to step back and see it from my perspective."

As much as I want to argue with her and tell her that I can give her everything she needs, I take a mental step back. I need to see everything the way she is seeing it.

Even though it is hard to admit, I can see where she is coming from. I can understand the feeling of wanting to know that you made it on your own. She wants to build something from the ground up that she worked for.

"I'll support you in whatever way you want. I won't invest in your company, but will you let me give you a bonus at the end of the contract? You've been dragged through the wringer for the last couple weeks, and I want you to know how much I appreciate you standing by my side."

She smiles. "You're not going to let me say no to that, are you?"

I grin and shrug. "You could try, but I would just find another way to give it to you."

"I'm not going to use the money for the business." She stands up and smoothes down her slacks. "You should know that before you decide to send me more money."

"Use it for whatever you want. You could use a new car. Yours is looking a little worse for wear."

Billie gasps, putting a hand to her heart. "How dare you say that about my baby?"

"Your baby is a rust bucket just waiting to roll over and die."

She laughs and heads for the door. "I'm going to get to work and I suggest you do the same. I hear the boss is a real hard ass."

I watch her stride out of the office, my heart swelling.

I'm going to marry that woman one day.

27

———

BILLIE

"So, the contract is over," Emilia says as we curl up on the couch and turn on a movie. "What are you going to do now with your life?"

"Well, Papa can finally be on his own, which means that I would be able to leave now if I wanted to."

Emilia smirks and turns to face me. "That sounds like there is a but coming."

I look around her apartment, taking in the pictures of her family that line the walls and trying to come up with the right words to describe how I feel.

Over the past few days, I've spent a lot of time thinking about what I want for myself. For the longest time, I was sure that leaving would be the answer. I would escape the mafia and then I would be free to start my life the way I wanted.

When I started falling for Alessio, that thought shifted. I began seeing a life where I stayed in the mafia. Where he would make changes to make sure the *famiglia* felt like a family and not just people who would kill each other to get ahead if they could.

"There is a massive but," I say, pulling my blanket a little closer. "I'm falling for him, and I don't want to leave anymore. I don't know what that says about me now, but everything I planned for myself has changed."

"You're giving up everything you wanted for Alessio?" Emilia shakes her head and reaches for her glass of wine. "Billie, that doesn't sound like you."

"When did I say that I was giving up what I wanted?" My back stiffens slightly as I stare at her. I know that she is coming from a good place, but the question still bothers me. "I'm not giving up anything. I'm still going to have what I want. It's just going to be in Atlanta instead of somewhere else in the country."

Emilia sighs. "Are you sure that's what's best? You know how things in the mafia are. Sure, Alessio is changing them, but is it ever really going to change? Are you ever really going to be happy with a man who is a career criminal?"

"Are you forgetting all the crimes that we've committed?" I take a sip of my wine. "I don't think it's fair to judge him entirely on the things that he's done. It doesn't mean that I hate the mafia any less, but he matters a whole lot more to me than the mafia."

"You sound like you're in love with him." Emilia smiles and reaches out to squeeze my knee. "If you think he is the one for you, then I'm happy for you."

"Thank you."

The butterflies in my stomach flutter their wings as I consider what it means to be in love with Alessio. We're going to work toward a future together. It's something that I didn't think would ever happen with anyone in the mafia.

That brings some complicated feelings with it. Even though I know that I've fallen for Alessio, there is also the sense that the mafia is always going to come before my future and dreams. I know that it is his legacy, but I'm also trying to create a legacy of my own.

He is going to give me the space to grow as I need. I can chase my dreams and be with him.

It's what I keep telling myself, even though there is a little voice in the back of my mind that tells me otherwise. I have to have faith in him, though. He has been nothing but supportive of my dreams.

I'm going to be able to have everything I want.

Christian glances up from the kitchen table as I get home late that night. He nods in my direction before glaring down at his phone. I see a thin bar come up across the screen.

"Girl problems?" I ask as I set my purse down on the counter. "You know, if you want to talk about it, I can help you."

He sighs and runs his hand through his hair. "Fuck it. I may as well get an opinion."

I grin and open the fridge, pulling out a couple of bottles of beer. He shakes his head, a small smile curving the corner of his mouth as I open them before handing him one.

"You know, this is going to be a massive mistake. I'm going to regret telling you anything."

Laughing, I sit down beside him and take a sip of beer. "Come on, tell Doctor Billie about your problems. I promise you won't regret it."

"I have had a few names of people in my cartel leaked to the Feds, and I need to guarantee protection for my people.

I was approached by a very prominent person with a very... unorthodox proposition."

"Oh?" I'm curious what he could mean by that.

"He'll protect my people from the law in exchange for protection for himself."

"Okay. Sounds reasonable. A good deal."

"You'd think so. The problem is that he insists the way to insure both sides play ball is through marriage."

I didn't think that there were arranged marriages anymore. Christian certainly doesn't seem like the kind of man who would willingly go along with something like that.

"What? Are you serious? Who is she? Do you even like each other?" I ask, crossing one leg over the other.

He shrugs as his phone buzzes again. "We have never even met before. That's why I said I'd think about it. He is pushing me for an answer. The wedding would be taking place about a year from now, because he wants it to be a major PR event for himself. But I have no clue how a marriage with her is going to work. Especially since my sister says I'm sacrificing my love life, so she is against it."

"I mean, if I was your sister and my brother was considering marrying a woman as part of a business deal, I would lose my shit too."

Christian takes a sip of his beer. "I know you're right. And I'd never consider it under different circumstances. But I have to protect my people." He shakes his head as he lowers it. "There are times that I think I never should have come back from Colombia. If I had stayed down there, I wouldn't be dealing with this right now."

"Then why don't you go back there after Paolo is dealt with?"

He shakes his head. "I can't risk my people. And I have no guarantee they'll be safe if I do that."

I'm about to ask him another question when Alessio walks in the room. Christian nods to him before getting up and heading outside with his phone in hand. I watch as Christian makes his way to the pool house, disappearing inside moments later.

"How was Emilia's?" Alessio asks as he stoops down to kiss me quickly. "Did you have a good time over there?"

"It was good, but it was a lot. I haven't seen her in weeks, and it feels like she doesn't want to talk much about her own life." I shrug and sip my beer. "It's alright, though. Just that season of life, I guess. We talked about my business a bit too."

"Speaking about the business, when were you planning on getting started with that?" He stands behind me and combs his fingers through my hair. "I know that you're planning on doing this on your own, but I have some contacts I could give you who would be useful while you're building the resort."

"I have to find a location first," I say, my eyes drifting shut at the soothing feeling of his fingers in my hair. "I'm not sure where I want to build. I think the other side of the city or a neighboring one would be a good idea. I don't want to be anywhere near the casino, though."

"I have a few realtors working for me. I could introduce you to one of them when you're ready."

With a sigh, I wonder how far he is going to push it. I know that he is just trying to help, and I appreciate it, but he keeps pushing.

"Thank you. I think I'm going to look for a realtor outside the *famiglia*, though. I don't want to be any more indebted to the mafia than I already am."

His hand stops moving through my hair. "What are you

talking about? You're part of the *famiglia*. You aren't indebted to it."

I turn to face him, my heart racing. This is toeing very close to a conversation that I don't want to have with him. I don't know how he will react if he ever finds out I was planning to leave and I don't want to find out.

"Alessio, the mafia has paid for my schooling. The mafia money pays for my housing. That money comes with a price. I'm not naive enough to think that it doesn't."

"I'm working to change things," he says, moving to sit beside me. "There is no shame in taking money that the *famiglia* has earned if you're part of it."

"But then I have to let the *famiglia* have a finger in my business. Do you think I want that?" I finish off the beer and sigh. "Can you honestly say that having the mafia involved in my resort is going to be the best thing for the business?"

His lips press into a thin line. After a long moment, he shakes his head. "No. I can't say that."

"Then you need to try harder to understand my position on this. I am more than willing to ask you for help, but I don't want that help to be tied to the mafia."

He closes his eyes and pinches the bridge of his nose. "I really think you should reconsider your position on this. I want to help you."

"And if you have help that isn't tied to the mafia, I will gladly take it. I know that you have amazing connections and want to help me. I just need to make sure that I'm not playing a game where I could lose everything if the police investigates."

My stomach lurches as I get up from the table and walk away. Even though I want to settle this tonight, I know it isn't going to happen. He just wants to help, but I want my independence in this situation.

I want to build something for myself that is going to last.

28

ALESSIO

I drum my fingers on my desk and think about my conversation with Billie last night. It's been difficult to see things her way when I have the ability to help her.

Of course, I never considered the fact that she stood to lose everything.

Hearing that was like a punch in the gut. She's right, though. If she uses any of the mafia connections to get her business going, it could be seized. If I go down, I ruin everything she's building for herself.

I can't do that to her. She deserves to chase her dreams without having to worry about whether they are going to disappear the next day.

My phone starts ringing, the sound echoing through my head and causing a dull pulsing in my temples. It's the start of a stress headache that doesn't seem to go away these days.

I've been trying my best to put an end to the Paolo situation, but Christian and I haven't been able to gain much ground without knowing where he is.

"Davide, this better be important," I say, turning on the speakerphone before flipping through several reports Billie put on my desk that morning. "I have to sift through the profit and loss statements for the last month and I can't do that if you're just calling to chat."

"No, boss. It *is* important." He clears his throat and I hear several voices in the background of the call. "We have a problem. I'm at The Hurricane and there is some trouble brewing outside. At least, that's what Carmello is telling me. I got here a few minutes ago, but I didn't see anything suspicious."

"Carmello is a greasy bastard. Stay with him until I get there to deal with the situation. Do *not* let him out of your sight."

I hang up and open the bottom drawer of my desk, grabbing out the two guns I have hidden in there. Billie enters the office with another stack of paper, her gaze distant as she looks past me.

"Billie, I have to go check out a problem at one of my clubs. I wanted to talk to you first but given the current situation, it's going to have to be quick."

She raises an eyebrow and puts the stack of papers down on my desk. "Alright."

"I should have listened to you the first time that you told me to back off but I kept pressing. I thought I knew what was best for you, but I didn't take the time to think about the consequences of using mafia money. I'm sorry. I should have listened to you."

"Thank you," she says, a smile spreading across her face. "Now, what's going on and why are you rushing out of here with two guns?"

I hand her one with a smile. "I doubt there is any chance that I'm getting out of here without you."

She laughs and checks the gun over before tucking it into the back of her waistband and pulling her blouse down over it. "No. If there's something you're about to rush blindly into, I feel like I should be there for backup."

"Let's get going, then. I think Paolo is at The Hurricane. If not, he's going to be there soon. Davide is there and watching over everything, but the club manager, Carmello, is someone I think would have betrayed me if there was a good opportunity presented to him."

Billie follows me out of the office, shaking her head. "Then why is he still alive or part of the *famiglia?*"

"I don't have enough evidence to do anything about it. We're probably walking into a trap, though." We get on the elevator, my mind already racing.

The club is going to be under attack when I get there. I already know it. Paolo has been quiet for too long and this would be the perfect opportunity for him to strike out. He's going to kill as many people as possible before moving onto the next place he plans to attack. It's what he would have learned how to do from my father.

As the elevator doors open into the parking garage, I take a deep breath. Hopefully, this will be the end of it, but Paolo is smart. I don't know if he will be at the club when we get there, but if he is, I have a bullet with his name on it.

I look to the ceiling as I unlock my car. Somewhere, my big brother is watching this entire situation unfold and he has never been more disappointed in me.

I'm sorry, Enzo. I have to kill him.

I HEAR THE GUNSHOTS BEFORE I SEE THE DEAD BODIES. I park the car in an alley around the corner from the club and look over at Billie. She has her gun out and looks like she is ready to kill anyone who crosses her.

"When we get in there, you need to stay back. If things get worse, get in the car and go home. Don't try and save the day," I say, leaning over to look at her. "Don't do anything that is going to get you hurt."

I kiss her, my tongue tangling with hers. If this is the last time that I kiss her, then I want it to be memorable. My hands sink into her hair and I hold her close, kissing her until we're both gasping for breath.

"Stay safe," I say before getting out of the car.

I take off running to the corner of the building with my gun drawn. Billie's footsteps echo behind me as we round the corner, keeping close to the buildings lining the street and making our way to the club.

Billie watches my back as I open the door to the club and see the front entrance littered with bodies. There is too much blood to distinguish if they are my men or Paolo's.

Davide is behind the bar, shooting everyone who heads his way. I run to join him while Billie takes off the other way, diving behind the DJ booth. Davide looks over at me with a grimace as we both duck down.

"What's the situation?" I ask, standing up enough to shoot a man in the head before crouching back down. "How many of ours are dead and how long do we have until the cops show up?"

"Cops are maybe ten minutes out. Most of the bodies are ours. We're losing bad. Paolo isn't here, but his second, Maximo, is. He's looking to kill as many people as possible."

Davide stands and shoots another man in the head before nodding to me. I get up and the two of us shoot down three more men. Through the door to the kitchen, more men come running.

"You stay here," I say, gauging the distance between me and the kitchen. "I'll go in there and take care of the men in there. You stay out here and make sure that nothing happens to Billie."

Davide's eyebrows raise but he nods. I take a deep breath before starting to make my way around the edge of the club. I stick close to the wall, hiding behind the big leather couches that are already riddled with bullet holes.

I make it to the kitchen and look around for anyone who might still be in there. It's only when I round the corner that the mouth of a gun presses against the back of my head.

"Turn around and drop the gun."

I drop the gun onto the counter beside me and slowly turn around, unsurprised to find Maximo staring at me. He smirks and presses the gun hard into my forehead.

"You really thought that you could come in here and win this battle?" Maximo shakes his head, chuckling to himself. "Paolo is more powerful than you could possibly know. If you keep underestimating him, you're going to wind up dead sooner rather than later."

"What?" I ask, my tone mocking even though I know it could get me killed. However, I didn't get to be the leader of a mafia by shrinking back when my life was threatened. "Your boss couldn't grow the balls to be here and kill me himself?"

"He has better things to do with his time. Besides, I'm not here to kill you. I'm just supposed to give you a reminder of what happens when you cross Paolo."

I scoff. "He crossed me when he decided to turn against the *famiglia*. You can tell him that he is a spineless fucker who should have been here to deliver the message himself."

Maximo whips the gun against my head and I see stars. A thin rivulet of blood trickles down the side of my face. I laugh and shake my head.

"Is that really the best that you've got?" I ask as he draws his hand back to crack the gun against my face again.

The sound of a gunshot rings out. Hot blood splatters against my face before Maximo's body collides with mine. I shove him to the side, trying not to get his blood in my mouth before he falls to the ground.

Billie stands behind him with a wild look in her eyes and her gun raised. Blood covers her clothes and stains her blonde hair.

I'm definitely going to marry her one day.

"What do you think Paolo is going to go after next?" Billie asks as we step beneath the spray of a hot shower a couple hours later. "You know that this is far from over."

"He's going to come after you." I run my hand through my hair, slicking it back as the water cascades down around us. "It's the only logical next move. You were at the fight today. He will know that you're more important than just some woman I won at an auction."

She runs her hands up my chest, making my cock stiffen as I step closer to her. The water runs pink with the blood washing away from us. I grab her soap and squirt some into my hands.

"You'll find him before then," she says softly as I lather up the soap before running my hands down her curves. "Nothing is going to happen to me."

I stare at her for a moment, my heart racing. Even the thought of something potentially happening to her is nearly enough to drop me to my knees. I don't know what I would do if I lost her.

"How do you have that much faith in me?" I cup her breasts, my thumbs drifting over her peaked nipples. "How can you have that much faith in me when I don't even have faith in myself?"

She links her hands behind my neck, her body pressing against mine as my hands fall to her hips. My heart is beating rapidly in my chest as she smiles.

"Because I know the kind of man you are. The man you hide away from the rest of the world. If there's anything that contract has taught me, it's that you aren't the person you pretend to be."

"I didn't think that I would ever find anyone I could see as my equal," I say, trying to speak around the lump that's lodged itself in my throat. "Until I got to know you. You're everything that was missing in my life. You push me to be the kind of person I want to be, and you challenge me when I need it the most. I love you, Billie."

My stomach tosses and turns as a pause stretches between us. I can't read the expression on her face, and it makes me nervous. Hell, telling her that I love her makes me nervous. I've said the words so infrequently in my life that saying them terrifies me.

But I know Billie is the right woman for me.

"You love me?" she asks, her eyes shining with tears. She reaches up to wipe away one that escapes before shaking her head. "You really love me?"

"I do. More than I ever thought I'd love anyone."

Her smile stretches across her face. Billie runs her hand along the side of my face, her thumb drifting across my cheek. "I love you, too."

Her words hit me hard, and as I look at her, I can see forever in her eyes. When I lean down to kiss her, it feels like the best thing I've done in my life. I moan as her hand slides down my body to grip my cock while the other sinks into my hair.

Her hand moves up and down the length of my cock while I kiss my way down her neck. She moans, tilting her head back and giving me better access. As I suck on the sensitive flesh, she swirls her thumb around the head of my cock.

Even though I want to take my time with her — worship her body the way she deserves — I need to feel her pussy milking my cock as I tell her I love her.

Billie laughs as I pick her up and pin her against the wall. Her ankles lock behind my back as the head of my cock brushes against her core. Her fingers sink into my shoulders as I bury myself in her pussy.

Her inner walls pulsate around me as I thrust slowly. Billie moans as I suck on her neck, nipping at her skin until she's writhing against me.

I rock my hips faster, driving deeper into her. Billie arches her back, rocking her hips and building friction between us. My fingers dig into her ass, hauling her against me as hard as I can.

"Fuck, I love you," I say as her pussy clamps down around me. "I want you to come for me, Billie. Right now. I need to feel your tight little pussy milking my cock."

"Fuck," she says, her voice breathy as one of her hands leaves my shoulder to toy with her breast. She rolls her nipple between her fingers, teasing it as her hips buck forward. "I love you."

I slam harder into her, groaning as she comes. Billie's moans echo through the shower as her legs tighten around me. I push her harder into the wall, needing to draw out her orgasm for as long as possible.

As her pussy pulses around me, I come hard and fast. I

hold her tight against me as she rolls her hips, teasing me while I come.

Billie smirks as I pull out of her and put her back down. She gets to her knees in front of me, her tongue darting out to lick the head of my cock clean. My cock is throbbing as she slowly drags her tongue along the underside of my length.

"Fuck," I say, pulling her wet hair back from her face so I can watch her tease my cock. "If you keep doing that, I'm going to come all over your chest."

She arches an eyebrow in a silent challenge before dragging her tongue along my length again. Her fingers disappear between her legs, circling her clit quickly until she is riding her hand while licking my cock.

The image alone is enough to have my cock aching for release. Her little moan as she takes my cock into her mouth is going to be my undoing.

As I rock my hips, driving my cock deeper into her mouth, she rides her fingers faster. Her moans get louder as she comes, coating her fingers with her wetness.

"Lick your fingers clean," I say as I pull out of her mouth.

She does as I say while I stroke my cock. All it takes is her little moan as her tongue flicks between her fingers to send me over the edge. I coat her breasts in come, moaning as she smiles.

"Looks like you're going to have to start over," she says, her tone teasing as she stands up and rinses off her chest. She teases her nipples, mischief flashing in her eyes.

"I don't know how I'm going to get anything done with you looking at me like that," I say, grabbing the soap again. "What do you say we get cleaned up and then go watch a movie."

Billie raises to her toes to kiss me before nodding. "It sounds like the perfect way to close out a horrible day."

Even though both of us know worse days are coming, I don't want to focus on that right now. All I want to do is to curl up in bed with the woman I love and watch a movie until we both fall asleep.

29
———

BILLIE

I SHAKE MY ASS TO THE MUSIC BLARING THROUGH THE speakers while waiting for the bucket of soapy water to fill up. The mop leans against the counter beside me while I dance and wipe down the counters.

It's the first time in a couple of days that I've had the house mostly to myself. Papa is in his suite, doing whatever he does in there all day while I clean up the kitchen. Christian has flown back home for a couple days while Alessio is working overtime, checking on all his businesses to make sure that Paolo is staying away from them.

I keep dancing as I toss the rag to the side and drag the bucket out of the sink. Water sloshes onto the floor and someone scoffs behind me.

As I spin around, I grab a knife out of the knife block and hold it out in front of me. Alessio's mother crosses her arms and clucks her tongue.

"You should have been long gone by now," his mother says, looking at the water on the floor. "You don't even know how to mop a floor properly. Why my son keeps you around and defies his own mother, I don't know."

"He has his reasons," I say, grabbing a towel and tossing it down onto the puddle. I put the knife back in the block, even though I want to keep it. I don't trust his mother as far as I can throw her.

She didn't become a mafia wife by sitting at home and doing nothing while her husband worked.

I would be stupid to think that she couldn't kill me if she wanted to.

"Oh, I'm sure that he does." She looks at me like I'm nothing more than dirt on the ground. "And I'm sure that it definitely has to do with how far you're willing to spread your legs."

I scowl at her, trying to keep my temper in check. She is Alessio's mother, and she does hold certain power within the mafia. However, I would be lying if I said that there wasn't a part of me that wanted to kick her out right now.

"Is there something I can help you with?" I crouch to sop up the water before tossing the towel into the sink. "I have some cleaning to get done and I can't do that while being called a whore."

"Funny, I would have thought that you were capable of multitasking." She smirks and takes a step closer to me. "As for what you can help me with, I want you out of Alessio's life. He lost his focus with the *famiglia* when you came around. I don't want to see that for my son."

"Did he lose his focus, or did he start to turn the *famiglia* in the direction he wants?" I stand taller, not backing down from her intimidation tactic. She can invade my space all she wants. I'm not going anywhere.

"He lost his focus. He is burning his father's legacy to the ground, and it only started when you showed up. Now, you can leave on your own or I will have you taken care of."

I arch an eyebrow, even as my heart starts to race. "Get out."

"Excuse me? Who do you think you are? You think that you can just kick me out of my son's house? That's not going to happen."

"You can leave now, or I will call Davide to come deal with you."

She glares at me. We both know that if I call Davide, Alessio is going to hear about this. If there is one thing I know she doesn't want to do, it's piss Alessio off. He will come home and remove her from his life. We both know it.

"You're going to regret this," she says as she heads for the door. "I will be calling my son and talking some sense into him."

"Good luck."

I follow her to the door and lock it behind her, wondering how she even got inside. After the last issue with his mother, Alessio had changed the locks.

Although, if she went to see Alessio before coming over here, she would have easily stolen the keys. I need to ask him about it when he gets home.

I sigh as I head back into the kitchen. Papa is sitting at the table with his arms crossed and his eyebrows furrowed.

"What was that about?" he asks, jerking his chin in the direction of the front door.

"Alessio's mother wants me out of his life as soon as possible. She thinks that I'm the reason his father's horrific legacy is being ruined."

He nods. "She has always been that way. Just don't let anything she says get to you. But you do need to think about what you are willing to put up with. I doubt that he will remove her from his life entirely. Is that something you can be okay with in the long run?"

"I don't know," I say, though I do know. I would put up with her every single day of my life if it meant I got to be with him. That's the last thing that Papa needs to hear, though. He is still trying to wrap his head around the relationship.

"Well, you need to think about it, Billie. I don't want to see you get hurt by that woman."

"I know." I turn down the music and stick the mop in the bucket. "Want to keep me company while I get the kitchen clean?"

Papa smiles and leans back in the chair. "I guess I can do that. Why don't you tell me about all these new plans you have for your resort?"

I get to work scrubbing and talking to him about the resort I want to build. As we talk, I think about the days when it was just us. There was nobody else in either of our lives. It was me and Papa against the world.

It's strange to think that there's somebody else in my life that I can rely on now.

Alessio gets home late that night. I'm sitting in the living room and reading a book when he walks in and immediately strips out of his suit. He makes his way to the kitchen in nothing but his boxer briefs, getting a drink of water before looking over at me.

"Damn," I say, my tone teasing as I close my book and make a point of checking him out. "If I knew that I was going to get a show, I would have closed the book a lot faster."

Alessio sighs and crosses the room. He sets his glass of

water on the coffee table before sitting down beside me. "Sometimes I feel like that thing is suffocating me."

"Well, I much prefer this look."

He laughs and leans over to kiss me quickly. "Of course. I would expect nothing less."

"You look like you had a hard day."

He nods and laces his fingers with mine. "It wasn't great. Especially after I found out my mother stole my keys."

"That answers that question."

He looks at me, his eyebrows furrowing. "What question?"

"How your mother managed to get in here today to call me a whore."

Alessio lets go of my hand and gets up from the couch. He storms over to where he discarded his suit and rummages through his pockets until he finds his phone.

"You don't need to call her and deal with this," I say, leaning back into the cushions. "It isn't that big a deal. I can put up with her bullying me a little bit."

"You shouldn't have to," he says as he dials her number. "She has got to learn to respect you. Clearly, she didn't learn her lesson the first time."

I sigh but I know that he isn't going to listen to me. I don't want to make his relationship with his mother any more strained than it already is. Though, there is a part of me that likes his willingness to stick up for me.

"I'm going to say this and I'm going to say it once," Alessio says, his phone pressed to his ear. "You are not to insult or harass the woman I'm going to marry. You are not going to come over to my house and pull that shit. You are not going to pull that shit in public. You are going to treat her as my future wife because that is what she is."

He hangs up and tosses the phone onto the counter. His chest heaves and his cheeks are red.

The world shifts out from under me as I look at him. My mouth drops open, and I don't know what to say for a long while.

He wants to marry me.

Happiness flows through me, but terror is close behind it. While I've thought about the future with him, I didn't think he had given it much thought yet.

I thought this conversation would be a long time coming, not something that was happening right now.

But as he said it, I realized I want to marry him. I'm not going to love anyone the way I love him. My future is with him.

One day, Alessio is going to be my husband.

I can't wait.

"So," I say, grinning as I try to lighten the mood. "We're going to be getting married, are we?"

Alessio lets out the breath he's holding and laughs. "I want to get married someday. But I guess that I should have asked you what your thoughts on marriage were too."

"I want to get married someday. I want marriage and kids, honestly. Although, a lot of people have told me that it won't be possible to run my own business and have children. A lot of people like to make it seem like it has to be one or the other."

He shrugs and comes back to the couch, settling into the cushions beside me. "I don't see why it would have to be one or the other. You're a bright and capable woman. If anyone is going to be able to get everything they want, it's going to be you."

"We have time to figure that out." I smile and lean closer to him. "Any news on Paolo today?"

"None. He's back into hiding after the attack. Christian will be returning in a few days with some of his men and then we are going to start turning the city over until we find Paolo."

"He's still going to come for me. You know he is."

Alessio nods and closes his eyes, moving to put his head in my lap. "I know. We're going to handle it, though. Maybe we'll get lucky and he will go after another person in my life to try to torture me with."

I run my fingers through his hair. "I doubt that, but we'll figure it out."

Even though I have no clue how.

30

───

ALESSIO

"I lowered your protection detail today," I say late one night, getting naked before jumping into the pool with Billie.

She is grinning from ear to ear as I surface. When she throws herself at me, we both go tumbling back into the water.

"You mean that I won't have a bunch of men following me around all the time?" Billie asks as we tread water in the deep end. "I can't believe this. You don't know how excited I am to not have people looking over my shoulder all the time."

I shake my head, though I can't help the smile that stretches across my face. "Close, but not quite. It only lowered from six people to four. I know that you're capable of handling yourself. Six people is overkill when you always have a gun with you. Hell, you might be a better shot than I am."

Billie is still smiling as she floats on her back. "That's better than six people, though. Thank you. I felt like I was being smothered when I went grocery shopping the other day. It was like all the eyes in the building were on me. I hate that feeling."

"I know." I grab her hand and pull her closer to me, towing her into the shallow end. "I just want you to be safe and protected. It might be overkill, but I would rather have you alive than running around without a security detail hiding in plain sight."

She sighs and stands up in the shallow end, running her fingers through my hair. "It's a good thing you're cute, otherwise I wouldn't be putting up with this."

"Oh? You wouldn't be putting up with this, would you?"

I lunge toward Billie and toss her over my shoulder. She is shrieking with laughter as I spin around before tossing her into the deep end.

When she surfaces, mischief is shining in her eyes. She reaches behind her neck and unties her bikini top, letting it fall away. Her hands slip beneath the water and she works the bottoms down her long legs, tossing the fabric to the other end of the pool and leaving it to float away.

"And what do you think you're doing?" I ask as she swims to the other side of the deep end.

Water glistens on her body in the glow cast by the moonlight and the pool lights as she pulls herself out of the pool and sits on the edge. Billie parts her legs, her pussy already slick.

"Oh, you think that you deserve a little action?" I ask, grinning as I swim over to her. "And what have you done today to deserve me teasing that pretty little pussy with my tongue until you come?"

"If you don't want to help a girl out, I have a perfectly good vibrator upstairs."

I drape her legs over my shoulders as she leans back on her forearms. She moans softly as I nip at her inner thighs.

"Your father isn't about to look out the window and catch us like this, is he?" I suck on a high point of her inner thigh, just to the right of her pussy. She rolls her hips toward me, begging for more.

"No. He went out with Christian for the night. Riding around with him, I think. I don't know. I didn't ask."

I slide my tongue along her wet slit, loving the taste of her. Billie hums as I slide two fingers into her wet pussy, feeling her inner walls squeeze me. I moan against her pussy as my tongue flicks against her clit.

"Yes," she says, her heels digging into my back. "Fuck yes. Just like that."

I move my fingers slower, taking my time to massage her inner walls and tease her. She writhes against me, one hand sinking into my hair to keep me in place.

I chuckle and move my tongue faster, sucking her clit before circling it quickly. Her hips rock in time with my fingers, trying to build the tension between us.

"You're being a tease," she says as I slow my pace.

Her pussy pulses around my fingers as I pull them out. When I slam them back into her, her grip on my hair tightens. I thrust my fingers quickly while my tongue flicks her clit, pushing her closer and closer to the edge of an orgasm.

When I graze my teeth against her clit, she comes. Her legs shake over my shoulders and her pussy clenches down around my fingers. I keep thrusting into her, feeling her pulse around me.

"Get back in the water so I can fuck you properly," I say, backing up to give her room to slide back into the pool.

Billie slides into the pool, draping her arms over my shoulders and wrapping her legs around my waist. My cock is aching as I inch it into her. Billie rolls her hips, trying to take me deeper but I hold back.

"I want you to beg for my cock. Tell me how much you love it and then beg me to fuck you."

Heat flashes in her eyes as she digs her nails into my back. I pull out of her, rolling my hips to brush my cock against her core. Her head tilts back as I kiss her neck and nip at her shoulder.

"Tell me that you want me to fuck you, Billie." I slam into her once, burying myself to the hilt before pulling back out of her.

She moans, her eyes squeezing shut. "Why do you have to be such a fucking tease when you know how much I love your cock?"

"Good girl," I say, inching into her again. "But I'm pretty sure that's not everything I wanted to hear from you. Are you going to keep being good, or do you want me to leave you aching and needy?"

She hisses as I pull out of her, one hand gripping the edge of the pool behind her while I massage her breast with the other. I pinch her nipple hard, my cock throbbing at her little gasp.

"Tell me that you want it, Billie."

"Please fuck me," she says, her voice breathy as her nails rake across my skin. "I want to come all over your cock. I *need* to come all over your cock. Please fuck me."

I groan as I thrust into her hard and fast. My cock is aching as her pussy clenches around me. I know that I'm not going to last long when she feels this good. I rock my hips faster, needing to feel her come around me.

As I thrust, I keep teasing her nipple, rolling it between my fingers and pinching it. Billie's back arches off the wall as she yelps, her pussy pulsating. I groan, burying my face in her neck as I come.

I keep thrusting as I lift her high enough out of the water to take her nipple in my mouth. She moans as I graze it with my teeth. Her hips rock faster as I suck on it.

When she comes, her nails dig deeper into my back. I'm sure that I'm going to have marks on my skin in the morning, but it's worth it to feel the way her pussy clenches hard around me.

Billie's chest is heaving as I pull out of her. I kiss her, lazy and slow, our tongues tangling as I cup her face.

"You know, a girl could get used to a life like this," she says as she breaks away from the kiss.

"Could?" I pull her closer to me as her stomach starts to growl. "*Will* get used to this. Bille, this is your life now. You're it for me. And if I haven't made that clear enough, then I need to step up my game."

She gives me a smile and combs my hair back from my face. "I know that this is my life now. Although, if we don't get a late-night snack soon, I might die from starvation."

I chuckle and let go of her. "Alright, let's go get some sort of snack going."

Billie takes off toward the house while I swim to the deep end to grab her bikini. By the time I get out of the water and get into the house, she is dancing around the kitchen in one of my button-down shirts, the music blasting. I grab a towel from the stack near the door and dry off before wrapping it around my waist. Billie winks at me as she hops up on the counter to grab something from one of the cupboards.

"What are we making?" I ask, looking at the oven preheating.

"I want chocolate chip cookies," she says, hopping down

from the counter with a bag of chocolate chips in her hand. "Don't warm chocolate chip cookies sound like the perfect late-night snack to you?"

"I'm more of a salty fan." I grab the container of sea salt flakes. "Top the cookies with this and some caramel sauce too?"

Billie's stomach growls in response. She laughs and nods. "Apparently, I like that idea."

"I'm going to go get dressed and then I'll be back to help." I kiss her temple and put the salt on the counter before taking off to my room.

When I make my way back into the kitchen, my phone is ringing on the coffee table. I sigh and pick it up, silently wishing for a night where nothing goes wrong.

"What is it?" I ask, not bothering with a greeting.

"Nothing good," Davide says as something crashes in the background. "The casino has been robbed. I just got here, but there is a lot of damage. The police are going to be asking for you when they get here. I've already paid them to ignore the silent alarm for an hour while we clean this up."

"That fucker." I run my hand through my hair, considering all the ways that I'm going to kill Paolo. "Alright. I'll be there soon. Pay the cops whatever it takes to keep them out of my business for now."

I hang up and look over at Billie. Her eyebrows are furrowed as she turns off the oven and puts the cookie dough in the fridge.

"I'm sorry," I say, turning to head back to my bedroom for a pair of jeans and a shirt. "I have to go to the casino."

Billie follows behind me. "I'll get dressed and meet you back down here in a minute."

I turn to look at her and shake my head. "You don't have

to come with me. I would really rather if you just stayed home."

"Not happening," she says with a bright smile. "We're a team. I'll be ready in a minute."

I watch her jog up the stairs. Even though I want to argue with Billie, having her there with me makes me feel better. More at ease and less likely to explode.

She brings a calmness to my life that I didn't know was missing.

That calmness isn't going to save Paolo, though. Once I get my hands on him, he is a dead man.

THERE IS A GIANT HOLE IN THE CASINO WHERE THE wall once was. The truck lodged in that hole is the first thing I see when we arrive at the casino. My blood starts to boil as I grip the wheel and try to take a deep breath.

"It's going to be okay," Billie says, reaching out to put her hand on my shoulder. "If that truck is still here, then I doubt whoever did this got away."

"We just have to find them before the cops show up," I say, my tone dry as I get out of the car.

Davide is standing in front of the building and several of my capos are surrounding the perimeter. He nods to me as I walk over to him, his hands in his pockets.

"Have you caught the person who did this yet?"

Davide shakes his head. "We've searched the building twice, but we can't get to the panic room in your office. We don't have the codes. The men are still sweeping the building, but we suspect whoever did this is sitting in that panic room."

"Kill the cameras inside the building," I say as I head for

the doors. "I want every camera turned off so they don't see us coming."

Several more of the capos are in the building, sweeping every corner and looking for whoever might still be in the building. A group of people huddle in the corner, paramedics leaning over them.

"You don't think that they're not going to call the cops?" Billie asks, nodding over to the group of injured people.

"They've been given a lot of money not to." I look around and get a sinking feeling in the pit of my stomach. We're going to be setting ourselves up to get shot. Whoever is hiding in the panic room is going to have the advantage. "This way."

Billie follows me to the staircase. We climb the stairs together, guns drawn and watching for Paolo's men. The higher I climb, the more I realize I'm tired of killing people. I want this to be over.

I want to have a month where I don't have to kill anyone. A single month where I don't have to feel like a monster.

Billie's hand presses softly in the middle of my back as if she knows what I'm thinking. I look over my shoulder and offer her a small smile.

"Let's do this," I say as we reach the office floor.

I open the door and wait for her to pass through it first. She nods to me when she is a few feet away and we head for my office. My heart is hammering in my chest and my head is on a swivel.

This feels like a trap.

Either a trap, or one really stupid person.

I take a deep breath and open the door to Billie's office, clearing it before walking into my own. As soon as I step inside, I nearly trip over the bookcase that's been pushed to the floor.

"Watch yourself," I say softly to Billie. "There's broken glass everywhere."

She nods and looks over at the wall. The hidden door to my panic room is fully visible and a bundle of hundred-dollar bills is sitting outside.

"They're going to start shooting as soon as that door opens." I lean down, keeping my mouth close to her ear so whoever in the room can't hear us. "I want you to stay to the side. They're going to be shooting in every direction possible. I'm going to be the main target, but you need to surprise them."

Billie nods and stands to the far side of the door, half hidden behind another bookcase. I take a deep breath before keying in the code to the panic room on the panel beside the door. There is a low groan before the door swings open.

The shooting starts immediately. I throw myself away from Billie, getting behind a couch. More gunshots echo out. I pop up over the couch and shoot the man in the knee.

He drops to the ground, screaming as he grabs his knee. Billie appears from behind the bookcase, keeping her gun pointed at him. I join them, kicking away his weapon as Davide and a couple capos flood into the room.

"Who the fuck is this?" I ask, kicking the man in the ribs.

Davide looks down at him. "Jones. Low-level dealer working for Paolo."

"Excellent." I crouch down beside the man, shoving my gun into his mouth. "Here's the thing, Jones, I could kill you now, but I don't think that's enough punishment for you. Davide here is going to take you away. Torture you. Make you regret the day that you decided to fuck with me. And *then* he is going to kill you."

Davide hauls Jones to his feet, ignoring his protests and groans. He drags the man to the door, hurrying along, though Jones is hopping on one leg. The gunshots stop as more of my men flood the room.

"We've won," one of the men says as he looks around. "The cleaning team is on the way."

"Good." I nod and put my gun away. "The capos will give further instructions. Billie, it's time to go."

She keeps her gun in hand as we make our way out of the club and back to my car. Billie's stare is a thousand miles away as she gets into the car and leans back in her seat. I stand outside for a minute, watching as the cleaning crew's van pulls up to the doors.

"It won't be long before the cops are here," I say as I get in the car and start the engine.

"I'm so ready for this shit to be over," she says as her eyes close.

"I know." I reach over and squeeze her thigh gently. "We're going to get through this together. We're getting closer and closer to Paolo every single day. Christian and his men are searching Paolo's properties and killing whoever they find there. We're going to end this soon."

When she opens her eyes, I hate the look she gives me. It makes me feel like nothing is being done, even though I'm doing all that I can.

The disappointment cuts me to the core, and I don't know what to do to make her feel better.

31

————

BILLIE

Dead bodies are sitting on the doorstep of the main house in the compound when we get back. Alessio looks ready to kill as he parks the car and gets out. I follow behind him, tucking the gun in my waistband.

After the shooting at the club, this is the last thing he needs to deal with. I hate how much stress he's been under lately, but there's nothing I can do to fix it.

I also hate how many people have to die over two men's egos.

Davide steps out of the main house with two capos flanking him. One of them carries a body and tosses it into the pile with the others. The man's head rolls back and Jones is staring up at me.

"Are you alright?" Alessio asks, glancing over at me. Davide's eyes narrow as he watches me.

He's like a shark searching for blood in the water. I can't show any sign of weakness, even if he's watching for it.

It's the one aspect of being with Alessio that concerns me. The consigliere and capos are always watching my every move. They want me to make a mistake so they can report something to Alessio. Win his favor while destroying my relationship with him.

"No. I'm fine. The men had it coming." I keep my tone cold and professional. The voice of a woman who doesn't let killing bother her anymore.

Alessio raises an eyebrow before turning his attention back to Davide. "What did you learn before you killed him?"

Davide shrugs. "Not much. Paolo is getting closer, but we already knew that. He thinks that Paolo's attention is going to be focused on Billie, but there is no true proof of that. He said that Paolo insists that she is your weakness and killing her will leave you open and vulnerable."

Alessio nods, his shoulders slumping. "So, nothing that we didn't already know."

"We have several more men downstairs in the cells," Davide says as he smooths down his bloodstained shirt. "I'm getting dinner and then I will continue with the questioning. I'm sure that one of them knows something we don't."

"Good. One of them will know something. Just make sure you get that information before you kill them."

Alessio turns and heads back to the car. I watch the men for a moment longer, giving them a cold stare. Davide matches my gaze but after a few seconds, he dips his head.

I say nothing as I get back in the car. I don't know what there is to say right now. While I know that the men they captured are killing our people, torture isn't anything I've ever agreed with. It's inhumane. Necessary, but inhumane.

"Now that we're alone," Alessio says as he starts the car. He twists in his seat to face me slightly. "Tell me how you're really doing and don't give me some bullshit like you're fine. You're not fine and I can see that much right now."

I look out the window, trying to gather my thoughts.

"It's shit like that pile of dead bodies waiting to be picked up that makes me want to leave this life and never look back. You told me that you were going to change things, but leaving those bodies there is monstrous."

Alessio is quiet for too long. When I glance over at him, he is facing the wheel again. His knuckles are white as he clutches it, his jaw set in a hard line.

It's only when I think about what I said that I realize my mistake.

I told him that I had been thinking about leaving. I told him about considering treason against the *famiglia*.

"Alessio, it's not like that. At least, not entirely. I did think about leaving. A lot, honestly. This was never the life I wanted for myself. It isn't the kind of life that I thought I could live."

He pulls away from the main house, taking the road to his home. "I thought that we were going to start a future together, but you haven't even slightly mentioned not wanting to be here."

My chest constricts. "I changed my mind. I fell in love with you, and I changed my mind, alright? I want to be with you. I want to spend the rest of my life with you, and I know that the *famiglia* is part of that. I know that there's no avoiding it."

He stops the car and puts it in park, turning to face me.

"*There's no avoiding it?* Fucking hell, Billie, you could have fucking told me at any point in our relationship. You could have told me that this wasn't the life for you. But no. You wait until I tell you that I love you and want to marry you!"

He starts the car again, driving the rest of the way home. It feels like the world has fallen out from beneath my feet.

The rules of the *famiglia* say that the punishment for treason is death.

Alessio won't kill me. I know he won't. We love each other and he isn't capable of that. He may have killed a lot of people in his life, but he isn't capable of killing me.

That's what I tell myself as we get out of the car and head into the house.

The silence between us is deafening as I follow him to the kitchen. This discussion is far from over. We both know it.

"I've got a trip to Savannah tomorrow night," I say, thinking that I may as well give him all the information he isn't going to like at the same time. After all, in comparison to treason, a trip to Savannah is nothing.

His face turns a bright shade of red while his lips press into a thin line. "You really think now is the time to go to Savannah?"

"Christian agreed to go with me. He and two of his men are going to be my protection while I'm there. I'm meeting with that real estate agent you recommended. There's a piece of property that would be a great place to build a resort and I have to act quickly."

He exhales slowly, leaning against the counter and crossing his arms. "I'm glad that you are taking people with you. Thank you."

My heart skips a beat as I watch him, waiting for the rest of the explosion. I know it's coming.

"But before you go, I need to get this straight. Not only do you have a trip to Savannah that you've likely been hiding from me, but you've been thinking about committing treason. You want to leave the *famiglia*? You want to leave *me*?"

I bite back the tears that burn in my eyes. I have nobody

to blame for this situation but myself. "I used to want to leave, yes. But never you. I love you. I don't want to leave you."

"So, you settled for staying because you love me? Is that supposed to make me feel better? Sitting here and knowing how unhappy you are? Fuck, Billie. Do you even know what an impossible situation you've put me in?"

"I know that this is horrible for you. I didn't plan on falling in love with you, though. I thought the auction would be a quick way to get money and get out of here. I didn't anticipate you coming that night. What was I supposed to do? Admit to the leader of the mafia that I want to leave? I'm sorry, Alessio. I'm really sorry. I should have told you, but we were in too deep. I didn't know how."

He shakes his head and heads down the hall. "You should have fucking told me once we started to fall for each other. Have a good fucking trip, Billie. I hope you get everything you want out of it."

I watch him disappear down the hall, swiping away the tears that fall once he's gone. This isn't the way I want to leave things before I go away. I need to make them right. I don't know what's going to happen when I'm gone. He could get into a fight with Paolo and die.

I don't want him to potentially die thinking I was still going to betray him.

As I follow him down the hall, I take a deep breath. My heart is still racing and I have no idea how to make this right. I can't lose him, though. He is the best thing that's ever happened to me.

Continuing through life without him by my side isn't an option I'm willing to consider.

He'll leave you for this. Everyone leaves. What makes him any different?

Voices echo from my father's suite down the hall. I stand outside the door, taking a moment to myself before I go in there and beg for Alessio's forgiveness.

"She stopped talking about moving away a long time ago," Papa says, his voice gravelly. He sighs. "You have to let this anger go. It's only going to poison your relationship."

"If anyone else finds out about this, they're going to expect me to kill her. The Marchetti mafia is blood in and death out, Arturo."

When I peek around the door, Alessio is pacing back and forth across the room. Papa sits in a chair, running his hand down his face. I duck back around the corner before either of them sees me.

I feel horrible about listening to their conversation, but I can't drag myself away either.

"I know. Are you going to do it?" Papa's voice sounds choked. "Billie has had a hard life. She's always blamed herself for her mother leaving, even if she says nothing about it. She thinks that everyone else will leave."

My stomach plummets to my feet. I've never spoken about any of that with Alessio and I didn't plan on doing it either. I try to avoid the topic of my mother as much as possible, and I've done a pretty good job over the years.

Papa shouldn't have brought her up.

"You can't kill her," Papa says, defiance in his voice. "She may not have told you the truth about what she was doing and planning for, but did you ever stop to think about why?"

"Arturo, I don't know if I'm going to be given the option to save her," Alessio says, his voice cracking. "I'll do every-thing I can to keep her safe, but you know there are prob-lems in the ranks. Someone may come for her when I can't protect her."

It guts me to hear him admit that I may still die for this. I know I put him in a horrible position but there was a tiny part of me that would think he wouldn't stick to the old ways.

He had me fooled. I thought that he was changing for the better. Alessio was becoming the man he's hidden deep inside of him for so many years.

And just like that, he's reverted to the ruthless man who puts mafia before family.

Before me.

I should have seen this coming. I should have known better.

I push myself away from the wall and head back down the hall. I can't listen to any more of this.

I need to get to Savannah and try to clear my head. Hopefully once I'm there, I can think through our situation rationally.

Our relationship may not be strong enough to survive this.

32

ALESSIO

"What the fuck did you do to Billie?" Christian asks, the sounds of punches coming from his end of the call. "I'm used to the woman who spends time busting my balls but right now she is punching the shit out of a bag like there is no tomorrow."

I sigh and lean back in my chair, staring up at the ceiling. "I didn't do anything."

"I have a hard time believing that. I thought she was going to snap the real estate agent's head off the other day when he looked at her the wrong way."

Guilt starts to eat at me. I didn't go to talk to her the other night after I spoke to Arturo, and I should have. I knew she was outside the room and listening to us. I saw her peek around the corner and look at me. I thought it would be a good way to teach her a lesson.

I've been feeling sick since she left. It's impossible to focus on the casino and the mafia knowing that she is mad at me.

She should have told me the truth about everything.

"Look, we got into a fight before she left. There is some

shit that she didn't tell me, and I'll be honest, I acted like an asshole about it. Did something I knew would hurt her. I should have talked to her before she left, but I was too busy licking my wounds."

Even as the words leave my lips, the guilt still tears at me. I'm not this man. I'm not my father. I love Billie and I'm never going to let anything happen to her. She's safe with me, but I made her think that she wasn't.

Sometimes all I see when I look at myself is my father.

The shit I pulled is something he did to my mother a thousand times. I always thought I would be better than him, but in the end, I'm the same monster.

"You better wear a jockstrap when you apologize to her. And I would suggest getting on a plane and doing it now. Set your ego aside and be the bigger person. You fucked up. It happens, but you're fucking up more by not working this out."

I get up and grab my keys from my desk drawer. "I'm on my way to the airport now."

"Don't forget your jockstrap." Christian laughs as there is a heavy thud in the background. "Actually, you might want body armor."

Great, I think as I hang up and head for the parking garage. *I'm going to apologize to her and I might get the shit kicked out of me.*

CHRISTIAN MEETS ME OUTSIDE WHEN I GET TO THE hotel, his mouth set in a hard line. He has men flanking him on either side and a gun on either hip, just barely concealed by his leather jacket.

"What's wrong?" I ask, crossing my arms and looking at

the men who are supposed to be watching over Billie. "Where is Billie? Did something happen to her?"

"She went for a run," Christian says as he jerks his chin in the direction of where my car is parked. "She hasn't come back yet. I got a message from an unknown number with a picture of her tied to a chair."

My phone starts vibrating in my pocket. As I pull it out, my heart is already sinking to my feet. I know what I'm going to see when I open the messages and it's going to tear me apart.

This is my fault. I should have gone with her. I would have been able to protect her from this shit.

Would I, though? Billie took Christian and a couple of his men. She knew that they would keep her as safe as they could. She did everything she was capable of to make sure that I would be comfortable with her traveling.

And Paolo was still able to get her.

I open my messages and see a picture of Billie on the screen. She's tied to a chair, but her glare is fierce. She looks like she's going to get out of the chair and kill him if she has the chance. Even as my heart swells with pride, terror seems to freeze the rest of my body. I know that she is going to do what it takes to keep herself alive, but I need to get to her before that.

Another message comes in with an address beneath it. I show the message to Christian before getting in my car. He stands beside the car as I start the engine and roll the window down.

"Call Jovan," I say as I put the address into the GPS. "Get his men on the border. Get your men on your border. Paolo is going to be with Billie. I know he is. His other men might try to make a run for it, though. Anyone who is captured is killed."

Christian nods and looks at his men. "We'll meet you there. I'll make the calls on the way."

As soon as the words leave his mouth, I take off. There isn't any time to waste. None of my men will be able to get to Savannah in time to help. The few that are stationed here are already searching the city high and low for Paolo and his men.

I race through the streets, my stomach tossing and turning. Car horns blare as I weave in and out of traffic but I don't care. I have to get to Billie before Paolo kills her.

I should have gone to her room and talked to her before she left. She should have known that I would never kill her. That I was just hurt, so I was lashing out. I can't believe I said that.

As I head to the edges of town, Christian's car behind me, two cars following along behind him, I breathe a small sigh of relief knowing that I won't be going in there alone.

Though I don't know what I'm walking into, there is no way that I will be walking out without Billie.

After a few more minutes of driving, I turn onto an empty street. Most of the buildings that line either side of the road are abandoned. Broken glass litters the cracked sidewalk. Graffiti covers crumbling bricks. There is an apartment building with an old man sitting on the front step, who looks as run down as the buildings.

The most stereotypical place to take a hostage.

I should have seen it coming. If I was paying more attention to Billie and had known her schedule, I would have known that she was planning a trip to Savannah. I would have looked at it from a critical standpoint and seen Paolo's ability to get her alone.

There are a thousand different things I could have done to prevent this, but I did none of them.

This is all my fault.

I peer out at the numbers on the buildings, trying to find the right one as the GPS tells me to stop in front of a group of three buildings. I park behind one of the warehouses across the street and get out.

Christian and his men join me behind the building. While they arm themselves, I pop open the trunk of my car and rummage through it for the weapons I brought with me. One of the many perks of owning a private plane is bringing my own car and weapons with me.

"Are you ready?" Christian asks just as gunshots crack through the air.

I feel like I'm going to throw up as I pull out my guns. I slide one into my boot and another in my waistband. I keep the third in my hands, my heart racing as I nod.

"Let's go in there and get my woman."

33

BILLIE

"The next time you run your fucking mouth, it's going to be you that gets shot," Paolo says, lowering his gun. The body of a man I don't know hits the ground. His blood stains his white shirt as my stomach turns.

My head still aches from the hit I took when Paolo knocked me out. I could use painkillers and an ice pack right about now, but my main focus is trying to survive.

At least until Alessio hopefully comes for me.

I glare at Paolo, my heart hammering in my chest. The rope tying my hands together behind the chair is starting to bite into my wrists.

Running alone was possibly the stupidest idea I've had in a long time.

If I had given it more thought, I never would have gone alone. I didn't think about it, though. I just knew that I needed a way to relieve some of the stress in my body and headed out.

I thought it was safe and I was wrong.

"Look, all I need to know is where your boyfriend is right now," Paolo says, crouching down in front of me. He runs the muzzle of the gun up my leg. "Just be a good girl and tell me where Alessio is. I won't hurt you."

As laughter comes from the shadowy corner of the room, the blood in my veins turns to ice. I recognize that laugh. I grew up with that laugh.

I feel like I'm going to throw up. As I bite back the tears that fill my eyes, I try to process what is happening. There is no way that she would hurt me like this. Absolutely no way. We've been best friends for too long.

I trusted her.

The betrayal cuts deep, like a knife rammed through my heart and yanked out the other side.

"Stop playing games with her, Paolo," Emilia says as she walks out of the darkness and into the dim light cast by the skylights. "We all know that you're going to kill her once she stops being useful."

He hums and nods his agreement. "Yes, but I don't need to torture her. Now, honey, you need to leave. The men are going to be here soon, and I don't want you to be caught in the crossfire."

"Traitorous bitch," I say, spitting on the ground at Emilia's feet. "Was this all a fucking set up? Was our friendship worth this?"

Emilia shrugs and crosses her arms. "I did what I had to do to stay alive. The Marchetti mafia is going downhill fast. Paolo has a vision for the future. He is a good man. You would do well to help him, Billie."

She spins on her heel and strides out of the room, her head held high. The betrayal hurts worse than the ropes biting into my wrists. There is no time to focus on that right now, though. The first thing I need to do is give myself a chance at survival.

I shuffle my wrists around, trying to find any give in the

rope. If I can get my hands free, then I can untie the rest of the rope binding me to the chair the moment Paolo leaves the room again.

A chair to the head will make a good weapon.

"Billie, I'm getting tired of playing this game. It could have been you at my side. You do know that, don't you? You are everything that a mafia wife should be." Paolo stands and presses the gun against my lips. "I could kill you right now but it would be a waste to the world."

"Fuck off."

He slams the gun into the side of my head. "Watch your fucking mouth. I might have sent my men out of here, but I don't need them to kill you. You would do well to remember that."

The taste of blood coats my tongue as I glare at him. Alessio is going to kill him when he sees the bruise on my face. Paolo seems to register that fact too as he looks at me.

"Now, you're going to tell me where Alessio's strong-holds are throughout Georgia. After that, you can sit in this room until I decide to kill you. Hell, if you cooperate, I might even bring you a sandwich later."

"I'm not going to tell you anything." I pull back slightly and glare at him. "And you can keep your damn sandwich. I rather starve."

He clicks his tongue and shakes his head. "Billie, I really need you to think about this. I know you are a loyal woman. It's why I want you. But you need to think about what you're doing. If you're loyal to me, you have an entire life ahead of you. I will make you my wife and you will get to live."

"I'd rather die than be your wife."

Paolo grins and starts to walk away. He paces back and forth in front of me while I free my hands. When he turns his back to me and goes to stand by the boarded-up window, I untie the rope but stay seated. I want the element of surprise.

There is a better chance of attacking him if he doesn't know that I untied myself.

"Billie, I thought that you would be smarter than this. I thought that you would know enough to not get caught. Though, if we're being honest, I was getting tired of chasing you."

When he slides his gun into the holster at his hip, I start to see my chance.

He grabs something from the windowsill and turns around. A long knife is in his hand, the blade gleaming when it catches the dim light. His smile stretches from one side of his face to the other.

"I know I said that I wouldn't torture you, but this could be fun. You won't need that pretty face once I'm done with you. I could start with removing it for you."

My heart freezes in my chest and a pit opens in the bottom of my stomach. I'm going to die here. Even if I can surprise him and attack, there is a good chance that I won't be able to get away from him.

Paolo is a large man, and it looks like he's only packed on more muscle in the time that he's revolted against the *famiglia*. He could beat me in a fight if it comes down to it. I'm small and fast, but I don't know if he really is alone in the warehouse. He could have people waiting outside that I don't know about.

He chuckles as he presses the knife against the side of my face. I feel the bite of the blade and blood pooling on my cheek. "Last chance to agree to be my wife, Billie. You know that we would be good together. I would give you everything that you've ever wanted."

"Go to hell," I say, standing up and slamming my head against his as hard as I can. When I hear the crunch of his nose breaking, I let the ropes drop to the ground. The dull headache that was there before blossoms with pain but I don't have time to think about that.

I need to stall for time until Alessio gets here. Though I don't know if he *is* coming, everything in my body tells me that he will come save me.

The knife cuts a little deeper before I shove Paolo back. He stumbles, grabbing his bleeding nose. I slam my foot into his crotch, sending him to the floor. Paolo groans and the knife falls from his hand.

I dive for him, taking the gun from his holster. Though I try to get back, his hand wraps around my ankle and he pulls me to the ground. My finger squeezes around the trigger as I fall, the gunshot deafening. I land with a thud, stars dancing across my vision as the door to the room slams open.

Two men rush in, though neither of them are men I recognize. They grin as Paolo gets on top of me, his hands wrapping around my neck. He starts to squeeze as Alessio rushes into the room.

"Get your fucking hands off her!" He aims his gun and pulls the trigger.

The gunshot cracks through the room, followed by two more. The last thing I see before Paolo's dead body slumps on me is Christian rushing into the room behind Alessio.

I scream and shove at his body, terror racing through me. I need him off of me now. It feels like the room is closing in around me. I can't breathe.

I'm still going to die here.

Just when I think that I'm running out of air, the body is lifted away and I'm pulled into a tight embrace. My throat aches and my head is throbbing. I don't feel like I can see straight as I look up at Alessio.

"Are you crying?" I ask, my voice soft as I reach up to wipe a tear away from his cheek.

"Yes." He cups my face gently and kisses me, the salt of his tears mixing with the tangling of our tongues. "I was so scared that I wasn't going to get here in time. I thought I was going to lose you."

"I knew you were going to come." I wrap my arms around his waist, clinging to him as tears stream down my cheeks. "I knew you would get here in time."

'I'm sorry," he says, his voice raspy. He kisses the top of my head. "I should have apologized to you. I let you think that I was going to let you be killed. I never would have let that happen, Billie. I love you so damn much. I was angry and trying to teach you a lesson and this happened because of it."

Shaking my head, I pull back to look at him. "No. This wasn't your fault. He got to me because I went out alone. This isn't your fault, do you hear me?"

He nods, but there is still a distant look in his eyes. More shooting erupts from outside the building. Alessio stands up, putting himself between me and the door.

"It's time to get out of here," Christian says, reaching down to help me to my feet. "Can you walk?"

"Yeah. It just feels like I've been shot in the head a dozen times." I give the men a small smile before taking a deep breath.

I grit my teeth and breathe my way through the pain as the three of us leave the room. Christian leads the way, shooting down two men who rush at us. The second we're outside the warehouse, we take off sprinting across the street.

"This way," Christian says as he turns a corner. We follow behind him, Alessio covering us as we approach the car. "There are men from Jovan's cartel here to help. Davide is sending more men. You two need to get out of here. I will stay and make sure that this gets dealt with properly."

"Emilia was part of this," I say, looking at Alessio. "She helped Paolo set this all up."

"I'll send Davide after her," Alessio says, pulling out his phone and typing out a message. "Now, get in the car, Billie. It's time to go home. That is, if you still want your home to be with me. You're free to leave if you still want to give up the mafia life. I won't hold you back. You can take the car and get to safety and carry on with your life."

I put my hands on either side of his face and gently force him to look down at me. "With you is where I want to be. Every single day for the rest of our lives together. I love you, Alessio, and I'm not going anywhere."

"I love you, Billie." He smiles and leans down to kiss me. The kiss is soft and slow, soothing away all the aches, pains, and fears in my body. "Now let's go home."

Home. Finally.

34

____

ALESSIO

By the time we finally get back to Atlanta, I'm still angry at myself. I should have been there to protect Billie and I wasn't. We drove back home after she was cleared by a doctor to travel, but the entire drive I was wondering whether she was going to leave me once we got back to the house.

"Come on," I say as I open the passenger door and hold out my hand to help Billie out. "Let's go inside and get you cleaned up."

"Can we take a bath?" Billie asks, her eyes drooping shut slightly. She winces as she moves too quickly to get up, one hand flying to her head.

"Of course. I'm going to call my doctor too. I want him to take a second look at you. Make sure that everything is alright."

She rolls her eyes as I help her up the front steps and into the house. "I don't need another doctor to look at me. I just need some painkillers and the longest nap of my life."

"Bath, then doctor, then we can talk about painkillers."

"Actually, fuck the painkillers." She leans on me as we

head for the bathroom. "I need a bath and then a stiff drink. Alcohol numbs the pain better than anything else."

I chuckle and kiss her temple, my chest constricting. "How about a bath and one drink? You shouldn't be getting drunk after what you've been through. We need to make sure that there is nothing wrong with your head."

She waves a hand as we stand at the edge of the tub. "I'm fine."

"One drink, Billie. And you're getting checked out by the doctor."

Though she sighs, she does nod and smiles up at me. "I'm glad that you're here. I don't think I would be able to wash the filth off my body myself."

"Funny," I say, shaking my head as I help her out of her clothing. "But there is no way that we're fucking tonight. You're bruised up and need your rest."

"Fine." Billie leans against me while I start filling the tub with the water. "You win this time. But next time, I'm winning."

I laugh and help her into the steaming tub before stripping down and sliding in behind her. "You can win for the rest of our lives if it means that you're safe here with me."

Billie closes her eyes and leans back against me. "I'm with you forever."

My heart soars.

I SIT BESIDE BILLIE AT THE EDGE OF THE POOL, watching as she swirls the water around with her toes. She takes a sip from her glass of bourbon and tilts her head back to stare at the stars.

We've only been home for a couple hours, but seeing

the doctor took longer than expected. While Billie is fine, there is a considerable lump on her head and dark bruises on her face and neck.

Even looking at the marks Paolo left on her makes me want to bring him back from the dead and kill him again.

"What are you thinking about?" Billie asks, her voice soft as I reach for my own glass of bourbon.

I swirl the liquid around in the glass before taking a sip. "I want to buy a house off the compound. Somewhere you and I can be without the mafia seeping in. I want to give you the life you deserve. I want to build us a life that we can love. I want to get you the ring you deserve and I want you to have the wedding of your dreams."

Billie looks over at me with a smile that makes my heart skip a beat. "I don't need any of that, Alessio. I'm happy to be with you. There doesn't need to be anything more than that for me."

I sigh and slide into the water. Even though I should be happy that my problems with Paolo are finally over, I can't stop worrying about Billie. She's fine, but she might not have been if I didn't get there in time. I could have lost her today.

"Billie, you almost died today. If I want to give you the world, then I'm going to do it." I wrap my arm around her waist and pull her close to me.

"And what happened to letting me win for the rest of our lives?" She smirks and tilts her face upward, silently demanding a kiss. I grin and kiss her slowly, savoring the taste of bourbon and Billie on my tongue.

"I did say that, but not about buying a house or a ring." I kiss her temple quickly before taking another sip of my drink. "You're the love of my life and I get to spoil you. Especially after everything that we've been through."

She gives me a playful roll of her eyes. "Fine. I guess you can win that one. Maybe a couple others in the future. We'll see about that."

I laugh and lean back, propping myself up on my forearms. "Why don't you tell me about what else is going to happen in this future of ours?"

Billie hums and turns slightly to face me. "Well, I was thinking maybe a couple kids. A wedding. Some nice vacations in countries I've never been to. Maybe the odd mafia job every now or then."

"And what about your dreams of owning a resort? Are you still going to make that happen?"

Billie nods. "Yes. Actually, I was going to talk to you about that when I got back. I'm going to be purchasing the property in Savannah. I won't have time to be your assistant anymore."

Pride fills me as she pulls her phone out of her pocket to show me pictures of the property. It's a stunning piece of land with beautiful views. Billie's entire face lights up with each new picture she swipes through.

"This is amazing, Billie. I'm so happy for you. If there's anything you need, let me know."

The smile that she gives me could melt the coldest heart. "Thank you. I appreciate the offer."

"Anything for you, Billie. Now, why don't you tell me more about how we're going to grow old together while we finish our drinks?"

She puts her feet on the edge of the pool and lays back to look at the stars. "I couldn't think of a better way to spend the night with you."

EPILOGUE
BILLIE

One Year Later

It's been six weeks since I shot my ex-best friend for betraying the *famiglia*. For betraying me.

Some nights I still shed a few tears when I think about it. Emilia was supposed to be here for the big moments in my life, but she chose the promise of power over friendship.

Only one month has passed since the last of Paolo's followers was tracked down. I was there when Alessio snapped his neck.

In that one month, life has only gotten better. It's amazing what Alessio has accomplished in such a short time. I know that we still have a long way to go, but the *famiglia* is starting to feel like an actual family. It feels like the kind of place where it is safe for me to stay and chase my dreams, which is exactly what I've done.

I take a deep breath as I stare at the bright red ribbon that stretches from one side of the white stone archway to the other. Wide and long steps lead down to the parking lot where dozens of reporters are gathered. Family and friends surround the reporters. Faces smile up at me as Alessio hands me the oversized pair of scissors.

"How do you feel?" Alessio asks, his voice low. He presses a kiss to my temple and smiles down at me. "I'm so proud of you right now, Billie. Look at all you've accomplished."

"I'm nervous," I say, plastering on a bright smile as I look out over the crowd. "I couldn't have done this without you."

He shakes his head, his hand pressing against the small of my back. It's a small gesture, but one that brings me comfort as the butterflies wreak havoc in my stomach. This is one of the biggest moments of my life and I need it to go well.

I'm finally opening the resort of my dreams. I spent the last year going over the designs with a construction company. Every inch of the interior from the ground up had my input and ideas through the work of a fantastic interior designer.

"You would have been able to do this without me," Alessio says. He waves to his mother who stands in the front row, smiling up at us beside my father.

For a long time, my relationship with her was strained. In the past few months, she's started to come around. I don't know if we will ever be friendly with each other, but she is trying.

"I wouldn't have gotten this done as fast and as well-built as I have without your connections." I hold the scissors a little higher as the man making a speech starts to take a step back.

I've missed most of what he said, but it doesn't matter. This is the moment that I've been waiting for.

I step closer to the ribbon and open the scissors. As I pause, smiling for pictures, I try to rein in my nerves.

This is everything that I've ever wanted and I'm finally getting it. I've got the man of my dreams and a career I've built for myself.

A year ago, I didn't think that this would be possible. I thought that Papa and I would still be on the run, trying to make sure we were well-hidden from the mafia before I started building my new future.

Falling in love with Alessio is the best thing that's ever happened to me.

"Thank you all so much for being here today," I say as I look at everyone in front of me. "Without your support, none of this would have been possible. I'm horrible at speeches, so that's all I've got. Now, I'm going to cut this ribbon and we can head inside and get the party started."

Christian cheers, clapping loud as I shake my head and laugh. We've only grown closer in the last year, but I know that he's going to stop visiting Georgia as much soon. The finalization of his arranged marriage is coming fast. He's going to be spending more time getting to know whoever he is going to be stuck with for the rest of his life.

I'm worried about him, but I can't focus on that now. Tonight is about having a good night and living life to the fullest.

I cut the ribbon and stand to the side as it falls. My new employees lead the way inside. The crowd follows behind them as I take another step back and wait.

Alessio joins me over at the side, pulling me into a big hug. He kisses the top of my head as the last person walks past us and heads inside.

As soon as we are alone, he steps back and gets to one

knee. He reaches into his pocket and pulls out a ring, the sun shining off the stones. My eyes water and my heart starts to race. Even though I know what he's about to do, it still doesn't take away from the excitement racing through me.

"Billie, I didn't know that love or life could be like this. Our relationship might not be the most conventional or have a beginning we can tell all our family, but it's perfect for us. The day you signed that contract was the day I knew my life was going to change forever. Every morning I wake up and want to be a better man for you and for me. I want to spend the rest of my life loving you and I want to do it with you as my wife. Will you marry me?"

"Yes!"

I fling myself at him, my heart racing. He laughs as he catches me, nearly falling over. As we kiss, I couldn't think of a more perfect way to spend the day. I get to show off my fiancé and my resort.

Although, the fiancé part is the one I'm most excited about.

"Come on," I say, standing up and waiting while he slips the ring on my finger. "Let's go celebrate with everyone."

Alessio takes my hand, linking his fingers with mine. "Alright fiancée, let's go party."

***

I laugh as we stumble through the door to the penthouse suite, Alessio's lips trailing up and down my neck. He leaves hot and wet kisses as he goes, sucking on the flesh until my panties are soaked.

With a low moan, he spins me around and pushes me up against the wall. His fingers trail across the bare expanse of my shoulders, pushing my hair out of the way. Fire ignites beneath his touch. A shiver runs down my spine as he unzips my dress.

The fabric pools at my feet as he grazes my earlobe with his teeth. I moan, tilting my head back.

"You know, sneaking out of the party to come up here is the best idea you've had in a long time," Alessio says, his voice raspy. "Fucking hell, Billie, I love you so damn much."

I turn around as he hooks his fingers in my panties and pulls them down, leaving me in nothing but an engagement ring and a pair of heels.

"I love you too, Alessio."

He strips out of his clothing, his cock hard and bobbing against my stomach as he presses me back into the wall. He nips at my bottom lip before he kisses me, his tongue tangling with mine.

I sink my fingers into his hair, trying to pull him closer. I need more of him.

Heat pools in my core as he picks me up. The head of his cock brushes against my pussy as I wrap my legs around his waist.

"Fuck, you're soaked for me already."

'I've been thinking about getting up here and riding your cock since you slid the ring onto my finger," I say, my voice breathy as he slowly pushes his cock into me.

My inner walls pulsate around him as he thrusts slowly. Each time he pulls his cock out, he leaves me aching and desperate for more. I need to feel him in me as I come.

"More, please." I kiss him, nipping at his bottom lip while his fingers sink into the flesh at my hips. "I need more."

He chuckles as he thrusts harder into me. Alessio buries himself to the hilt before pulling out and slamming into me again. My legs tighten around his waist as my hands move to his shoulders. My nails dig into his skin as I arch my back. He drives into me faster as my pussy pulsates around him.

Alessio pulls us away from the wall, carrying me over to the bed. He sits down on the edge with me in his lap before leaning back. I position myself over his cock before he grabs me by the hips and holds me in place.

"I want you to ride my face first," he says, his voice husky.

Wetness coats my thighs as I move to straddle his head. He reaches up, toying with my nipples as his tongue slides along my wet slit. I moan as his tongue flicks against my clit.

Alessio teases my clit until shudders start to roll through my body. Just when I'm on the edge of an orgasm, he sucks on my clit and sends me over. I come as he continues to tease me with his tongue, drawing out the orgasm until I'm gripping onto the headboard to keep myself upright.

"You taste so good," he says as I move back, kissing my way down his body.

I give the head of his cock a teasing lick, swirling my tongue over it until his hands are in my hair and he's moaning.

He uses his grip on my hair to guide me until I'm hovering over him. His cock brushes against my pussy before I sink down onto it, moaning and arching my back. I toy with my clit as I ride him, loving the feeling of his hands working their way down my body. He rolls my nipples between his fingers as I rock my hips faster.

His cock is throbbing as he thrusts upward, filling me as he comes. I roll my hips, taking every inch of him that I can while I work my fingers faster over my clit.

My orgasm comes hard and fast as Alessio pinches my

nipples. Shockwaves roll through my body as I continue to rock my hips until my pussy stops pulsating.

I slump to the bed beside him, rolling onto my side. Alessio grins as he wraps an arm around my waist and pulls me closer to him. I put my head on his chest, listening to his heart race.

"Today has been a perfect day." I kiss his chest before closing my eyes. "I don't know how tomorrow is going to top it."

Alessio laughs and runs his fingers up and down the curve of my hip. "I don't know. I'm sure that I'll be able to find a way to make tomorrow special for you too."

"Every day with you is special." I open my eyes and look up at Alessio, only to find him already staring at me. "Thank you for everything. I know that this has been a long year for both of us, but I can't wait for the rest of our lives together."

He kisses me, soft and slow, before pulling back. "Tell me about our future together."

Smiling, I tell him everything I've already told him and more. Over the last year, we've sat beneath the stars countless times, talking about our futures. Every time, the conversations start the same way.

Tell me about our future together.

As we lay together, talking about the future, I know that the mafia is both the best and the worst thing that's ever happened to me.

The last year of our lives has been hard, but it's only brought us closer together. It's the same year that's been filled with more love than I could ever imagine.

Even though it's been difficult at times, I would go through the years of trials and triumphs over again if it meant I still got to be by Alessio's side for the rest of my life.